Seraphina's Awakening

BOOK ONE IN THE SERAPHINA SERIES

SHEENA HUTCHINSON

Dedication

This book is dedicated to anyone who has ever felt lost, to those who feel as if they don't belong in their own skin. This book is for you. It's intended to remind you that everything happens for a reason. You are just in a dormant stage, awaiting your Awakening.

Introduction

Seraphina was eighteen the first time it happened. She awoke and remembered everything about the dream she had just experienced. It's as if she lives one life during the day and upon closing her eyes on this world, wakes in another. She's gotten used to it over the years; her dreams have actually become something of an escape from mundane life. During the day, she's a normal, everyday receptionist, but at night, she becomes something else—something important.

It's not always images, either. Sometimes her dreams are blank, and she's only experiencing emotions and sensations. Don't get her wrong—the illusions can be scary sometimes. Laying her head down at night, she never knows if there will be good dreams or bad ones. The good ones tend to make her feel empowered and strong, while the bad ones result in waking up in a pool of her own sweat, screaming or even shaking in fear.

The dreams are what some would say started everything. However, for those that understand, who know that she has been a thousand years in the making, her dreams were just the beginning.

This is a strange tale; one with no real beginning or end, for the battle between good and evil is constant. This particular legend is Seraphina's Awakening.

Erika

Seraphina's
Awakening

Follow
Your
Dreams!

Dena
Hunter

One

Nathanael

THE SUMMONS COMES MID-DAY. Little did Nathanael know, his life would be forever changed. It arrives as the setting sunlight glistens through the reflective amber stones of his home. A tiny trumpet flares to life outside the window before a young cherub swoops in on its little wings, dropping the scroll on the ivory desk before zipping back out through the open doorway. Unrolling the scroll he reads: *Report to the Throne Room.*

Directions, that's all the Lord ever sends. The tone, as always, is immediate and commanding.

He rises to his feet and heads through the arched entranceway toward the River of Life. His wings spread and slowly they begin their rhythm, bringing him into the air.

Michael passes, his wings glistening in gold behind him. The Archangel avoids eye contact as he flies straight past. Nathanael's fists clench in response, knowing it's not Michael's fault Nathanael was involuntary relocated into a position within the seven Archangels. If he had his way, he would have stayed a Throne. Guarding the Throne of God was all he had ever desired. The water from the River of Life glistens beside him as he forces the thoughts deep down. He needs to right his mind before entering the Throne Room. The Lord can read him like a book. The choir grows increasingly louder as he finally lands atop the endless steps into the columned temple. Raziel meets him at the door, blocking his way with his full wingspan.

"I was summoned," Nathanael responds to Raziel's stern glare.

"Nathanael, it seems like only yesterday we were in opposite positions."

His fists clench once again. *Keep it together, Nathanael. He's just trying to rouse you before your audience with the Lord.*

He offers only a nod when he passes Raziel. Nothing is going to ruin his day. He has been nothing less than exceptional since the first demotion. He almost choked when he heard the announcement of his transfer from the Throne of God to become an Archangel. One of the main things he took pride in while being so close to God, was not being tainted by the filth of the secular world, the Earth. Archangels aren't so lucky. Their entire job is to meddle in secular matters or Sec-matters, as the Heavenly community calls them.

The columns of the altar room spread up all around

him, going higher and higher, disappearing into the clouds above. This will be good news. He's been dreaming about this promotion. It's going to happen today. His steps quicken as he draws closer. If it were allowed, he would spread his wings and fly to the throne, his feet never seem to get him anywhere fast enough. Especially, right now. Pausing on the three ivory steps to the Throne Room, he throws his shoulders back and with a deep breath, climbs the steps.

He only makes it a few strides before the glory of God brings him to one knee. Cherubs fly around with harps and horns playing nothing but praise. His eyes dart everywhere but directly at the light of God. The paintings lining the walls seem brighter than he remembers. How long has it been since he was here? Time is incalculable in the graces of Heaven, but it seems like forever in his soul. This was his favorite place. He was standing in this exact spot when he protected the Lord from the second century invasion. The Throne Room had become his sanctuary, the one place he meant something. Now, he has no place.

"Nathanael." A booming voice sends the cherubs flying out of the room. The voice echoes in the space between them.

He bows. "Yes, Lord."

"You have an assignment."

Nathanael attempts to hide the smile in his bow, but it's obviously written across his face. A female Virtue with hair pink as the sunset brings him a scroll. Taking it in his hands, he slowly unrolls it to read his next assignment:

Notice of Reassignment

Archangel: Nathanael

Assignment: Guardian to Human

Report immediately to Coordinates: 42.3064' N, 78.0164' W

"I... I don't understand." An Archangel sent to guard a Sec? It's ludicrous and unheard of!

"Report immediately." The Lord's voice calls his entire body into action; spine straightening in response.

"Yes, Lord." He lowers his head, suddenly losing his excitement. Without another command, he turns and leaves the Throne Room. With every receding step, his shoulders slump a little more. Raziel is still outside the temple entrance. The scroll in Nathanael's hand incinerates, sending ashes onto the ivory floors of the coliseum as he approaches his rival.

"Bad news?"

Nathanael attempts to straighten his posture. "I'm to report to Earth."

"To Earth?" Raziel scoffs, "For what?"

What does he have to lose? Word of his reassignment will spread eventually. "To become a Guardian."

Raziel breaks into laughter, collapsing over to lean on his knees. "A Guardian?" he cackles. Each sound echoes in Nathanael's head only to come back and mock him once more.

"I have to go." Nathanael turns and descends the steps.

"My how the mighty have fallen," Raziel boasts from the

edge where he looms above.

His fists are so clenched, his nails make marks in his palms. If he could feel pain, they would probably ache. He wanders down the pathway alongside the river by foot. Mindlessly, he walks through the Pearly Gates, not even bothering to waive to Saint Peter before his feet pause at the edge of the clouds. Below him lies a completely different world—Earth. He was only sent there twice over the past few months—earthly time—on assignment as an Archangel.

Now, he takes in the winding roads and the cloud of smog humans have created in an otherwise perfect realm. His first time to Earth, he took one whiff of the air and didn't breathe until returning to Heaven. Secs have a way of destroying everything Angels work so hard to keep thriving. Secs, the Secular world, Raziel is right. The mighty have fallen.

Before he can change his mind, his wings burst open. There's no way he's going to ruin everything he's ever worked for. Even if it appears to be hopeless now, the Lord always has a purpose. He will prove his worth—if it's the last thing he ever does. His feathers twitch, anxious for the air. With one last breath of the clean, fresh air of Heaven, he dives toward the surface.

His wings carry him lower and lower. They spin him around in circles causing his usually perfect hair to flap all about. This long descent is the best part of this whole thing. It's the most air he's ever experienced, making him feel like a dove: determined and free.

He begins to lose some of his excitement as the trees below grow bigger and bigger. Just as he's about to enter the first few branches, he pulls up and straightens out flying over them instead. He's just not... ready. The line of trees cease, and an endless sight of houses sprout up underneath him. His wings spread wide and flap up and down causing him to hover above the town.

What am I doing? I need to report. Responding to his thoughts, his wings turn his body around, taking him back toward coordinates 42.3064' N, 78.0164' W.

Nathanael's feet pace their way across the pavement for the hundredth time before turning to do it over again. The coordinates took him to a blue farmhouse nestled along the tree line.

The house is still, sitting on a quiet, dead-end street with nothing but the sound of the woods around. A hooting owl in the distance makes him jump slightly. He will have to get used to sounds like that down on Earth. He takes one more look down the bleak street. It's so... *dark*, how can he ever get used to it here?

Finally, he succumbs to reality. This is his life now, whether he likes it or not. Time to get to work before he's even further demoted—if that were possible. However, if he's learned anything in this life—it's that anything is possible. With one last deep breath, his long, plush wings extend from his back with one swift movement. They sprout out past his arms in a glorious, pure white not visible on the secular plane. With one gust, they make him airborne and with a few more, his feet land on the roof. The shades in the room below him are drawn, but a dim light emanates from behind them. A sigh escapes his lips as he closes his eyes and swings down from the roof. He takes a step into the exterior wall. His body goes rigid, the blue siding of the house shimmers as he enters. The vortex pulls him completely through, the smell of wood lingers on his nose as he opens his eyes on the other side.

Whoa. It's apparent he's not in Heaven any longer. This Sec confines herself to a small room—like a prison. It's crowded with pictures, books, and piles of clothes that make it feel even smaller. Looking at all the clothes this Sec has, he stands there, wondering why anyone would need so much clothing. Angels only ever wear robes. Nathanael continues to wander around the room before making himself comfortable at a desk in the corner. Propping his feet up on the top, he tosses an arm over his eyes to block out the light and begins to mentally prepare for the mundane earthly life he's just tumbled into.

The door opens. He doesn't even bother to lift his arm off his forehead. The rules state all he has to do is protect the subject. That is all. He doesn't have to get involved past that. A thump causes his arm to drop. Her purse now sits on the floor, its contents strewn all over the ground, but she doesn't appear to care. His attention gravitates to her bright auburn hair. It's so vibrant. Not even the Angels of Heaven could compete.

"Like, are you kidding me?" she mumbles into something

at her ear while pacing across the floor. "We both know I deserved that raise!" She whips around to face him, her hazel eyes alive with anger. He's certainly happy he's invisible to human eyes. He can't imagine her giving him that look.

She continues, "I know, my time will come, but Amanda, it's a promotion to Florida. I just wanted a change of scenery; I thought this might be it."

The other end of the thing begins erupting in muffled voices. The Sec continues, "I know, I'll miss you, too. However, some things you have to do for yourself." She pauses. "All right, I'll see you tomorrow. Bye."

She hits a button on the small rectangular object in her hand. Her legs still pace until she collapses onto the edge of her bed, a sigh escaping her lips.

Another thing Nathanael hates about Secs, they have a flair for the dramatic—always whining and crying when things don't go their way. Instead of working for something, they attempt to pray it into existence. He's witnessed the power of prayer first hand, but he harbors no sympathy for those that don't fight for what they want. This one seems to be in the latter category. Throwing his arm back over his eyes, he zones out while this new charge of his rummages around her room.

It only takes her a few hours before she turns all the lights out and climbs into bed. The next couple of hours should be a breeze. He was always semi-fascinated with the idea of a secular body that needs periods of rest to recharge. The idea of wasting hours upon hours of the day sleeping just seems strange for a being the Lord created an entire planet for. Watching the girl sleep, he realizes that he has all the time in the world to study it now. The Almighty has a sick sense of humor sometimes.

Nathanael remains in the shadows of the room for most of the night. He picks up nothing but the sounds of the girl's shallow breathing in this small room. The night outside is quiet as well. It's strange not to constantly hear a background chorus of worshipping music. The quiet is almost eerie. That's why, when the Secular girl turns her head and mutters something, he hears it. A strange word that shouldn't even be on her lips—a word that makes Nathanael furious and energized all at once. One word that will wake him up and put him on high alert. The only name that is dreaded above all others in the clouds of Heaven.

Lucifer.

$\mathcal{T}wo$

Seraphina

A few months later...

SERA'S HEART THRUMS IN HER CHEST as she wanders along the busy street. Huge buildings sprout up all around her. They loom above, shadowing her in their massive wake. Her eyes dart across the numbers over the storefronts. *Where is it?* Her hand wraps around the vial dangling from her neck, and she continues to look around. People pass her without a second glance. She hears a few snickers or sighs as she ambles into their way.

She turns to a lanky man in a suit, "Excuse me, can you—"

The man passes by without even glancing up from the phone in his hand. Discouraged, she turns around and attempts to grab the attention of another. As Sera opens her mouth, the woman pushes past her as if she weren't even there. *Will no one help* her?

She twists around, glancing at the passing faces until they turn into a blur, and the numbers on the stores make no sense. Everything swirls into a massive tornado of confusion.

A bump from behind causes her to tumble forward. Her knees break the fall and her hands feel like they will have gravel engrained in them forever. Sera rocks back onto her heels and climbs to her feet, attempting to wipe what looks like gum off of her hand. A glare of light sparkles in her eye and takes her attention from her dirty palm. She glances up to meet the light dancing back and forth across her face.

The sea of suited people part and cause her eyes to focus on a lone figure. He's fussing with a watch on his wrist, causing the glare to shift back and forth across her eyes. Behind him, the sun is setting between the buildings casting a romantic orange hue around him. His other hand pushes a stray hair back as he turns her way.

Their eyes meet. A smile slowly spreads across his face, his blue eyes alive with a light brighter than the sun behind him.

It's him.

She makes her way toward him, finding her hurried New York pace. She quickly becomes the one that pushes her way through people. He watches her, amused, and she rushes up the street toward him.

Sera is a few feet away from the handsome stranger when he extends his arm for her. Her fingers outstretch, reaching for him. Her hands twitch, begging to graze their way across his strong jawline, and she stares up into his beautiful blue eyes that put *the Caribbean Sea to shame. Before she can reach him, he too, becomes only a blur of the orange and red hues of the sunset.*

"Mm, No! No. No," Sera mutters, rubbing her face back into the pillow. "Just a few more minutes. Just a few more." The harder she tries to return to the dream, the more awake she feels. It's the dream about that guy again. She dreams of him frequently—at least once every night since she turned eighteen. Sometimes she will spend all night just trying to find him. Just like all dreams, it must come to an end. With a sigh, she lets the mysterious stranger with blue eyes vanish.

The light purple walls of her room come into focus when she rolls onto her side. Sera is still reminiscing about her dream. It's so hard for her to wake up sometimes. Maybe she could sleep forever. She finds herself wishing she could live in the other world, the one her subconscious has created. She's still contemplating this when her alarm clock blares to life behind her. Sighing to herself, she rolls over and out of bed to begin the routine that is her daily life.

Sera climbs over her little stool and settles onto it. Her fingers begin gliding foundation across her skin. She blinks rapidly, finally focusing on her reflection. Her head tilts in a curious manner, leaning closer to the mirror. Those bags under her eyes seem to be getting darker. No matter how many hours of sleep Sera seems to get a night, it will never seem to be enough. If she didn't know any better, she'd wonder if she were actually participating in those dreams of hers. Although, she wouldn't mind participating in the ones involving the handsome stranger. His eyes are bluer than anything she's ever seen, and they seem to haunt her even at night. Her fingers move her auburn hair behind her ear. Even that seems dull under the morning light. She twists a strand between her fingers, inspecting those split ends of hers. Before her fingers fall to the necklace at her throat, they trace their way down the little vial before dancing along the silver cord at her collarbone. It's the only piece of jewelry she ever wears. She never even takes off, not even to shower.

The cell phone beside her chimes to life with an incoming text. She jumps. *Whoops*, if that's Amanda it's probably because she's running late, again.

By the time Sera's white sedan pulls up to Jack's Coffee Bean, she has shaken the thoughts of her dream and replaced it with a hint of anticipation. When she notices her parking spot right in front is free, she realizes this might be one of the good days. There seem to be so few of them lately. One look at the small shop with the green awning and big welcoming windows and things just seem better. Lately, the coffee house is the only place Sera seems to feel at home. It quickly became her favorite place—besides her subconscious—a few months ago. It's quiet, relaxing, and their coffee is pretty addicting. Not surprisingly, it's the only coffee shop in the little suburban town of Angelica, N.Y. Angelica is the kind of town that's just far enough from any city to not have a corporate coffee chain, but just big enough to not know everyone you went to high school with. The small, homey feel is what makes her like it that much more.

Her smile deepens when she notices Jack is behind

the counter today. Jack and Sera seem to have developed a little flirtatious banter ever since he opened the small shop. His back is facing her as he puts the finishing touches on a customer's drink. His curly, golden hair and tan skin are stunning even under the florescent lighting. He epitomizes the whole California-surfer look. Sera doesn't miss the way his back flexes when he places the lid on the cup before turning around to hand it to the woman in front of her. His blue-green eyes meet her gaze as soon as he turns, his face lighting up in a smile. Secretly, she's had a crush on him for months now, but she's too shy to actually admit it. Besides, a bad break up almost a year ago has caused her to take dating off the table, but maybe for him, she'd make an exception. Her fingers twist slightly as Jack makes his way to the register. Redness creeps into her cheeks, and she glances away pretending to read the menu behind him.

"Good morning, Sera, What can I get for you? The usual?" A huge grin covers his face as he leans his hands on the counter expectantly.

Sera can't help but return his big smile. She's flattered he even remembers her name, let alone her drink. "Am I here that often to have a usual? Oh Lord, I'm going to have to switch up my routine then."

"Nah." He turns, grabbing a cup off the counter and flipping it high into the air before catching it, now facing the other direction. "I wouldn't have it any other way." His last words are just barely audible as the machine next to her groans when he flips the nozzle. She attempts to distract herself, by glancing down at her cell phone. "Headed to work?"

"Yeah." A deep sigh escapes her lips.

"Aw, come on, it can't be that bad." His eyes echo his smile when he hands her the latte.

"Do you ever just have one of those days where you think to yourself, if I see one more cup of coffee…?" Her fingers wrap around the cup, only Jack doesn't seem to release it right away. Their hands meet, both holding the coffee, when he leans in slightly smelling of the wonderful coffee that always fills her with comfort.

"What are you doing after work?"

After months of daydreaming about it, here it is: one simple question. Stunned, all she can manage to stutter out is, "Uh, nothing."

"Someone called in sick, I've got to work a double. You should stop by after work and keep me company." His fingers slowly slip through hers, finally releasing the coffee to her. Jack then leans his elbows on the countertop intently awaiting a reply.

"Yeah, I'm sure I can stop by later." For some reason, she's finding it hard to wrap her mind around the fact that he wants to see her again. It's been a while since she's been hit on. She hides another blush before starting to leave; all she can think about is making it safely to the car before she does something completely embarrassing.

"Maybe I can prepare a snack… or dinner or something? I mean you're going to be starving coming from work and all," he calls after her, drawing her attention. The group of high-school-age boys in the corner begins to snicker at them, if she wasn't scarlet before—she is now.

She glances over her shoulder. "Sounds great, I'll see you later," she tells him, hoping that it sounded causal before walking out the front door. Jack's eyes are on her back the entire way. She can feel them through the window. Once she closes the door of her car, closing her into a cocoon of safety, she finally feels like she can breathe again. Her hands grip the steering wheel before resting her head in between them.

"Oh. My. God. Did Jack just ask me out?" she mutters to herself her fingers toying along the necklace at her throat. *I have to tell Amanda.* The last thought is what gives her the drive to get to work on time, for once.

The oval driveway feels longer than usual as she navigates her way up toward the office. The three-floored, glass medical building sits atop a freshly manicured lawn. The morning sun reflects on the windows and glares into Sera's eyes while she continues her journey up from the employee parking lot. Sometimes, she hates going to work. It seems like she can hardly get herself out of bed anymore. The only thing keeping her going today is the gossip she has for Amanda and her pseudo date with Jack. Once through the automatic double doors, she's hit with the sharp scent of antiseptic. Ducking her head and holding her breath, she heads straight for the elevators. Stepping inside the elevator, she presses the button for level three. Normally she can deal with a small space, but elevators are the one thing that makes her heart race. Just something about a rickety tin can held up by a pulley system that doesn't sit right with her. The metal doors close and the contraption clangs to the top. By the time it reaches the third floor, she releases a sigh.

The third floor is the billing department of the Angelica Medical Center. Situated in a horseshoe pattern are cubicles that section people like cattle. Oh, they decorate them with pictures and festive holiday figurines, but it doesn't make the place feel any less suffocating to Sera. She veers off down the right side to head for Amanda's cubicle. Her closest friend is also her complete opposite. Whenever Sera thinks she has things figured out, Amanda seems to prove her wrong. Amanda has always known what she wants and stops at nothing to obtain it. Sera finds herself a little jealous of her friend at times. Even though Amanda's younger than her by a year, (okay, two) she appears to have the world all figured out. Meanwhile, Sera has always felt life was like getting off a ride at an amusement park—fumble around until you catch your balance. Amanda's main concern now, besides boys, is nursing school. In an effort to help her ambitious friend, Sera finds herself doing all that she can to help her get there, including correcting ten page papers until three in the morning. Being total opposites doesn't hinder the two at all. If anything, they mesh better that way. If there was one person to get Sera to break out of her shell, it would be Amanda. That's why she needed to tell Amanda this juicy news since she has been trying to get Sera to go out on a date for almost a year now.

As Sera approaches Amanda's desk, she finds it empty as usual. Amanda would probably be flirting it up with one of the new interns down in the break room on the first floor. Winter break always brings fresh meat, as Amanda liked to call them. Bursting at the seams, Sera slips into the cubicle anyway. Plucking a hot pink Post-It note out from the top drawer, she leaves her a message. *Come see me when you get in.* She sticks it to Amanda's computer screen before reluctantly heading around the bend to her own desk.

Amanda doesn't make it to Sera's desk for another couple hours, leaving Sera's mind reeling until she is finally able to pull up some work and get lost in the mess of codes and charges. Amanda sneaks in like nothing had happened and props herself on the edge of Sera's desk, crossing her long, lean legs. Her short, dark hair swishes across her shoulders as she goes on and on about a hot orthopedist she met downstairs.

"You don't understand, Sera, he's so dreamy!" Her dark doe-like eyes drift off into the distance, reminiscing about the wonderful five minutes the two shared.

"Oh really?" Sera finds Amanda's antics amusing like always.

"I think he may be my soul mate. Can you imagine me, a doctor's wife?" Her hands press together almost like she's sending out a silent prayer to the universe. Amanda leans her long slender frame against the wall of Sera's cubicle and she can practically picture her best friend mentally piecing her new life together in her head.

"Oh please, you said that about our waiter at Bob's Bang'n Burgers just last week," Sera begins to reason with her, although there is no point.

"You don't understand." Amanda must have caught Sera rolling her eyes because she squints her own in response. "He *gets* me." There's a slight pause before she adds, "And he's totally hot!"

"Oh, he'll *get* you alright," Sera mumbles under her breath.

"Did I mention he's a doctor, I mean it's like meant to be, right?"

"You seriously don't see anything wrong with this picture?" Sera reasons, "I mean you work in the *same* building."

"I know, isn't it perfect? He's the smoking hot doctor, and I'm the sexy secretary. It's like every guy's fantasy." She's biting the edges of her perfectly manicured nails now. In typical Amanda fashion, she has bypassed all logical reasoning and gone straight for the 'Hot' factor.

"Really?"

"What, Sera-Crusher-of-All-Dreams, what do you want to say?" Their eyes finally meet in a playful testing of wills.

"Let me just paint you a little picture here." Sera takes a deep breath. "Dr. Hot-Stuff and you are hot and heavy for a while. Then he breaks up with you for no rhyme or reason. You come into work the next day and have to stand side-by-side in the elevator for a few seconds, or eat lunch across from him downstairs. Is that what you really want? To be walking on eggshells at work?"

Amanda gives her a familiar glare. One that means: you're lucky I love you. "You're right… as usual." Her shoulders sag in defeat. "Can't a girl dream?" Slipping off the desk, Amanda turns to leave; probably to get a second opinion, when Sera finally gets her chance to catch her off guard.

"So, I might have a date tonight." Her voice is low, but Amanda stops in her tracks all the same. Her head whips back to Sera sitting at her desk hiding a smile.

"What?" she almost screams before sliding back on top of the desk. "You? The I-Will-Never-Date-Again-Sera?" Once she's situated with her legs crossed, she commands Sera with one word, "Dish."

"Jack from the coffee house kind of told me to stop by after work." Sera grows sheepish.

"Sexy-Coffee-Jack?" Amanda shrieks, clapping her hands together several times. A few of the older women toward the back pop their heads up to see what all the commotion is about.

"Shh, Mrs. Valentine will hear you." The truth is, Sera doesn't care about the tedious lectures from the boss. She just doesn't like to participate or be the subject of workplace gossip.

"Oh, no. I did not wait a year for this moment for absolutely nothing, tell me every juicy detail."

Sera's mouth opens to begin, but the more she thinks about it, the more she realizes maybe this isn't a date. "He just asked me to stop by after work. He did mention something about dinner, but maybe he was just being social. Maybe—"

"Nonsense, Sera, you get hit on all the time you just don't know it." Sera doesn't even bother to hide the rolling of her eyes as Amanda continues, "You've got that mysterious, good-girl aura about you."

"Why is being a good-girl mysterious? Maybe you should try being a little more *mysterious*."

Amanda pauses for a second. "I see what you're trying to do—stop changing the subject. What are you going to wear?"

"What do you mean? What's wrong with my outfit?"

"Nothing for work, but for a date, you want something that says, 'Hey, Jack, I'm a mysterious good girl, come and find my naughty side.'"

"A-man-da."

"What, I'm just trying to help you out. We both know how long it's been."

Sera shoots her a look that Amanda can read like a book. A look that screams I-know-damn-well-how-long-it's-been-stop-reminding-me.

"I'm not going home to change, he just asked me to stop by after work, so that's what I'm going to do." That's what Sera deduces on the outside, but internally, she is singing a different tune. If it is just casual, why is her heart beating expectantly? She knows she should listen to Amanda; she's definitely more *experienced*. Sera's been off the market for a while, mentally and physically, so she could use any advice given. Stubbornly, she sticks to her guns instead.

Silence grows between the two girls. If they had been strangers, it would be awkward, but Amanda knows better. She's waiting for the right moment to say what she's been meaning to say from the start. "Sera, do you think Jack has been waiting all these months to ask you out for nothing? Of course it's a date."

"How do you know he's been wanting to ask me out?"

"I told you—he likes you. He memorized your drink and your very unusual name, but he can't remember that I like my coffee cold, not hot. There's something up with that guy. Plus, I was turning up the charm last Thursday, and he couldn't tear his attention from you. I swear his eyes follow you around like a lost puppy."

"You're exaggerating."

Amanda shrugs. "Fine, don't believe me. Go another twelve *months*!" At that, Sera winds up for a swift jab to her arm. Amanda's laughter drifts off and her face grows serious, those manicured nails are now twirling around the tips of her hair. Sera knows that face means she's trying to think. "Now, what are you going to wear? We need an outfit that says I-just-got-out-of-work-but-I'm-still-sexy-casual."

Sera just stares at her. "I don't even know what that means."

"Don't worry about it." Amanda shakes her brunette tresses about and adds, "Leave it to me." With a twirl of her hand, she indicates she has everything under control. Amanda once again scoots off the desk and turns with her hand on the edge of the cubicle. "And I want to hear all about this date *and* Jack's beanstalk."

"Amanda!" she reprimands. If she had said it any louder, half the floor would have been all over the gossip like a lion devouring its prey. Their mouths salivate at the slightest notion of drama or information. The pen in Sera's hand goes flying past Amanda's head, and she ducks just in time. Her laughter echoes behind her all the way back to her desk, leaving Sera to stare blankly at her computer screen for a few seconds before scooting her chair in and returning to work. If she doesn't keep busy, she'll be stuck reminiscing about the possibilities of tonight. It seems like that's all she ever seems to think about, the possibilities of what could be.

Three

First Dates

A LONG DAY DOESN'T EVEN BEGIN to describe the kind of day Sera has had. She's happy to leave it all behind as anticipation begins to bubble up inside of her. Despite Amanda's unending knowledge of the dating scene, she decides against changing. If Jack would be donning his work clothes, so would she. Keeping the tan dress pants and white collared shirt, she did happen to stop home and apply some extra makeup before making her appearance. She parks her white sedan in the spot in front of Jack's Coffee Bean for the second time that day. Sera flips down the visor to double check that she resembles what Amanda calls 'sexy-casual' before running her fingers through her hair. With one last nod of courage to her reflection, she exits the car and heads toward the door.

Approaching, she notices all the blinds are down and the

lights are dimmer than usual. A weird feeling settles into the pit of her stomach when she reaches the door. The sign on the door reads: 'Closed', but the hours posted along the bottom clearly indicate otherwise. Looking around nervously, Sera starts to chalk this up to a dating failure and starts to leave when she spots Jack springing through the double doors of the kitchen. One more deep breath and she knocks softly. Hearing her knock from a few feet away, his eyes immediately meet hers. He appears to visibly relax, and his lips curl into a smile. Within seconds, Jack is holding the door open for her, welcoming her inside. Sera's eyes greet him shyly before glancing about to notice the whole ambiance has changed. The holiday music is replaced with something sultrier. The lights are all dimmed, and the brightest glow in the place emanates from the tea light candles scattered all about. The tables and chairs are moved to the side until all that remains in the center is a small table for two. Even Jack has spruced up, wearing a black-collared shirt with khaki pants. She catches a whiff of cologne upon entering.

"Wow," comes tumbling out of Sera's mouth as she continues to gawk. Tugging at her shirt uncomfortably, Sera realizes then, maybe she should have listened to Amanda. To be honest, she's a little taken aback by the spread. The way he asked was so… casual.

"So, I figured you'd be hungry, and I've made us a little something to eat." Jack breaks the growing silence.

"Well, you were right—I'm starving."

Jack places his hand on the small of her back, guiding

Sera to the center table. "Let me check to see if it's ready."

Disappearing through the double doors again, Sera uses the time to take one last gaze about. Garland wraps all over the walls and candles glisten back at her. "Oh. My. God," she mouths to herself before Jack reappears with two plates of his famous Panini's. He brings them to the table on one arm with a steaming latte that smells like warm caramel in the other. His arms gracefully place the plate and coffee in front of her before slipping into the remaining seat. Jack's eyes scan Sera, enveloping her like a warm summer day. She glances away nervously trying to look at everything and anything to draw the attention off her.

"I'm happy you came."

"Why wouldn't I? This place is my favorite."

"I'm happy to hear you say that, you know this is a new business venture for me."

"Well, you picked a good one." Headlights shine through the blinds causing Sera to jump. Thankfully, Jack doesn't appear to notice, because he's uneasily looking up from his hands.

"It took me a while to work up the courage—I mean look at you." His hand motions toward her.

"Me?" Sera responds after her first bite of the Panini.

"Yes, you. Sera you're—" But she never gets to find out what she is, because he abruptly stops talking and looks at the blank space beside her. If Sera didn't know any better, she'd swear he shook his head minutely.

"Jack?"

He blinks. It's almost like he forgot she is sitting only a few inches away. "Sorry, what was I saying?"

"I don't remember." That's the truth, because she starts to get this cold shiver down her spine, like an ice cube is dripping down her shirt. Her skin prickles. She looks around the shop once more. It appears different somehow; darker. The candles dim and the December night's coldness creeps in. Something is off here, she's not getting that homey and welcoming vibe—instead it's almost eerie and creepy.

"Sera, can I be honest with you?" Jack's question startles her before meeting his blue-green eyes. There's that feeling again, the strange one in the pit of her stomach. The one that tells her something is wrong.

"Of course." Her hand reaches for the coffee, desperate to chase away the chill.

"There's something about you." He leans in, placing his elbows on the table. "I'm drawn to you for some reason." One of Jack's hands slips inside hers. Words escape her as she stares down at their clasped hands. For months, she had been fantasizing about this moment, yet deep down, she knows it doesn't feel right. Saving her from having to respond, something clatters to the floor in the kitchen. They both jump when it echoes.

"That's weird." Jack rises to check it out, leaving Sera sitting alone, staring after him apprehensively. A cool breeze sways past, causing another shiver to rack through her. When Jack reappears from the double doors, she doesn't miss that he's rubbing his arm. "It was just a pot that fell, must've piled them too high." His tone indicates there is nothing to worry about, but his eyes depict otherwise. Those blue-green eyes scan the air around them and the tables behind where she's seated. His body language is making Sera so anxious, she attempts to change the subject.

"The Panini was delicious as always."

"I knew it was your favorite." By favorite, she can only assume he meant it's the only one she's ever ordered. Forcing a smile, she can only assume it is a joke. Jack walks toward the table, looking back only once. He's still mid-squat when the cash register behind the counter starts beeping incessantly. He freezes. The drawer clinks open, and they are both on their feet this time. Jack swings around the bar, but Sera approaches the countertop apprehensively. He inspects the machine, pushes a few buttons, and closes the open drawer. The register falls silent. Their eyes meet across the counter once again dark with fear. They have met like this millions of times, but tonight it's different—Jack is hiding something.

"Well, that was weird." He tries to joke to dispel the awkward tension.

"I'll say." Her eyes dart about feeling the hair on her arms stand on end. Something weird is definitely going on here, and she doesn't want to stick around to find out what exactly it is. Quickly, she racks her brain for an excuse to leave as Jack comes around the counter. He walks determinedly up to Sera and places his arms on her shoulders, looking into her eyes. He looks rattled, too. He seems... tense.

"This isn't going as planned."

"You planned for me?"

"I tried."

"Things happen, Jack, don't worry about it."

"You're being a really good sport. I'm glad you came…"

Despite the strange happenings, she has to say that she's happy, too. Her first date in a year was long overdue. She needed this to get back on the proverbial horse, so to speak. Even if nothing comes of tonight, she had to know. "Me, too."

His lips crack a smile before he takes a step closer, leaving their feet toe-to-toe. His eyes close, and his lips purse slightly. Sera holds a breath, unable to move, when commotion springs to life in the kitchen once again. The clanging doesn't stop, pots and pans bang around, beeping starts, and a crinkling sound begins. Sera is on Jack's heels as he dashes for the back door, not bothering to hide his alarm anymore. He attempts to block her view, but Sera pushes past him to get some answers. The kitchen is in shambles; everything is thrown about like a tornado hit. The timers all beep repeatedly, food is tossed this way and that, pots scatter the floor, and doors hang off their hinges. She's starting to think the ovens are on as well because there's an intense heat emanating from the room.

Sera turns to Jack whose face appears genuinely shocked. Whatever is going on with him, I don't think he was expecting this. Sera's instincts start to kick in; she sneaks past his rigid body heading back into the store. This isn't right, she thinks shaking her head.

"Sera?" She turns around to respond when the fire alarm

blares to life in a deafening roar. The sprinklers extend almost automatically before raining water on the two of them. Sera glances down, almost unbelieving as the water soaks through her shirt and pretty much everything else around. Their eyes meet again; Jack's eyes are as wide as his mouth. He's frozen in the same stance as when the sprinklers started. If Sera didn't know any better, she would say he looks just as stupefied as she must.

Pure unrelenting laughter bursts from Sera. What are the odds? Jack's shoulders visibly relax at Sera's reaction before also cracking a smile. He then walks beside her, placing a hand on her shoulder blades this time, guiding her toward the door.

"I'm sorry our first date was such a mess." His ringlets drip, but his eyes hold a sincerity she finds endearing.

"Well, when Amanda asks, I'll tell her that it was so hot the fire alarm went off." That gets a laugh as he holds the door open for her, his cologne filling her senses. The sirens from the approaching fire engines become increasingly louder. Jack escorts her all the way to her car out front when suddenly his demeanor changes.

"I'm sorry this had to happen tonight, I hope you'll give me a second chance."

"It's not a big deal, Jack, my clothes will dry. I'm worried about your store." Water has begun to pour out from under the front door and snake down the path toward the parking lot.

"Don't worry about it; it's just a glitch somewhere."

He rubs his arm again, which Sera is beginning to realize that the gesture shows he's lying. "You should go home and dry off before the firemen get here and this date gets really embarrassing."

"So this *was* a date?"

"I was hoping it would be…" His eyes gaze down at his feet. "But, maybe we shouldn't count this as a date."

"Maybe." Her fingers swiftly slip into her pocket and deftly pull out the car keys behind her back. Jack's eyes study her face, trying to read her, but she spent a year schooling her features so that no one can.

"Well, this was… eventful." Her eyes glance down allowing the keys to jingle from her hands. "I'll see you tomorrow."

"I hope so." His expression tries to hide disappointment before he closes the gap between them.

Sera grows increasingly nervous. The end of the date, the uneasiness of how to say goodbye flushes her cheeks. She can feel his breath on her face, feel his heart beat through his shirt; it has been a while since she's been this close to a man. "Definitely." Her arms quickly wrap around him in a hug, and she tilts her face to give him a gentle kiss on the cheek. "Goodnight, Jack."

He watches her slip inside the car before closing the door behind her. Only when she straps her seat belt on and shoots him a shy wave, does he finally step back onto the curb.

Sera pulls away from the shop before glancing back in the rear view mirror just as the fire trucks begin to pull up. Jack's eyes are still staring after her sedan. Should she have kissed him? Jack is gorgeous, sweet, and owns his own business. So why does she still have goose bumps on her arm and the feeling that something is off? Her mind reels the entire drive home.

By the time she pulls the car across from her house, she's still no closer to answers. The weird feeling in the pit of her stomach has passed, and she finds herself wondering if she imagined it all. It could have been nerves, only it wasn't like any butterflies she's ever experienced before. That combined with the goose bumps and her hair standing on end make her wonder what Jack could be hiding. With a shake of her head, she exits the car, not able to bear thinking about it any longer. Her feet take her up the walk of the blue farmhouse she shares with her parents. When she returned home from college, she didn't have the funds to move out and now, quite a few years later, she finds she doesn't have the heart to. Her parents are the best 'roommates'. Her father is hardly ever home, working long hours in the city while her mother spends most of her time grading papers from all of her high school students.

She opens the door quietly, but there is no need. Her mother is still awake. She's curled up in the living room reading her latest adventure novel wrapped on the comfy (and dare she call ugly) recliner her father just had to have. Her curly auburn hair is up in a bun with a few stray strands spiraling free as her eyes intently scan the new Kindle she received for her birthday only a few weeks ago. It's safe to say she has become a little obsessed with it. Can't say Sera can blame her. She herself escapes to a different world every time she's asleep and has become a little infatuated with it as well. Bianca Cross looks up from her retro reading glasses when she hears the front door close.

"There you are. Where were you all evening?" It seems like no matter how old Sera gets, her mother will always be protective of her. A smile plays on Sera's lips when she enters the living room.

"I kind of had a date after work," she says, sitting on the edge of the couch across from her.

"Oh?" Her mother's head picks up; Sera has her full attention now. "And how did that go?" Her glasses slip low and she eyes Sera's wet clothes. Ever since Sera turned twenty-four, her old fashioned parents have begun hounding her to settle down and get married. They didn't hide their disappointment when she broke up with her high school sweetheart a year earlier. To be honest, to this day, he still comes up conveniently in conversation with her parents. She knows they mean well, they just feel she should be getting on with her life by now. Looking into her mother's dark almond-shaped eyes, Sera can't bear to admit she doesn't think there will be a second date. So instead, she switches to her go-to response—sarcasm.

"Oh, you know," waving her hand and scooting off the arm of the couch, "The kitchen exploded, the sprinklers went off, the cops came, the usual." Sera's footsteps slosh their way toward the stairs.

"Well, as long as you had fun," she says, shaking her head at Sera's antics before returning to her book. Sera notices she is leaving a trail of water in her wake when she climbs the stairs and slips into her room. Peeling off the wet clothes, she tosses them in the corner before throwing on an oversized tee shirt and collapsing into bed. After the day she's had, she's completely ready to escape to her alternate universe. Closing her eyes, she hopes that sleep will come quickly.

Four

Delusions

Nathanael

WIND BRISTLES THROUGH THE TREES as the moon casts a ghostly glow over the silent woods. The sounds of the Earth make their way to Nathanael while he's sitting on the edge of the windowsill with one knee bent. His skillful eyes survey the black trees surrounding the little farmhouse. The peaceful street causes him to relax, leaning slightly off his knee. His nose rises to meet the breeze. The air has changed. The cold has actually turned into a scent: crisp and earthy. The edges of the leaves have started to turn a shade of red. A grunt brings his attention back inside the room. Placing a leg on the ground, he examines the tree line one last time for good measure before climbing to his feet. If the Lord is testing him, he sure doesn't plan on failing.

Sera begins to toss and turn on her bed. The covers tangle between her legs. This happens every once and a while. Sometimes he'll catch her mumbling something, but tonight she just rolls back onto her side. Gibberish escapes her lips. Nathanael takes a few steps closer, propping himself onto the foot of her sleigh bed. He assumes his crouched position, always ready to pounce. Things on Earth are so... unpredictable. His eyes dart over her shadowed furniture.

With another groan, her head flips to the other side. "Demons," she gasps, loud enough for him to make out. His wings extend in response to the word. The heat swirls inside the palm of his hands readying himself. It only takes one swooping flap of his wings before he is airborne, hovering above her.

She never awakens. Her auburn hair flings from side to side as she thrashes about. He glances around the cluttered room again trying to remember the protocol: *Do not step in with Earthly affairs, unless your subject is in danger.*

His fists clench at his sides. He struggles to contain himself. There's this powerful urge inside of him to take action.

Again, he surveys the room preparing for everything, anything. Guarding the Throne has made him a little... paranoid. Here on Earth has proven to be a little monotonous in comparison. Regardless of what he was once responsible for, he will take pride in whatever position he's granted.

The order came from the Lord Almighty, himself. He continues to remind himself, shaking his head. Although, as the days go by he finds it feels less and less like a demotion.

After a few minutes, her thrashing calms and her murmuring halts. His wings retract, causing him to land on the edge of her bed. Her dreams have grown increasingly vivid over the past few months. *What could she possibly have been dreaming about that involved… demons?*

Seraphina

THE NIGHT IS SO DARK, Sera can barely see her hand in front of her face. The streetlights are either broken or nonexistent. She wanders deeper through the city streets looking for the blue-eyed stranger. There's a chill in the air causing goose bumps to sprout up along her bare shoulders.

Tin slams to the ground behind her causing her to burst into a run. She dashes down the street and around the corner before ducking into an open cast-iron gate. Sera slips low behind a bush to make sure no one is following her. The street is silent, not even a car on the road. It's strange for New York City, she thinks. The stores across the street are vacant, the apartments above are all void of movement. What is going on?

That's when she feels it. A breeze tickles her skin from behind. She jerks up onto her feet, heart beating wildly inside her chest.

The church looms high above, hiding her in its ghostly shadow. The moon hides far behind it, lighting up only the tips of the gothic spindles. The arched doorframes mimic the thick wooden doors underneath. On each corner sits a stone gargoyle with a small round head and paws like lions, but what really shakes her are those paper-thin wings, almost like a bat. The statues look down upon Sera. They seem aware she's intruding on their territory, their eyes intense and locked on her, while their paws seem to lean over the edge.

A growl breaks through the silent night. That definitely wasn't in her head—these gargoyles just made noise!

With one last glance above her, she can see the wings along the backs of the gargoyles have spread and their eyes are now glowing a luminous, ruby color. The stone of the church crumbles as they break from their posts. Chunks of rock come tumbling down around her. She whips around to the cast iron gate again. She closes it for good measure before dashing across the vacant street. The gargoyles slink down to the ground like shadows. Their ghostly figures thin to air, slipping between the spindles of the gate. Slowly, their bodies form back to terrifying, demon-like stone figures. Their paws move silently as they stalk toward Sera across the street. The gargoyles have her right where they want her. Her eyes scan the silent street for an escape. Something. Anything.

The deserted city offers no escape. The closer they reach, the colder the air feels around her. The hairs on her arm stand on end and a cloud of air puffs from her open mouth. It only increases as she backs up into the dark alley across the street. Sera can't help but think this is it. This is how I'm going to die. My parents will be so proud to find me shredded to pieces in a dark alley.

The alley soon fills with the scent of old garbage. Her back finally hits the brick wall indicating the end of the stone backstreet.

Pressing her lids closed, "Please God, don't let it end like this." She offers up a quick prayer before opening her eyes to the approaching shadows.

A thump comes from somewhere behind the darkness. The ruby eyes growing larger and larger are all that encompass the alley. Suddenly, a crack echoes the tight space and the red eyes of one of the gargoyles grow bigger before it falls to the ground. The stone creature is silent as it writhes there for a minute. Even its companion pauses in shock until the shadow gargoyle vanishes.

A man comes into view dressed all in black. With his long sword, he slices the head off the other gargoyle in front of Sera. A scream echoes in the alley as it too, begins to writhe in pain. The man glances up from the tip of his sword as the creature vanishes. The blue eyes shine through the dark alley. I know those eyes—it's my dream guy.

"Where did you come from?" Sera calls across the alley. Strangely, the enclosed space is beginning to grow brighter by the second. "What's your name?"

The stranger loops his sword back into his belt. He doesn't seem at all concerned with her questions. His hair moves from side to side as he glances up and down the street.

Sera's legs finally snap out of their trance and walk toward him. "What were those things?" she tries once more.

His eyes finally meet hers again. They soften slightly at her ignorance and he offers her only one word. "Demons."

Unexpectedly, the world around them shakes and blurs. The brick buildings around them fade into the darkness. The moon shines high above, like a spotlight, until he is all she can see.

Those piercing blue eyes envelope Sera, drawing her in like a moth to a flame. As his eyes focus upon her, he reaches his hand out, and she finds herself walking to him. When they are chest to chest, he wraps one arm around her waist, and she takes the opportunity to run her hands up the length of his side before stopping at his biceps. She feels a sense of home and safety in his strong arms. Glancing up to his face, she tries to memorize everything from his jaw line to every last eyelash. Holding her protectively, his eyes dart around the darkened space around him. This leaves her plenty of time to indulge in all his glorious features. His dark hair is long enough to run fingers through, but not long enough to put behind his ears. The color reminds her of a dark cinnamon, making his blue eyes stand out just that much more. His smooth skin is pale and flawless. Her eyes are once again drawn to his. Sadly, there are no words to describe them. They can only compare to a cerulean blue, but they have a translucency to them that a crayon color could never replicate.

He must feel her eyes on him because their eyes finally meet. Sera freezes, transfixed by his beauty. She finds that she can't move a muscle. He has a spell on her. This handsome stranger glances down to her lips, and she loses her breath, his hand reaching up to the tip of her chin. Tightening his grip around her waist, he draws her even closer against his firm physique. Upon contact, there's a pulse of electricity firing through Sera's entire body, beginning from where he touches her waist and shooting out to her toes, fingertips, and every red strand of hair on her head. His fingers begin to dance across her chin and up her jaw and cross her lips before they find themselves back under her chin. When his eyes meet hers again, he pulls her closer and kisses her softly. The contact of his full lips against hers, shock her yet again. Her knees go weak, feeling as though her whole body is beginning to tingle with a deep fire. The kiss deepens, his other arm tracing its way down her spine to meet its companion at the small of her back. Sera can't help but get the feeling he's been waiting for this moment for a long time as he groans against her lips with passion. Surprisingly, she feels the same way. Her fingers find their way up his arms to the nape of his neck and finally entwine in his hair. She feels like she has found something she didn't know was missing. She feels… whole. The last piece of the puzzle is finally complete. Then he pulls back, everything beginning to slip away, his beautiful face fading, blurring…

Five

Prophecies

THE MORNING SUN STREAMS ITS way through the blinds, slowly creeping across the carpet until it remains on Sera's face like a spotlight. The light is a gentle reminder that it's time to wake up. Sera rolls over to face the wall and escape the sun, which is growing brighter and brighter by the minute. She finds herself unable to wake from this new dream. For months, the handsome stranger was just out of reach, and now she can feel him somewhere within the deepest parts of her. She refuses to let that go. Not soon after she rolls away from the impending morning does she begin to hear the raucous noise of the garbage truck hunkering its way down her dead-end street. Sera clamps her eyes shut. Tin garbage cans are thrown around and the truck screeches into her gravel drive before it turns around and putters away.

She's allowed a few blissful moments of silence before her alarm clock clicks on, blaring the news: "It's a gorgeous, brisk December morning in Angelica, the temperature at an all-time low like the county hasn't ever seen. Makes me wonder, Diane, if this is all going to catch up to us at some point." Sera sighs loudly, rolling onto her back to face the blank ceiling. "I sense a monster storm coming on. These quiet days are leading up to something, I can feel it."

"Alright, alright, I'm up already!" She slams her palm on the off button. Her feet drop to the floor, and she swings out of bed. Sera hates waking up in general, but this dream—it was just getting good.

Sera's white sedan idles in the parking spot in front of Jack's Coffee Bean. Her fingers tinker with the keys a few times, debating whether to go inside or not. Sera tends to avoid awkward situations and confrontation in general, so her knee jerk reaction is to flee. Finally, she reaches across the console for her purse, grabs the cell phone, and types out a message to Amanda. Should she play hard to get? Should she just act normal? Should she swoon? What the heck is the protocol anymore? The message is only a few sentences long but her finger pauses, hovering over the send button.

This is insane. Shaking her head, she tosses the phone back into her purse. *I need to man up. I can do this, it's just Jack.* The car door swings open with a gust of bravado. Sera briskly walks to the door, swings it open, and steps in before she can change her mind.

Once inside, she relaxes slightly, pausing to take in her surroundings. Something's strange. The shop is completely back to normal, not even a drop of water on the floor, the sprinklers have retracted, and there's no music playing. To add fuel to the weird fire, the store is completely vacant. According to her cell only moments ago, it was a few minutes after 8:30 a.m., prime-coffee-time. There's been mornings she had to wait in line twenty minutes for a cup of Jack's special coffee. That's not the case today. Sera uneasily makes her way to the counter, glancing back over her shoulder a few times almost expecting someone to enter soon. The shop is eerily silent; one could hear a pin drop. Anxiety bubbles inside her once more. She turns to leave, and Jack bursts through the double doors. They flap back and forth behind him as he pauses for a second with one hand on his hip and the other tangled in his curls. His face is blank when his eyes meet Sera's before a look of surprise and relief flood into his posture. Without a word, he walks over to her.

"Sera," he breathes like a silent thank you to the universe. "I didn't think you'd be back anytime soon." Sera revels in the fact that she is braver than they both thought.

She doesn't have the heart to tell him she almost wasn't. It might be the softness behind his eyes, or the way he appears just a little bit more vulnerable to her. The sexy Jack she idolized is no more. Now he's a china doll she feels will break with one wrong move. Sera doesn't like the feeling; there's something about that kind of power she feels uncomfortable having. "Well, after the excitement of that first date, it makes a girl wonder what could possibly happen next time…" She lets the sentence drift off between them. Jack's face brightens, but his hands are still hidden in the pockets of his apron. She turns her gaze down toward her shoes.

"Sera, I'm really sorry about last night. Never in a million years did I see our first date happening quite like that." His eyes barely meet hers when his hands slip out and clench at his sides. The silence between them thickens. Almost like a reflex, she reaches out to comfort him. Her fingers touch his bicep.

"Don't worry about it."

"No, I'm serious." His eyes meet hers, blue-green, and deep like the sea.

"Jack," Sera's voice breathlessly calls from somewhere in the room, but it didn't come out of her mouth. Jack doesn't appear to question where the voice came from, but his eyes search hers expectantly.

"Don't worry about it." Sera shrugs it off, trying to shake that chill again. Maybe the radio was right—there's a storm brewing. "Trouble seems to follow me wherever I go." That's the truth. Since she was little, Sera would drive her mother crazy. Walking around the mall, she would take in lost toddlers, and while playing in the street, stray animals would flock to her. It wasn't her fault they followed her. What was she supposed to do with them? There was also that time a hurricane blew through. Hurricanes in New York are rare, but it's not unheard of. Actually, the weather seems to be getting increasingly unpredictable.

Dark weather makes her uneasy as it is. The one memory that still haunts her is that time she spent during the hurricane. Young Sera got caught in this storm walking back from the bus stop. Her high school had a problem with closing unless there was a state of emergency. She still remembers how the winds whipped her hair around and stray garbage cans rolled past as the rain drenched her clothes. She made it to her street just as the storm peeked. A tree dropped in front of her, cutting her off halfway down the dead-end street. To this day, she can remember the way the Earth quaked under her feet and the crunch of glass when the tree slammed into her neighbor's Buick less than a foot away. The tree was huge, blocking her off from the safety of home. She turned to head back down the street to a neighbor's house when the second tree fell, missing her by inches. The air from the fall was fresh on her face as branches wound into her hair like snaky fingers. She curled up in the space between the two trees, trying to regain her composure. Sticks and branches scattered around her, trapping her legs between branches under the tree she rested, dry and silent until the storm passed. The branches cradled her close, almost protectively. It took twelve hours before they found her in the misty heat. The cops sawed the tree and pulled her out from between the branches. The town newspaper ran the headline: *An Angelican Miracle: Girl Survives Outside During Hurricane*. A miracle, that's what they called it. Seraphina Cross – the miracle child. No one could believe she had survived in the storm for as long as she did. Even with the proximity of the fallen trees, they said she was lucky she wasn't a pancake. Sera didn't feel lucky. She remembered the fear, the anxiety, and feeling fragile between the two trees. The time spent with no space to move, has made her a little self-conscious in enclosed spaces to this day. Goose bumps sprout along her arms whenever she remembers falling asleep to faint singing. She's not aware where it came from and wasn't even familiar with the song, but the melody still comes to her sometimes. When it does, it becomes stuck in her head until she can't help but hum it.

"You're not kidding," Jack mumbles. Her eyes blink toward him, standing across the counter. How long had she zoned out? "So, Sera, what can I get you today? I hear through the grapevine you had a bad date last night."

"Oh," she giggles, "I had a date like you wouldn't believe."

"That good, huh?"

"He wishes." The harsh sarcasm tumbles out before she can stop it.

"Ouch!" He pretends to stab his heart with an invisible knife. The laughter allows the awkwardness to dissipate between them, returning to their friendly, fun banter once again. "What can I do to help make this day better?"

"A cup of your world famous coffee should do it."

"Ah, you sure know how to make a guy blush." She stands back, admiring Jack making her latte in the sexy way only he can, while he turns every so often to shoot her a smile. His biceps bulge when he shifts the machine's handle down and up again, causing Sera to turn her head to hide the blush from her own face. When he places the cup on the counter between them he states, "It's on the house."

"No... Jack."

"You're money is no good here," he says with a shake of his head.

"I want to speak to the person in charge." Sera leans over pretending to look for a manager and taps her fingertips against the counter top. "You seem to be giving me a hard time."

"I'll relay the message." He leans close, "But I'm pretty sure he'll agree with me." Jack winks, the sweet smell of coffee beans radiating from him to Sera. "You can pay me back by letting me take you on a real first date."

Something unsettling anchors in her stomach. What is wrong with her? This is Jack, the same person she's been flirting with and daydreaming about for months. Only, the remnants of their date lay uneasy on her heart. If she didn't know any better it's as if he were keeping secrets from her.

Maybe she can give Jack one more chance; last night wasn't completely his fault, right? Furthermore, what does she have to lose? "Well, I guess I gotta do what I gotta do to keep this place in business, seems like everything is falling apart around here as it is," Sera calls over her shoulder and retreats toward the door. Jack's laughter fades as she opens the shop door. The December morning air clears her head while she walks to her vehicle. She rounds the edge of her car and something tells her to glance back. Jack's eyes are still on her through the front window of the shop. His back tenses when their eyes meet, Sera shoots him a wave before climbing into the car.

Throughout the morning, Sera finds herself reminiscing about touching the handsome stranger from her dreams. Those eyes haunt her, piercing through her until she returns to admire them again. She doesn't think she will ever be able to forget them as long as she lives. There's something about them, almost like he is trying to tell her something. She's wondering what his voice would sound like when Amanda breaks up her private party.

"Okay—you don't stop by my desk all morning and you have a cup of coffee." She points to Sera's coffee cup sitting beside her on the desktop. "So, you did see him again." Her eyebrows rise with her tone, "I'm dying here! Are you going to tell me about the date, or do I have to pry it out of you?" She's sitting with her perfect legs on her desk once again, hands braced on the edge, knuckles white with anticipation. "Because I'm not above a tickle war, or beating it out of you—or I could tell Nancy, she'll get it out of you."

"No, no, not Nancy!" Sera's hands fly up dramatically announcing defeat. "I'll tell you, just keep Nosey Nancy out of my business."

"Spill."

Sera collects herself, trying to remember the date through her web of daydreaming about kissing the handsome stranger. Maybe her dream boyfriend is the reason her date with Jack felt odd. Her auburn hair falls from her bun from slightly shaking her head at the turn her thoughts have taken.

"That good, huh?" Amanda has started biting her nails now, impatiently waiting. Sera blinks, realizing she was staring for a few seconds longer than normal.

"Sorry, I just don't know where to start," she covers, trying to figure out a way to put things into words, well words *Amanda* would accept. "Um, you were right." She shoots a look that screams I-told-you-so. "He closed the shop early, there were holiday lights, and a table for two—"

Amanda begins cooing and kicking her desk in excitement causing Sera to pause. "Go on! I need more deets!"

"He made Panini's and coffee. He told me he's wanted to ask me out for a while—"

"I knew it!"

"Will you let me finish?" Sera scolds and Amanda pretends to slide an invisible zipper across her thin, perfect lips before her arm sends an invisible key flying over the cubicles. "Then weird things started to happen after that."

The mention of 'weird things' make Amanda's eyebrows quirk up, her interest peeked. "Weird how?"

"Pots and pans fell in the kitchen, the register kept chiming, then a fire broke out in the kitchen, and the fire alarm went off." An uncontrolled shiver escapes Sera again.

She takes a few seconds to collect herself, but Amanda breaks into hysterical giggles. Sera's eyes bore into her, but Amanda continues to slap her knee, bubbling over in laughter.

"Oh," Amanda says through more giggles, "Oh my—Sera, your first date in ages, and it's a total fail!" The laughter continues to rack through her. True, it's mildly ironic. Slowly, Sera breaks into laughter alongside her best friend. One giggle leads to another, until their boss Mrs. Valentine passes by shooting them a stern look. The girls shape up, pretending to talk about a patient's file.

"So, Mr. Green, we need to re-bill with a letter of medical necessity and..." When she is out of earshot again, both girls cover their mouths to hide the remaining snickers.

"But seriously," Amanda gets herself under control first, "I made an appointment with a psychic today at lunch, you should come with me."

"What? No, you know I don't like that kind of stuff. It's true; my parents raised me believing witchcraft is wrong. No one should know the future but God himself."

"Oh come on, just come with me, and check it out. I don't want to go alone."

"I don't know."

"Please." She gives Sera the doe eyes again. Damn it! How does she always manage to get her to cave to her whims?

"Fine."

"Yesss!" She slinks back to her desk in victory knowing if she stayed, Sera would end up changing her mind. Sera's eyes return to her computer screen. The codes swim before her because her mind once again retreats to the eyes of the handsome stranger from her dream.

How does Amanda always manage to talk Sera into these things? God only knows, but here they stand in front of a tiny brick building located halfway down 'The Avenue,' between work and the mall. A plaque plastered above the door reads, Amazing Anna with a half-moon crescent painted lavender. Amanda pestered her via text message for the remaining hour until lunch break about the possibilities her future could hold. Between Amanda and her own daydreaming, Sera didn't get much work done, which only made her that much more anxious to get back on track.

Sera pauses on the sidewalk taking in the small store with royal blue curtains draping across the front windows. The door chimes when Amanda opens it and disappears inside, waiving for Sera to follow suit. Sera lets out a sigh and follows her into the dark shop. She just has to survive ten minutes of this junk, and then she can get back to work. Walking inside, Sera's immediately hit with the aroma of incense and lavender. It soothes her slightly, on the outside. Her insides have been doing weird backflips since she walked in.

"Good afternoon, lovelies, what can I do for you today?" An older woman approaches, her voice soft like clouds and eye shadow as bright as one.

"Hi." Amanda's excitement renews, "I have an appointment with Daphne."

"That's me, dear, and your friend?"

They both glance back at Sera, touching a figurine of a black cat on the desk. She snaps up immediately, caught. Amanda leans in closer to whisper, "She says she doesn't believe in this stuff."

"I can hear you," Sera mutters, looking at the glass display case of pentagrams.

"Oh well, dear, the *arts* aren't for everyone," Daphne whispers back, no hint that she's offended at all. "Well, come with me, dear—I will tell you all you need to know."

They slip through a beaded doorway and leave her alone in the small lobby. The shop is tiny, cramped. The room would be more spacious if it didn't have these ridiculous displays of incense, voodoo dolls, potions, and crystals located all around. Sera feels slightly overwhelmed. Eventually, she plops down onto a red velvet couch sandwiched between two, three-foot displays of glass figurines (mostly of black cats). This is not at all what she expected. She had pictured a creepy, middle-aged lady donning a headdress, telling Sera to gaze into her crystal ball. Then again who knows, maybe that's what Amanda is doing right now.

Above the store counter, holding a cash register that looks like the first one ever invented, sits a painting that grabs Sera's attention. It's a simple painting, midnight blue with one perfect circular moon in the center. It's boring by normal standards, but something in the way the painter swirled the brush strokes around inside the moon speaks to her. Breaking her train of thought, the beads rattle as a woman passes through and walks behind the counter. She doesn't pay Sera any mind, and she digs below for something. When she finally pulls out an embroidered shawl, the woman wraps it around her tall, slender frame. Sera watches as her back straightens, shoulders tensing slightly. The young woman slowly turns to face her. Their eyes meet, and Sera feels herself tense in response. The uncomfortable expression on Sera's face must be apparent, because the dark eyes of the slender woman soften as she makes her way around the counter.

The woman is strikingly beautiful. Long, dark hair drapes down her back and big, dark eyes have a wisdom behind them that seems impossible for her age. The woman slips onto the couch beside her. Sera begins to fidget her hands in her lap. Even sitting, the lady has to glance down at Sera, trying to make eye contact again.

"I know I'm being forward, but I feel like I must talk with you."

"Oh, I'm just here for my friend. I don't want a reading, thank you." She tries to be as polite as possible, but she still comes off as dismissive.

"I don't mean to alarm you, Seraphina, but I think it's best if we talk."

At the sound of her full name—the name not even her parents use anymore—Sera's head whips back to meet the strikingly beautiful eyes of this psychic vixen. "How do you know my name?" Her stomach constricts, preparing for the answer.

The woman's smile is shy as she responds, "Not all of us

are a sham, you know?"

She extends her hand forward, "My name is Anna, and your energy is calling me."

"Well, I'm sorry—I'll tell it not to do that next time."

She giggles. *Damn, even her laugh is adorable.* "I can see what all the fuss is about." She shakes her head. "The spirits are all worked up around you. I'm getting so much." Her eyes close, the smile still on her face. Sera can only curiously stare. Goose bumps have begun to spring up along her arms, when suddenly Anna's eyes fly open. "I've never witnessed anything like this! It's so inspiring."

Sera's nerves lately make her a little anxious, but she can't help but also be curious. "Well, you already know my name. What else is my aura giving away?"

"Your aura is bright, like a sunset with beautiful yellows, pinks, and oranges. It tells me you are beautiful on the inside and outside. You are very fun, humorous, and generally a happy person. Like a sunset, people are drawn to your beauty." She pauses; her eyes close lightly as her head twists to one side. "But I think it's more than that. Your spirit, it calls them, too. There's something unique and special about it, almost like they can sense your destiny."

Sera's eyes are wide. This girl is good; she'll give her that. She can see why they call her *Amazing* Anna, but if she thinks she will get ten dollars out of Sera for a reading, she has another thing coming.

"It's crazy, I get this great feeling of protection over you; this force protecting you from harm. I think it even goes back to before you were born." She takes a deep breath before continuing. "Because people flock to you, you tend to amass many friends and even a few boyfriends, but none have made you feel the same toward them. You crave a deeper connection and yearn for not only love, but a fire and passion that you want to believe exists." She pauses once again, glancing around the small shop. "Don't worry. You will find it." Her eyes meet Sera's again, her smile returning before her eyes glaze over and she resumes. "What I really want you to be aware of is the black cloud encasing your aura, hindering your beautiful energy with thoughts of doubt and depression you're experiencing. However, you must be careful. Your energy is attracting both good and bad attention. Like most heroes with great destiny, there also requires great sacrifice. You will be no different. There will be times you must choose between your past life and your destiny."

She allows the last sentence to sink in. Sera is trying her best to remember everything Anna says, although, she can't figure out why she should. This stuff is baloney, right?

"This is so exciting!" Anna squeals with her eyes shut again. "Let's go into a room for some privacy, I'm curious what the cards will say. Immediately, she disappears through the beaded doorway. Sera hesitates and glances around the shop one last time. Eventually, she gives in to curiosity and follows Amazing Anna through the draping beads. They rattle together behind her and she finds herself in a windowless space with three alcoves. Hushed murmurs come from the alcove on the left, but it's enclosed with a sheer navy curtain. The light is dim inside, probably candlelit, and Sera can just vaguely make out Amanda's silhouette.

"In here," Anna calls from the alcove to the right. She lights a few candles on the candelabra on the wall, shedding dim light in the space. Sera pulls back the sheer curtain and slides into the booth, placing her hands on the round table.

Anna reaches for the cards on the center of the table. They are a vibrant royal purple with yellow stars on the back in a diamond-shaped pattern. Her dark, all knowing eyes take Sera in before sliding the cards toward her. "I want you to shuffle the cards. As you shuffle, have a question in mind. The more specific the question, the more specific your reading will be."

Sera takes the purple cards between her hands. They feel almost heavy against her palms. The cards make her fingertips tingle slightly. Anna notices her reaction, eyeing her carefully. To shake her from thinking about Anna's stare, Sera cuts the deck in half. She has to come up with a question: Will she ever find true love? That question has plagued her since she was first introduced to Disney movies. Although, it's something deeper than that. When she really reflects deeper into the innermost desires of her heart, she wants to know that her life will have purpose. Will she ever truly feel... whole? Shuffling a few more times and placing this question on the forefront of her mind, Sera opens her eyes and hands the cards back to Anna.

Anna's face remains amused, her head cocking to the

side slightly. If Sera didn't know any better, it appears as though someone is speaking in her ear. Anna's thin fingers flip over the first card of the deck, sliding it to the center. The image is of a cherub holding a large sun, only it's facing Anna—not her.

"The Sun. Presently, you feel lost and in a state of depression." The psychic's words cut through Sera to her very core, and she has to hide her shaking hands under the table. "You're letting your thoughts and worries thwart you and it's holding you back."

She flips over the next card laying it perpendicular over the first card. "Temperance." The card depicts an Angel, wings outspread holding two cups. "Your biggest challenge is patience. You must relax, everything will unfold in due time. Worrying is not going to make your destiny happen any faster."

The next card falls parallel to the first on Sera's right. It's an older gentleman with a long, white beard. He's draped in a cloak and holds a staff in his hand. "The Hermit. You are looking for answers, making you somewhat of an introvert. You've been shying away from people and even friends. Originally, it was an attempt to discover yourself, but it hasn't helped has it?" The analysis causes Sera to swallow hard before shaking her head. "That's because self-discovery happens through experiences, not introspection."

Anna flips the next card and places it below the first two facing Sera. It's a moon with several wolves howling up at it. "The Moon. Oh, you are having visions!" She leans closer, suddenly intrigued. "Have you been developing weird dreams?"

Anna's face is innocent and curious, but Sera's hair stands on end. This is hitting a little too close to home. "I mean, sometimes; doesn't everyone?" Sera attempts to turn the questions around; putting on her best poker face. Her facial expressions have to be giving her away.

"You, my dear, are not everyone." She breathes as a shadow crosses over the table. Sera blinks and the lighting returns to normal. Candles are flickering slightly. That had to be a trick of the light. Sera gets that sensation she has sometimes; the feeling as though someone is watching her. The impression her life is a secret television show and people are always observing. It makes her adjust herself in her seat, pulling her blazer closer.

"Well, Seraphina, trust your instincts. Those dreams may be more than they appear." Sera opens her mouth to ask Anna to expand, but she's already flipping over the next card above the cross of the first two cards.

"The Hanged Man." The man on this card is hanging upside down. "This indicates the best case scenario, and indicates you will be victorious in your search—but not without letting something go. Like I said before, some sacrifices must happen." Without further thought, she flips over the next card placing it on the left this time, creating a cross pattern of cards in front of her. "Judgment," Anna reads, "I see a rebirth in your near future. This indicates the beginning of a new chapter in your life. There will be several new changes and adaptations to endure, but they will help in the quest for your inner calling."

Her words slice through Sera. Did she tell Anna the question? The tears build behind her eyes and Sera takes a deep breath to prevent them from falling. *Poker face, remember.* Anna pretends not to notice and continues to flip over another card, sliding it all the way to Sera's right. It sits millimeters from Sera's shaking hand. She reads it aloud as Sera reads it internally.

"Strength." A breath escapes Sera's lips. The card depicts an angel taming a lion. She finds herself wondering what someone would need that kind of strength for. "You're going to develop this innate sense of, not only strength, but courage as well. Within you, lies the patience and control to handle any situation thrown your way."

Anna draws another breath and flips over yet another card. She places the card above the last one, her hands begin to shake a little. "The Devil." The hairs on the back of Sera's neck stand at attention. *That can't be good.*

Anna clears her throat. "The Devil," she repeats again pausing slightly, "This card indicates external factors that will affect you, but it doesn't literally mean the Devil himself will be one of those factors." Her tone is reassuring, but Sera doesn't sense that it's genuine. "It implies some kind of bondage is holding you back. It could imply a materialism to Earthly things or an addiction that is keeping you from achieving your goal."

That doesn't sound right, is reading from a script? Out

of this entire experience, Sera could tell this was the only information that felt... fake. Anna immediately flips over another card, quick to move on. Above The Devil, she places The Lovers.

"The Lovers. You hope for true love. I'm sure he will find you, drawn to you like the rest of us." She smiles, glancing at the empty space between them. Anna's demeanor changes, her smile slowly wanes. She leans over the table, her dark eyes locking with Sera's, looking for understanding. "This next card indicates the inevitable outcome of your question." Anna pauses, internally collecting herself before releasing another breath, she flips the last and final card. Sera vaguely hears a gasp and Anna's voice whispering, "Death."

Her back hits the pillows behind as her eyes focus solely on the grim reaper card sitting atop the table. Silence settles in the alcove. Dread fills Sera, and if she wasn't so focused on the grain in the table, she might have felt a disturbance in her spirit.

The woman finally snaps back. "This also isn't literal, only indicates the end of something. A new beginning or transformation, which I also feel beginning inside you."

"Anna, be honest with me. How often does 'Death' come up as the outcome to someone's reading?" Foreboding fills the emptiness in her stomach; everything about this reading puts something inside her on edge. It's like she is speaking about someone else, at another time, in another world. This can't be her, can it? The Sera that still lives with her parents and can't even ask a boy out? These things are not her. There's no way she can have this huge destiny like Anna keeps saying. Then why does a piece of her, a piece buried deep, deep inside, tell her this all makes sense. The piece that tells her there's more to life, much more.

"Seraphina, I must be honest with you. I've certainly not had a reading so… clear before and never had anyone pull *all* Major Arcana cards either!" Her hands indicate the spread of cards in a cross pattern and a line on the right before me on the table.

"What does that mean?"

"Well, a reading with mostly Major Arcana cards reveals a path to spiritual self-awareness. It depicts the search for greater meaning and understanding of themselves and their world. They usually hold deep, meaningful life lessons."

Her big brown eyes explore Sera's face until she uncomfortably states, "I don't know what to say…" It's Anna's turn to lean back, taking Sera in with her all knowing eyes. "Everything about you is astounding. The spirits and aura around you are strong and powerful. I want to express how inspired you make me and have reaffirmed why I decided to pursue my gift in the first place." She sighs, "It's not about the ten dollar palm reading or proving the skeptics wrong, it's about the spirit—the world untouched that speaks to me. Then with you around, I feel the gates open." Her face admires Sera with a simple smile. Sera doesn't believe in this, she has to remind herself. This is wrong. This can't be. I'm not going to die; this is all a sham. She starts glancing away through the curtain, because let's face it, that's what she does.

When things get uncomfortable, Sera flees. The old saying, 'what would you do – fight or flight'? Well, Sera would run. As much as she wants to be this big, strong, and fearless person, she knows she's not. Maybe she was in another life.

Sera can hear Amanda still deep into her own talk behind the curtain across the way. Running isn't going to be so easy when your getaway driver is busy.

"Do you mind if I do a quick palm reading?"

"Actually—"

"Please." Her eyes plead with Sera, speaking to the burning curiosity bubbling inside of her; answers dying to get out from years of oppression. Sera's unable to turn this woman down. Maybe, she has more powers than she thinks. She releases her right hand from where she had both clasped together and places it face up on the table in front of them. Anna spreads out her fingers so they lay flat before she leans back, inspecting it carefully.

"I see your lifeline," Anna's smooth voice finally speaks. Her finger points to a crease between Sera's thumb and index finger. "Strangely, if you look close, there are points where it pauses or stops."

Her lifeline stops? Sera whips her hand back and stares in disbelief, willing the wrinkles in her hand to magically fix themselves.

"Seraphina, they are only breaks. The lifeline does not stop, so it indicates a rebirth of some kind." Anna's eyes comfort her before reaching for Sera's hand once again. Sera lies her hand face up on the table and Anna continues. "You will marry once and only once. I have an overwhelming feeling you will find way more fire and passion than you can ever dream of. You will have a single child, a boy—unexpected, but he'll quickly become your one true purpose in this life."

Sera's hand twitches slightly as the sound of her heart's deepest desires echo inside. Anna pretends not to notice. "Hmm, you have the Ring of Solomon." She points to a circular crease under Sera's index finger.

"You put others before yourself, are very protective, and selfless. Be careful, I sense that will lead to your undoing." Anna's eyes glaze over while she continues to stare at Sera's palm. Sera glances around, growing increasingly uncomfortable as the silence continues. The flames on the candle sconces flicker higher, causing weird shapes to dance around the enclosing walls. Sera's heart beats wildly. She can sense something not seen. She reflexively pulls her hand back causing Anna to blink, breaking her from the trance she was in. The candles return to normal, producing Anna's blank face.

"That's all I am able to get from your reading. Your friend should be finishing up, we should go." Anna rises from the table, leaving Sera to stare after her. Why is she suddenly so dismissive? The truth is, Sera doesn't mind. She wants to get out of here and shake this weird feeling in the pit of her stomach.

As Sera steps out from behind the curtain, Amanda is doing the same, hugging Daphne. "Sera!" she squeals, catching Sera red-handed. "Did you get a reading?" Sera glances down in defeat. Clapping her hands excitedly. "Oh, I'm so proud. I'm really getting you to loosen up, aren't I?"

She turns to Daphne, "Only took a year."

"I can still hear you." Sera shakes her head, turning toward Anna. She is staring between her and Amanda, "Thank you, Anna, I—"

Anna immediately pulls Sera into a hug, holding her. She whispers in her ear, "No, thank you, Seraphina. Thank you for your sacrifice. Stop worrying, you will fulfill your destiny. The path has already begun." Anna starts to pull away, but locks eyes with Sera once more. Holding her at arm's length she whispers, "Seraphina, if you love your best friend, you will keep her away from all of this."

Sera opens her mouth to ask what exactly Amanda needs protection from, when Anna pulls away. "Be strong." With Anna's parting words, Sera nods and pulls away to leave. Walking back to Amanda's black coupe, her stomach ceases the back flips and her hands are still. Amanda is blabbing on and on about her reading and how Daphne really 'captured her essence.' Is that what Anna had done, captured her essence? Her words seemed so accurate, so final. Sera tries to calm her mind as the scenery of their small town passes by on the way back to work.

$\mathcal{S}ix$

The Necklace

Nathanael

SERA HAS SPENT THE REMAINING hours after lunch, diving into work. Sometimes he would catch her staring at the computer screen, but for the most part, she kept herself distracted. She's numb to it all. That's why when she pulled into the coffee house parking lot, he didn't even care.

He's been here countless times with her before. The past two days have been different. Sera is changing. He can't figure out whether he likes it or not; and can't for the life of him understand what this feeling is in the pit of his stomach, tying itself into little twisting knots repeatedly. By far the strangest feeling he's ever experienced.

It's a habit when he hovers behind her while she orders.

The tension between Jack and Sera is palpable. Jack always has that slick smile on his face; the one he only saves for her. Nathanael hates it. The way he looks at her, says her name, knows her drink, and watches her while she works on her laptop at night. It makes him uneasy. It makes him… mad.

"Hey, Sera. How was work?" Jack's voice is cheery as ever. One would think after that first date was a bust; he would be a little more withdrawn. A proud smile spreads across Nathanael's lips.

"Just like my life: long, uninteresting, and mundane," she responds.

"That good, huh? Anything I can do to make it better?" He leans slightly over the register. Nathanael feels the need to step in and glide through the counter. The machines shimmer as he shifts through them to wind up behind the bar. Bending over, he grabs hold of the rubber floor mat and flips it out from under Jack.

Jack wobbles before falling onto his back. Quickly, he dusts himself off and stands. His smile, a little less perky than before and his cheeks redder than the apron he's wearing.

"Whoops, it's just a little wet there." He attempts to recover.

"Are you okay?" Nathanael's heart stops when Sera looks so concerned.

"Uh," Jack rubs the back of his head, "Yeah, that was weird."

"Appears a lot of weird things are going on around here lately." It's Sera's turn to glance around, uneasy. Her hand reflexively flies to the vial at her chest again.

Not that he blamed her. Strange things are going on around here. He suspects something happened in that psychic shop she went to at lunchtime. Anger inside bubbles at the memory. For some reason, Nathanael wasn't able to enter the shop. A strange force stopped him. It must have been some form of shield protecting the building from everything supernatural. The only thing that could have done that would be powerful spells. *What is a powerful being like that doing here on Earth?* What is it they could be hiding? Above all things, what could they have possibly said to Sera to make her so... jumpy?

Nathanael leans on the window ledge of Jack's Coffee Bean. Beside him, sits the green chair where Sera is typing away at something on that portable computer. The longer he remains here, the more he begins to comprehend their many purposes, not that he would ever know how to work one. The world now revolves around these devices. Not one human seems to walk around without some kind of technology with them. The Angels of Heaven are going to be so entertained with all his stories when he returns. Some have never been to the surface. Those Angels are the most curious, hovering around the outskirts by the clouds, hoping for morsels of the secular drama. The unknown can tempt even Angels.

Sera stirs, mumbling something to herself and glances off into the distance. Her hand automatically reaches for her chest. She does that often. The necklace hanging there proves to be a source of comfort for her.

The vial on her necklace brings his attention lower. Situated between the curves of her breasts, sits a powdered substance that glimmers in the sunlight. He scoots off the ledge, coming in closer for a better look. That's not just any vial.

It pulses at her throat in tune with her heartbeat. Whatever it is, it is somehow *connected* to her. He can feel the power radiating from the necklace the closer he gets. This is something supernatural.

How did she get a hold of this? His hand reaches for her neck, the pulsing increases.

Sera's breathing increases as the vial thrums against her. He can feel the power the closer his hand gets. That's Angel dust around her neck. His fingers dance along the edge of it. What could this be?

She gasps, wraps her slender hand tighter around the pendant, and sits back in the chair, escaping him. "Why are you so connected to this necklace?" He asks rhetorically, staring at the hand at her chest. "And how are you able to touch something *spiritual?*" He glances up to see her hazel eyes staring into the space where he's standing or would be if she could see him. He freezes; his hand still extended, reaching for her.

They stay like that for a few seconds until he can sense her heartbeat slow. With a shake of her head, she bites her fingernails and melts back into the chair.

That is… strange. It's as if she can *feel* him there with

her. The more he comes to know about this girl, the more mysterious she becomes. She has hidden secrets, unknown to even her. He doesn't even know them yet, but he will find them out. Maybe that is why they sent him for her, maybe she is somehow important. He was given this assignment for a reason, the Lord entrusted him with her for a purpose. He intends to find out all of her secrets... and figure out what is going on around here.

Seraphina

SERA PULLS HER FEET UP onto the comfy green chair, her hand still clutched around her necklace. She could have sworn it just jumped. That's absurd. The necklace is just a vial filled with powder. As much as she reiterates that detail to herself, she can't keep explaining away the fact that it's... it's been feeling weird lately. Things appear to happen when she wears it—like glimmering slightly when she looks at it sometimes, and she can swear occasionally it fills her with this sense of security, like that blanket she carried around as a baby.

Climbing to her feet, her hand still holding the vial, she picks up her purse and heads for the door.

"See ya, Jack!" She waves and slips out before he has a chance to reply.

All she can recall is the necklace was among her presents on her eighteenth birthday. A little box, settled on the top of the pile—the only one without a card. She's on a self-imposed mission to finally figure out where this necklace came from.

Her mom's car is in the driveway, perfect. She pulls up across the street and hops out, not even bothering to lug her laptop inside with her. Barely making it inside the house, she hollers, "Mom!"

"In the sunroom, dear," her mother replies from deep inside the house.

Sera makes her way through the hall and kitchen to the back door. Her mother is sitting in a white whicker chair, papers spread out in front of her and a smudge of red ink on her cheek. Sera hides a giggle, opens the door, and slips into the seat across from her mother.

"You have a little something there." Sera points to Bianca's cheek.

Bianca rubs the spot vigorously, yet unsuccessfully. "Oh, I'm so behind in grading these." She picks up another packet and places the red pen between her lips as she returns to her task.

"Do you need any help?"

"Do you mind, dear?"

"Nope." Sera pulls a packet onto her lap. She reads the first sentence before needing to pick up a pen. "What grade are these kids in?"

"Tenth."

"Well, this sophomore just used the word 'gonna' in a sentence."

She sighs before rolling her eyes. "I swear '*the* texting' is the worst thing ever invented for the English language."

Sera smirks. "Is that why you refuse to participate?"

"Yup."

They return to their papers, but Sera can't hold it in any longer. "Hey, Mom, can I ask you a question?"

"Anything to distract me from this nonsense." Bianca Cross peeks up from her winged-retro, red reading glasses.

"Do you remember where you got this necklace from?" Sera pulls the vial between her fingers, bringing it to the front of her blouse.

Her mother looks over her reading glasses. "Uh, I don't believe that was from us."

"Are you sure?" Sera glances back down again. The vial between her fingers now shimmers in the setting sun through the large sunroom windows.

"I'm sure. Maybe it's from one of your aunts?"

"Hmm, I'll check."

"Why do you ask? You've had that thing forever."

"A few years," Sera admits. "It's just getting a little tarnished; I wanted to purchase another one."

"Oh, well do '*the* texting' to your aunt."

"'*The* texting'?" Sera stifles a giggle.

"You know what I mean." She looks up again, her brown eyes appear bigger behind her reading glasses.

"Okay, I'll do '*the* texting.'" Sera giggles one more time before returning to the paper in her lap.

Every so often, while reading through the rest of the

papers, her hand would reach for the vial at her neck—
the mystery behind it suddenly becoming imperative to
figure out. How can a necklace fill her with such a sense of
comfort? How is the vial something that is such a big part of
her, and she has no idea where it came from? It's something
she resolves to figure out.

Nathanael

NATHANAEL HOVERED OVER where Sera stood, watching
her compute things onto her tiny phone. Again, with this
technology, communication is faster than ever. People are
available at the press of a button.

Her phone chimes as someone responds. He leans close
to her ear. Her back stiffens, and she tugs a little at her
shoulder but doesn't look over at him.

A necklace? No, doesn't ring a bell. He reads the response
from the tiny screen. Damn it.

"Well, it couldn't have been Aunt Kathy—she usually
gives me cash," she mutters to herself. "Who else was there
that night?" She paces the floor still tugging at her necklace.

In spite of everything, he has noticed that once she gets
her mind on something, she always sees it through. He has
started something here. He can feel it.

The necklace pulses again at her throat. She clutches it
tighter, glancing around the room.

Once more, he hovers over her shoulder and watches her

pull up a new window on the phone. Her fingers slide over the square until a list drops down from the top. Most have job titles in the search bar. She bypasses all the job search websites, and she combs for "*Necklace vials.*" A bunch of pictures litter the screen. Maybe not all secular ideas are so bad after all.

She scrolls super fast through a bunch of them. "No. No. No. Too small, too big, too gold," she utters to herself as the screen swims in his vision and forces him to glance away. There are so many. How can one person find something so small in the masses of that search? Maybe, it's not something that *she* can find. What if this necklace isn't of this world? His eyes gravitate to it once again. The necklace between her curves glimmers, agreeing with him. It only makes his decision official. His new self-imposed mission: find out the origin of the mysterious necklace.

That night she went to bed without any answers. The night is warm, at least that's what the box called a 'Television' announced this morning. A breeze brings with it a different scent. One he's not familiar with yet. Sera has been asleep for a while now. The only thing to keep him company is the sound of the woods surrounding her house. A cricket chirps, and the wind rustles between the leaves.

Nathanael turns away, swinging his legs onto the floor. The room is quiet as he glides over to her bedside. The gentle curve of her cheek is calm, relaxed even. Maybe this is all in his head. Maybe this is normal for Earth.

Just then, her brows furrow in her sleep—her head

flinging to the side. *Maybe not.* Movement above his head draws his attention. The shadows from the tree branches are growing, stretching across the ceiling closer and closer to the bed. His arms fling outward preparing for an attack. The shadows elongate farther, creeping like fingers reaching for her.

Something is strange, yet he can sense no evil around. What is going on? Sera whines in her sleep, tossing and turning now. Not having anything else to do, Nathanael reaches out for her. His hand touches her shoulder and Sera stops struggling; her face peaceful again. A light outside the window causes the shadows to slowly dissipate. The light grows brighter and brighter. Curiously, Nathanael approaches the window.

Lampyridae, or lightening bugs as Sera calls them, have begun to flock to her window. They float in a growing swarm suspended in the warm winter air.

Suddenly, Sera jumps halfway up in bed. The spell breaks, causing them to scatter. Her eyes dart around the room. With a sigh, she rolls over clutching her blanket against her chest.

The night returns to normal. After a few minutes, Sera's breathing evens out. Nathanael wanders over to her bed again. She stopped at the touch of his hand. This keeps getting even more curious. He attempts to touch her again.

Her skin is warm, too warm, feverish for a human. She doesn't look uncomfortable though; her sleep even seems peaceful. These things only happen when she is asleep. This girl has no idea she's even doing this. The Lord has placed him here for a reason. He finally understands his purpose, to dissipate the cloud of mystery surrounding the fiery red headed dreamer.

$\mathcal{S}$even

Calamity

Seraphina

$\mathcal{S}$ERA COULD FEEL AMANDA approaching before seeing her short, quaffed hair over the edge of her cubicle. She doesn't feel the need to lower her search window, even though she knew she would have to explain herself. Instead, she continues searching until Amanda catches her.

"Job searches?" She snickers low, knowing Mrs. Valentine has a way of popping up at the worst times. "What the hell are you looking at Sera? We both know you're not going to leave me," she jokes, but her smile falters.

With a sigh, Sera turns her chair to face her best friend. "Don't you ever just get tired of things, A? Don't you just want a change? Do you ever feel like you have a destiny bigger than this?" She gestures to the space around her.

"More than a simple job, 401K, weekends and holidays off, and a team of doctors at your beck and call? No, I think we have it pretty stinking good here, girl. What more do you want?"

"I don't know," Sera mutters, "I just feel… bigger than this place. I want to feel more important, like my job actually means something. I want to feel like I'm a piece of something bigger than myself. I just sense I'm wasting my talents on this place."

"Sera." It's Amanda's turn to sigh. "If that's really how you feel, maybe you should leave. You've changed, and aren't happy here any longer. I don't want to keep you at this job for my own selfish gain."

"Well, when have I ever listened to you anyhow?"

"True."

"I just want to make sure I'm making the right decision before I jump off the cliff."

"Please don't jump off a cliff."

Sera cracks a smile. "Okay."

"Promise me you won't make any rash decisions."

"I promise—but something is going to happen soon. I can feel it."

"Just keep me in the loop."

"You got it—loop Amanda." Sera makes a check mark with her hand in the air.

"Okay. Now, let me get back to work before I have to job search, too."

Amanda leaves her best friend at her cubicle around the

corner, glancing back only once. Sera contemplates what she would do without seeing her best friend everyday—maybe actually get some work done.

HER EYES GAZE AT THE LEATHER stitching of her steering wheel. She doesn't recall making the decision to come here, but Sera finds herself in the back parking lot of the coffee house. She must have subconsciously driven here out of habit while she was yet again distracted by her talk with Amanda. It was on her mind all afternoon, she found herself obsessing over it, as the patient names on her screen appeared to blur into one.

Forcing a deep breath, she convinces herself she must go inside, slips out of the car, and heads toward the front entrance. The side window comes into view; anticipation floods her veins as she sneaks a peek. A sigh escapes her lips when she notices Jack isn't there. With added assuredness, she walks inside. The blonde behind the counter wipes her eyes and shoots her a smile before asking for her order. Her green eyes are a little puffy like she's been crying. The bags under her eyes tell Sera it's been going on for a few days now. The barista turns to craft her drink, and she takes the time to admire the way the tips of her blonde ponytail form a perfect hot pink V. Sera has always wanted to have the guts to do something crazy to her hair, but, let's face it, she's the play it safe type of girl. When the barista turns to hand her the usual latte that always calms her soul, her eyes glisten greener than usual. It's crazy how the ugliest things can bring out the beauty.

Once Sera pays for her drink, she turns, debating whether to sit and get some paperwork done—she couldn't exactly focus on work earlier. That's when she hears her name.

"Sera?" Jack is coming up the hallway that leads to his office in the back. His messenger bag is slung carelessly over one shoulder. His tousled, golden hair looks like he had been fussing with it while he paid invoices.

"Hey, Jack," she responds, trying to distract herself from her thoughts.

"It must be a long day if you're here again." His entire face comes alive with one smile.

Once again, she is sucked into Jack's friendly banter despite the disastrous date, and the strange sensations she receives around him. No matter how much she knows she should stay away, a part of her can't seem to follow through. "You have no idea." Her hard exterior cracks, allowing her to smile.

Even though there is an unspoken elephant in the room, she finds it nice to still be able to joke around with Jack like nothing has changed. It makes Sera believe that no matter what happens between them, they will always be close.

"Are you staying?" His hand extends toward the green chair in the corner window.

"Uh, no. I was just headed out," she lies.

"Me too, let me walk you to your car." His excitement is apparent with every word. As he ushers Sera out the door, he waves to the barista. "See ya tomorrow, April."

"Stay out of trouble, Jack." Her sarcasm makes Sera hide a smirk. Jack holds the door open for her, and she follows him while sipping her coffee. She finds herself zoning out as Jack begins telling her about the investigation into the date-night-failure—a glitch in the wiring of the kitchen, which in turn, caused the melt down. Sera was there; that was no glitch.

"That's crazy," she finds herself mumbling in between his sentences.

"It's crazy it had to happen *that* night, of all nights, but, I'm glad you're okay." His arm wraps around Sera's shoulders. As they walk closer and closer to her car, his footsteps get shorter. His body seems closer. Sera glances around, feeling those eyes once again. Her hazel eyes scan the small, half-empty parking lot, from the dumpster to the low hanging tree… everything seems quiet, anticipatory.

They finally reached Sera's car, and she tries to dig into her pocket for the car keys. The nervous anxiety is building inside her once more. Before her fingers can grasp the key ring, he pulls her into an extra tight hug. Her fingers slip from her pocket, eyes wide with surprise. When he finally pulls away from their embrace, both his hands are on her shoulders.

Looking up into his face, his eyes are on her lips. She's

frozen as his hands slowly trace their way up to her neck, then her face, until he finally brings her chin to his and plants a soft kiss against Sera's lips. Her limbs grow cold, ice cold in an instant. Her eyes immediately shut and her mind floods with every daydream she has ever had about Jack. Like some corny movie trailer, Sera sees the months of flirting, the way she smiled in the candlelight, and the first kiss just now.

Abruptly, Sera hands push him against her sedan, deepening their kiss. Her mind is numb, her fingers don't feel like hers as they climb up his washboard abs and wrap around his neck. Her tongue doesn't feel like hers as it teases his. He moans against her lips, enticing her even more.

The branches in the tree above them shake. A terrible crunching sound eventually breaks the spell. Jack's lips reluctantly pull away, and he spins around to face the noise. Sera finally snaps out of it, doubled over as the cold seeps out of her body. She stands with her hands on her knees, trying to get her mind back with the deepest breaths her lungs can muster. No matter how much air she inhales, she can't catch her breath.

"My truck!" Jack's voice makes her finally look up. His black pick-up truck sitting only two spaces from hers has a dent in the fender the size of a deer. The angle indicates it fell from above, like the *tree?* The only suspicious thing is… there is absolutely nothing around. The parking lot is dark and empty; they are the only ones around. Jack is too busy inspecting his truck to realize what is going on with Sera.

Just as she starts getting her breath back, she doubles

over again. Something inside her has snapped. She feels like all the wind has forcefully exited her—like someone has come along and punched her in the stomach. She grips her shirt when the pain rises into her chest. Something is wrong. Something is missing, leaving. She falls to her knees, fighting a scream welling up in her throat and reverberating through her entire body. Finally coming to his senses, Jack turns.

"Sera? Are you okay?" He kneels before her, placing his hands on her shoulders.

"I…" she tries to form words to explain the pain inside of her, "I don't feel well."

"You don't look well." Jack's nimble hands brush her hair to the side. Her skin has grown cold, her face slowly draining of color.

"I need to go home."

"You are definitely not okay, let me drive you."

"No," she states, maybe a little too harshly. However, she needs to be alone, needs to get away from him. This isn't the first time strange things have happened around Jack, and she has a feeling he might know more than he lets on. "I think I've got it now, Jack." With every shred of adrenaline, she forces herself to stand up. Sera takes another deep breath before stumbling to her car and collapsing inside. When she turns for the last time, Jack's face is skeptical. A fake smile and a wave is all she offers him before she turns the car on and veers the hell out of there.

Driving home, she tries to focus on the road, but her mind won't cooperate. Tears fill her eyes. She's driving down the lonely, deserted road; staring out the windshield through her tears. Sera notices the scenery resembles what she feels inside, alone and dead. It's just a normal December night outside, but she can feel it coming for her—the darkness and depression creeping up on her like a monster in the night.

She pulls up to her house, puts the car in park, and pauses for a second. She sits with her hands on the steering wheel, staring down the empty, dead-end street, not hearing the radio blasting. Breathing in the darkness, she finally accepts the depression that is coming. Tears, actual tears, are streaming their way down her face now, and smearing her mascara. Resting her head on the steering wheel, she allows the tears to stream down her pale cheeks. She can't control all the emotions swirling inside her now, not like usual. Something has broken. Her last shred of self-control, lost like a needle in a haystack. All she can do now is release these emotions, allowing her mind to wander.

Her mind finally focuses on the weird feelings she felt on Jack's date to those of her dreams, and then the psychic encounter comes to mind, and the thoughts cycle again. She can't help but feel like this world will never be enough; she will never be truly whole because a piece of her lives in another realm. On top of it all, she has the overwhelming feeling that she is waiting for something, something else, something... more.

Sera blinks and she's in her room. Her eyes dart around surprised; she doesn't remember coming inside. She must have, because she lies in bed, fully clothed, with her shoes still on. The tears surge behind her eyes again and slowly begin to fall, eventually turning to sobs until she can't stop. Tears dripping down her face, she looks to the ceiling and shakes her head. She hasn't cried in years, and now she can't seem to stop. What is happening to her?

She just can't put her finger on what exactly is so upsetting. She's distraught, that much is obvious, but why? She always struggles to put her feelings into words. For some reason, she has never felt more... alone. *That's it; I'm lonely.* However, that doesn't seem to fit the range of emotions. She doesn't mind being alone. It's more than that. She's not lonely, she feels... *lost.*

Sera is completely lost in her own thoughts, wants, doubts, dreams, and desires. She feels misplaced, undecided, and dormant. There has to be more to life. She has to be missing something. Purpose? Maybe. Direction? Mostly. True love? Definitely. She is searching for answers in a world she decidedly doesn't belong.

She needs space, air, and time to think. The walls of her room are closing in around her, as if she's under that tree again. She jumps to her feet and runs out of the house. Once Sera reaches the porch, she pauses momentarily before deciding to just start walking. Walking has always been a way for her to get her mind right, but she's never gone this late at night and never in the middle of winter. Common sense doesn't currently seem to be at the top of her mind. The truth is, she can barely feel the cold while she trudges along. When she arrives at the end of her dark, dead-end street, she turns left toward town. Her emotions continue to run wild. The tears threaten to fall again, and she suddenly bursts into a run. She's running to somehow escape the feelings overwhelming her conscious mind right now. Sera whips past intersections and landmarks, but she doesn't put much thought into her destination. It's not like she can get lost in this small town anyway. She's lived here, in Angelica, her entire life; knowing the area like the back of her hand. She runs as fast as she can until her legs develop a deep ache and her lungs catch fire. Dashing into the town park, she jogs until seeing a bench by the jungle gym before collapsing with her head in her hands. All her worries and sadness seep into her again, she weeps harder. *I don't belong here.*

The tears dry against her cheeks, and her breathing turns to hiccups. By the time she blinks, the world becomes visible again. Once her heart calms to a normal pace, her breathing evens out, and the hiccups eventually cease. Although her mind is still a mess, she can't sit here all night. Her fingertips have already begun to go numb with cold. Sera climbs to her feet and walks out the main entrance to the park. She wipes away the remaining tears from her cheeks. Her foot is barely off the curb when she sees it. Two lights whipping around the corner, blinding her. She's frozen. They came out of nowhere. Now fully comprehending the term 'deer caught in headlights expression', because she's so shocked she can't move... and then—the pain. The careful, play-it-safe Sera has never broken a bone in her body before, but now it feels like every single one of them broke at the same time.

Excruciating pain vibrates throughout her entire body until finally she goes numb. Everything turns black.

FLUTTERING OF WINGS IS THE *first sound her ears comprehend. She feels afraid for some reason, but doesn't remember why. Wind is whipping her hair around her face, but she can't see anything. Darkness is crowding her vision; she can't tell if her eyes are even open, because her mind can't focus. All she is sure of is that her body feels ice cold. So cold, her whole body goes numb. The only sensation her mind can process is a tingling working its way through her body. The only reason she is aware, is how it feels like scorching fire flowing through her. It traces its way around her heart, down to her toes, and back up to her heart, only to trace its way down her other leg. Her mind is weak and fading, but the fire is coursing its way through her veins. The strong wings still flap around her. The sway of them pumping up and down lulls her back to unconsciousness...*

Eight

Awakening

SERA SITS STRAIGHT UP IN BED, gasping for air like it's the first breath her body has ever taken. Her blinds are open so that the sun, high in the sky, is shining directly in her face. That's when she realizes she's tucked into her own bed. *Huh?* Instinctively, she frantically runs her hands all over her body. Counting every rib, poking every muscle for pain, broken bones, any reason for the agony she remembers from the night before. She's still wearing the same outfit from last night. Her fingers pick out a tiny shard of glass from her light pink sweater. Ripping the covers off, she reveals the rest of her body. Her eyes widen as a gasp escapes her lips—there's dried blood all over her. The dress pants and sweater she was wearing look like they soaked through before they dried to a crusty red color. Yet, Sera finds no wounds. Not one ounce of pain on any part of her body; not even an ache from the running she attempted. *Is it crazy that I actually feel... good?*

Sera slips off the bed onto her feet, reluctantly at first, expecting all the pain to hit her again... it never does. Her toes wiggle into the carpet before she steps in front of the full-length mirror on the back of her door. Sera strips down to bare skin and throws her destroyed clothes in the garbage can behind her. She turns around and thoroughly inspects every inch of herself. Over and over, she turns, almost expecting something to appear—it never does. Her skin is spotless, even the birthmark on her stomach is missing. *Am I losing my fricken' mind? I feel... healthy, strong... why do I remember excruciating pain?*

Collapsing to her bedroom floor in a heap of confusion, she scoots against the bed frame for support and stares at the palm of her hands face up in her lap. *What the hell is going on with me?*

Sera blinks a few times as her hands come back into focus. She must have zoned out for a little bit. Like when a computer is on overload, it has to shut down to get things right again. That's how she just felt. Things aren't exactly clear, but it somehow doesn't make her too upset now. The sun is even higher in the sky, the warmth radiating into her feet against the carpet. Her body finds its way onto her feet again. She steals one last glance at herself in the mirror before the idea comes to her.

Go for a run.

Yes, that sounds great. Spinning on her heels, she digs

through her closet for a pair of yoga pants and a navy sweatshirt. By the time she has her sneakers laced up, she is practically dancing around in her little square room. Her body is firing with such pent up energy flowing through her every vein, she just has to release it. The feeling is beyond words, they seem to escape her. A fire has ignited inside of her. It feels as though something deep within her has finally awoken. She feels alive, awake, and excited all at the same time. She feels as though she's had six cups of coffee and three of those energy drinks.

Opening her bedroom door she takes off down the stairs two at a time, unlocks the front door, and jumps off the porch steps in one bound. Once her feet touch the concrete walkway, she's hit with an array of strange scents and noises that immediately bring her to her knees. A bird caws in the distance and echoes inside her ears. It pounds through her head, vibrating her eardrums. Next, she picks up a crunching that sounds like dead leaves underfoot, but then that too is background noise to an annoying drip. Drip, drip, drip—the droplets continue to fall from a leaky pipe in the backyard that has yet to be winterized. The sounds become too much and she places her hands over her ears, fighting off the noises that hound her all at once.

Then, her other senses come to life. Her nose inhales the first scents of winter. The smell of cold in the air, the nauseating garbage from the truck around the corner, even the candle in the kitchen that smells like peppermint wafts to her nose. Sera looks up and her gaze becomes enraptured by the fact she can see a spider burrowing under the bark of a tree branch, ten feet above her head.

Still hunched over with her hands on her ears, she decides to get a handle on things. Taking away all stimuli, she closes her eyes, and blocks out the smells and sounds, while trying to focus her mind.

The thought comes to her like a fleeting sentence inside her conscious.

You are stronger than this.

She can control this. Taking a deep breath, she calms her concern. Slowly, one by one, she focuses on the sights and smells. Her mind forms a mental filing cabinet where she archives them all away into categories. Just as suddenly as they appear, she finds she can control them as well. She continues with the mental-filing and the deep breathing until there is nothing overpowering her. Sera finally releases the death grip on her ears and climbs to her feet. One glance around tells her that things are different. The cold in the air has shifted; winter was teetering on the edge before— now the barrier has broken and brisk air is upon the small town of Angelica. It whispers through the trees, winding its way to her in a swirling vortex of natural energy. It's like the world around her is alive in a way she never thought possible before. She shifts her weight from one foot to the other as her energy begins to return. Without warning, she breaks into a run, dashing down the dead end street and around the corner toward civilization.

Sera only gets a few blocks before her hypersensitive

senses overpower her again, but instead of giving into them and falling to her knees, she tries to acknowledge them, study them. Every different bush smells different to her, exhaust from a passing car, donuts in the local bakery. She catalogs each one, somehow knowing it will make her better in the long run. Focusing her mind on something feels good; it keeps her from going mad. Her mind needed something to do. Instead of flinching at the slightest noise, she finds herself trying to determine what made it, where it is coming from, and why. Her body craves answers, thirsts for knowledge like never before.

Her vision is extremely enhanced; she was blissfully unaware of how blind she was until someone gave her glasses. Insanely detailed and practically x-ray vision glasses, but enhanced all the same. Everything seems so much clearer to her now, visually and mentally. It's like she has cleaned out the cobwebs of her soul. Things just seem to make sense, like her love for her friends, her sense of duty, and the overwhelming feeling of lost purpose. This is what Anna was talking about; this is how she should see the world, her rebirth. Anything is possible. She is possible. She is alive.

The minutes tick away and Sera barely realizes how long she's been running. She has circled the outskirts of the town about three times—her body showing no sign of fatigue or ache. She is bounding around another corner when her ears pick up a crunching sound. It puzzles her as she fights to figure out what it could be, until she almost runs smack into another runner. Time seems to slow and she reflexively dashes around them in record speed that even her own eyes could barely follow. From behind her she hears the runner let out a startled gasp as the wind from her ballerina twirl finally hits him. He's looking around now to see where it came from, but she's already gone. *Well, that was different.* She shakes the thoughts out of her head, no this 'New Sera' isn't going to over think things.

Running along 'The Avenue' now, it finally catches up to her that she hasn't had to stop and rest, her body doesn't even crave refreshment—something has definitely happened to her. She feels as though she can go on forever, pushing herself into a sprint she decides to test that theory. Her legs take her faster and faster, the scenery of the small town that she spent her entire life in is blurring past her. Her hands pump up and down until they, too, become a blur. The fire inside her is filling her with adrenaline, making her push harder and harder. Testing limits she didn't even know were possible. Until, she subconsciously begins to slow.

The pounding in the pavement softens, and her feet begin to slow to a walk. She stands before the green street sign. 'Florence Street,' it reads. The same street she remembered crossing the night before, the scene of the crime, so to speak. Hesitantly, she presses further down the street, her overactive mind once again craving answers. One foot carefully placed in front of the other until she is standing at the entrance to the park. The first thing she notices is the dark spot on the ground. It's long, and a shade of dark burgundy. Something crunches under her sneaker and she slowly lifts her leg to find glass. Actually, now that she looks around there's glass *everywhere*.

She must be in something like shock, because even now, it takes her a few minutes to realize this is blood. Her blood. Last night was not a dream, it wasn't a crazy figment of her imagination—it was real and somehow, she survived it. She tosses her head from side to side causing her auburn ponytail to swish behind her softly at first, then gradually more violent. She's trying to shake all the bad memories out of it. Whipping around, she breaks into a run back the way she had come. She sprints the entire way home without ever looking back. When she finally collapses on the porch steps with her head in her hands, she allows herself to process what she had just seen. It started out a joke, that she was losing her mind… but now, the things she has seen in the past few hours alone make her think otherwise. Her mind is close to overload again as thoughts flood her mind. On the verge of yet another re-boot, she finally shakes herself out of it. There's no way she's going to come to some solid conclusion right now. Her hands slap against her thighs, the only thing she can do is live her life, wherever that may take her—she has a feeling the answers will come to light.

Pushing herself to her feet again, she notices a stir in the woods across the street. Her eyes study the bushes with her new sense of sight, but it turns out she doesn't happen to have x-ray vision. After a few more moments of staring at a bush, she finally decides there is nothing there and turns to head inside.

Sera makes her way through the hall, her stomach growling like it never has before. Bianca Cross's humming makes it's way to her from deeper inside the house.

"Mom?" Sera calls.

"In the kitchen, dear."

She walks in the kitchen and finds her mother is behind the newly renovated island. The house is old, old enough to have been in the family for centuries. When Sera's parents agreed to keep it, her mom had one condition—an updated kitchen. She can survive without air conditioning in the summer, the creaky floorboards, and a leaky roof, but an outdated kitchen was not going to cut it. It only took one month to get it Bianca-Cross-perfect. Brand new white cabinets keep the farmhouse vibe, but the sleek new granite countertops and sleek metal appliances bring this ancient home back into the twenty-first century.

"And where did you go this early on a Saturday morning?"

Sera's head is deep into the fridge as she mumbles her response through the grapes in her cheeks, "I went for a run."

"You? Running?" her mother retorts before bursting into laughter. Obviously, Sera had never really been the athletic type (to put it nicely). Unless walking home from school constitutes athleticism.

Sera's father comes strolling into the kitchen drawn in by the laughter. Sera is shoveling yogurt into her mouth when her mother feels the need to fill him in.

"Edward, dear, did you hear that? Our Sera just came back from a run."

He has to lean on the granite island for support as he cracks up alongside of his wife. Maybe un-athletic was a little generous.

"Ha-ha-ha," Sera mocks, "I guess I just wanted to get back in shape since I'm dating again, but go on laugh." The statement was a joke, trying to put her parents in their place. She scoots up onto the counter top with a bag of chips in her lap.

"Oh, good," her mother mumbles, "You know, Sera, we were starting to worry about you…"

"What do you mean?" The joke is apparently on Sera.

"Well, it's been a while since Caleb and, it's just that you haven't even looked at another guy…"

Sera sucks in a sharp breath at the mention of her ex-boyfriend's name. It's been a while since she's heard it. It's a ripple of guilt every time she thinks about him. They were serious for a good while, but something told her it wasn't right. So, when he went away to college, she let him. Sera got into the same college, but she couldn't shake the feeling that here is where she's meant to be. Instead, she received a full scholarship to North Commons University, one town over from her little farmhouse. The full ride included housing so she was able to get the best of both worlds—the college experience and still close to home.

"… And you've been very distant and aloof lately," her mother continues.

"You know, Sera, when your mother and I were your age, we were already married and little Sera was on the way,"

Edward Cross feels the need to chime in.

This is Sera's cue to leave. She swings down from the island, "Okay, I'm done with this conversation." Her hands fly up in defeat. Before she turns to leave, she steals one of the ham sandwiches her mother has just finished making and walks out of the room.

Sera is finishing up the sandwich, but when she climbs the steps toward her room, her stomach still growls for more. *It's crazy*, she thinks, *I exercise one time, and I'm ravenous. Get a grip body*. She pats her abdomen for emphasis.

Once she closes the door to her room behind her, she finds herself pacing back and forth, desperate for something to do. She can't seem to sit for too long. Her eye catches a book she's been wanting to read. Reading hasn't exactly fit her mood lately. In one swift motion, she grabs the novel off the shelf, jumps into bed, and opens to the first chapter.

Less than an hour later, she tosses the finished book down and slips back downstairs for yet another snack. Coming out of the kitchen with a spoon to a tub of peanut butter, she catches sight of her mother's Kindle lying on the coffee table in the living room, unattended. With one glance around, she slips into the recliner and downloads the next book in the series.

The large mahogany grandfather clock in the hall chimes its tune. It's only chimed three times since she started reading. The tune echoes up through the house and reverberates through her ears. Staring at the words *The End* on the Kindle in her lap, she blinks in disbelief. She has finished the remaining three books in the series, in record time according to the percentage statistics on the Kindle. Her eyes flew across the pages at record speed and yet, she can still recall every line with insane precision, every plot twist connects. It seems that all her cognitive processing is moving at an incredible rate, just like her body. *Whoa.* Her fingers run themselves through her hair and she tries to contemplate this new phenomenon.

Finally, climbing out of the ugly recliner she makes her way back upstairs for her cell phone. It's on the bed where she left it. Clicking a few buttons, she calls Amanda.

Barely waiting for the second ring, "Oh my Sera, I was just going to call you! I met this really hot stud yesterday, and he wants to meet me at Chaos tonight." She breathes in. "Please, please come. Don't let me meet a strange hottie in the big city all by myself."

Sera's not fully inept when it comes to dating, but even she knows that guys only meet girls at clubs for one reason. She doesn't have the heart to break the news to her friend. That and a part of her needs an excuse to get out. "You read my mind—a night out sounds great right about now."

"Really?" The disbelief is clear. "Okay, who are you and what did you do with my best friend?"

"I thought you'd be happy. Can't a girl be in a good mood?"

"I am, I am! Let me go get a new dress—pick me up at ten-thirty; it's going to take a while to get to the city. Okay, see you later." Amanda hangs up without another peep from

Sera, apparently trying to hang up before she would have the option to change her mind. With a smile, Sera places the phone down, Amanda is absolutely nuts, but she couldn't imagine her life without her.

Glancing at the clock, she has two hours—what the hell could keep her busy until then. A nice relaxing bath should be just the ticket to get her in the mood for a girl's night. It's been a while since they've gone out. Usually, Netflix and wine are the kind of nights they have together. Sera has learned the hard way that going out with Amanda is an adventure in itself. Especially, when there's liquor and boys involved. For some reason, deep down, Sera has a feeling tonight is going to be a good night.

After digging through her drawers, she finds a bath set she received from a crazy Aunt one Christmas. *Perfect.* Ripping open the packaging, she treks her way into the bathroom. Her nimble hands draw a bath in the cast iron tub, turning the nozzle to the hottest temperature it will go before tossing in the lavender bath soap. The bubbles ripple out automatically, filling the small bathroom with the relaxing scent. Sera slips out of her clothes with not even an ounce of sweat on them, before tossing them into the corner. Before the tub is even full, she finds herself testing the water with her toe. The heat doesn't bother her remotely. She climbs over the edge. Carefully lowering herself into the depths of the tub, she expects the heat to eventually become too much—it never does. As she slips into the tub and rests her head on the edge, she allows the lavender to soothe her. She continues to soak, lifting her legs a little; she's not even remotely sore from the longest run of her life. How is that possible? How can she have such mental clarity and yet still have no idea what's going on with her own body? Her last thought—maybe it's because the reason is nothing believable.

Sera lowers her face into the hot water, allowing her thoughts to dissipate out of her mind as she reemerges again. Her head returns to the lip of the tub and rolls to her shoulder. Glancing out at her arm propped up along the edge of the tub, she notices the water beading up on it. It fascinates her for some reason; she continues to watch as it drips back down into the water below. With a blink, she notices her skin seems to be shimmering. Her skin is giving off a slight glow. Her eyes focus closer, like a microscope it clicks closer, closer until she can make out perfect pale skin. It looks unreal, almost like a porcelain doll.

That just exceeds the amount of strange happenings in one day. She sprouts up and pulls the stopper out of the tub. Her arms reach up and turn the shower on before grabbing hold of her apricot scrub. She pours a huge wallop and starts scrubbing her entire body vigorously. Struggling to hold back the frustration, she scrubs out all her confusion, all the creepy things that are happening to her. When she's on the verge of breaking down, she turns off the shower, grabs her towel off the rack, and practically runs out of the bathroom. Her wet feet leave tiny puddles in her wake before she closes the door to her room and whips the towel off her naked body. She then commences another full body inspection; starting from top to bottom, front to back, and side-to-side. If anything, her skin is glowing, firm, and vibrant. She climbs to the edge of her bed, resting her head in her hands. There's no trauma, no bruising—how is this possible. Her hands fall to her sides. *How is this possible? Was I hit by an alien rock? Did a radioactive spider bite me? What the hell is going on with me?*

Breaking her out of her thoughts, her cell phone chimes to life. Without looking, she automatically answers, "Hello?"

"Sera? It's Jack!"

"Oh, hey Jack…" Sera replies, not exactly returning his enthusiasm.

"I," he pauses, "I just wanted to make sure you were okay, you didn't look so well last night."

She almost feels guilty, "Yeah, I'm feeling a lot better today. You're sweet for checking up on me."

"I just had to make sure." His voice is starting to lose its twinge of concern.

"Thanks, Jack, I don't know what came over me." It wasn't a lie, but she still felt guilty telling him.

"Good," he whispers almost to himself, "Good. I'm glad you're better."

That's when Sera gets the feeling Jack sounds a little too relieved, almost like he knows something she doesn't. Or a worse thought, maybe he is the one responsible for it.

"Jack—" she starts.

"What are you doing tonight?" he interrupts. "I'm sorry,

what were you going to say?"

"Oh, nothing—never mind. Amanda and I are going to Chaos, that new club in the city. You know, the one with all the posters plastered everywhere."

"Oh, my friend mentioned something about that place, maybe we'll see you there?"

"Yeah, maybe. Well, I have to start getting ready..."

"See ya."

Sera hangs up the phone and lies back on her bed. There's just too many things going on with her now, she doesn't want to add boys on top of that.

Sera allows herself to take her time while getting ready. She scoured her closet for the hottest outfit she could find. After about an hour of trying stuff on, she finally finds something that fits her mood—naughty. Of course, Amanda bought her the shirt last Christmas. The tags are still dangling from the sleeve. The old Sera would never have worn something so, revealing.

After coming to a decision on the outfit, she takes a straightening iron to her naturally wavy hair so that it falls down her back. Digging deep into her drawers, she pulls out her makeup; liberally applying more than she's normally comfortable with. Dark eyeliner coats the top of her lids and lavender shadow makes her hazel eyes pop with color. It takes a few seconds for her to recognize herself in the mirror. Amanda was right, who is this new person?

The icing on the cake is black knee-high boots. Sera

zippers into the boots before grabbing her little black clutch off the dresser. She takes the time to admire herself in the mirror. A glimmer of her neck brings her attention downward. Her necklace. It just doesn't seem to fit the outfit. Her fingers reach up to the clasp behind her neck. It takes a deep breath before she unclasps it and places it down on her desk. Without it, she feels slightly naked. She debates putting it back on when her phone chimes again breaking her out of her thoughts. She has to go. Instead, Sera grabs the necklace and stuffs it in her tiny little clutch.

Stealing one more glance into the mirror, she smiles at her reflection before heading out of the house for the night.

Pulling her car up to Amanda's apartment ten minutes later, she runs up the three flights of stairs and lets herself in with her key. She finds her closest friend in the bathroom still applying her makeup, typical Amanda, on her own time clock. Amanda's jaw (and eyeliner pencil) drops when she turns to greet her. Her dark eyes look her up and down, starting from the knee high boots, up her tight skinny jeans, and finally the low cut black shirt. Sera gives her a little twirl while she finishes her assessment.

"You like?" Sera playfully pushes Amanda in the arm. Amanda continues to take in her long, auburn hair framing her face which is accentuated with dark eyeliner and lavender shadow making her eyes appear jade green tonight.

"Wow, I thought you were losing your mind on the phone, but this—" Amanda points to all of Sera. "This? Who would have thought there was a major hottie in there this whole time? And…" She takes a step forward. "She even appears to be a little slutty." Her finger drops to Sera's low cut shirt.

"Hey, you bought me this shirt!"

"Exactly, takes one to know one." She winks at me. "Wait, where's your necklace?"

"I left it at home. It didn't exactly go with the outfit."

"Are you trying to show off the goodies?" Amanda bites her lip from laughing.

"Maybe." Sera shrugs."

They share a laugh before things fall quiet again. "But seriously, Sera, is everything okay?" Her face flashes with concern.

The truth is Sera has no idea, but she answers as honestly as she can, "Yeah… I just feel, *good.*" Her fingers run themselves through the length of her hair.

"Okay, good enough for me." She shrugs picking up her eyeliner pencil from the sink and finishing her other eye. "Let's go get our groove on hot stuff." She playfully smacks Sera's bum and pushes Sera toward the door before grabbing her own clutch on the way out.

$\mathcal{N}$*ine*

Chaos

THE DRIVE TO NEW YORK CITY is bursting with laughter and belting out songs on the radio at the top of their lungs. However, things quieted as they drive through Manhattan as the girls stare all about them in awe. Buildings Sera has to press her face on the glass to see and so many people wandering back and forth.

Then she notices steam spiral out of grates on the sidewalk. Trash piled so high they look like buildings themselves. She is starting to think New York City isn't all it's cracked up to be until the car finally drives into Times Square, which is lit up with probably more lights than her entire town could ever hope to power. The billboards flash and draw her eyes in. A yellow M&M waves to her as they pass and all too suddenly, the streets dim again. All Sera can do is stare. Amanda is of course, un-phased.

"Small town girls in the big city, watch out New York." Amanda hums to herself to the same tune as the song on the radio. She weaves the car through a few more turns. How she is veering in and out of lanes while avoiding the million pedestrians, Sera will never understand. The GPS keeps blaring directions and Amanda obeys every single one, even from the wrong lane. Ignoring the gasps escaping Sera and the obscene gestures she's receiving from other drivers, her best friend continues cutting people off like it was in her DNA. It's like she belongs here. Sera steals a look at her closest gal pal. Drop dead gorgeous with a what-the-hell attitude. It's a shame she was born a small town girl, when everything about her screams tough-skinned-city-chick.

Finally, the black sedan pulls up to an industrial neighborhood and miraculously, finds a spot a few feet from the brick single floor building with Chaos scribbled in green graffiti. Splotches of paint splatter around it in assorted colors.

"Are you sure this is it?" Sera turns to her friend. There's no windows, no line out front—nothing to indicate that this is indeed a nightclub.

"Yup, looks like the website."

"Oh." She finally climbs out of the car glancing about with concern. *Because, websites are never wrong.* Uneasiness settles in her stomach, something inside of her is telling her things are too easy.

She ignores her sudden unrest; this is going to be good night she reminds herself.

The bouncer gives their ID's a passing glance before allowing them entry.

Definitely too easy.

With one last glance behind her, Sera turns to the black curtain and passes through. On the other side, the club comes into view. The ambiance holds true to its name— Chaos. The whole place reeks of sweat and booze. Music thrums through the speakers above cascading down onto the dancers as they gyrate against one another. The opposite side of the club is where the huge bar lies, with mismatched stools and a bar lit up from the inside with a black light. The bottles lining the wall are also lit up from underneath, highlighting the premium bottles in ranging color scheme. Amanda begins weaseling her way to the bar.

"Are we late?" Sera screams into her ear to be heard over the music.

"Just in time." Amanda is still facing away, but Sera can still hear her with precision. Amanda continues to squeeze through two guys before turning back, "Oh, excuse me." With a push, Sera moves her forward.

They finally reach the bar swarming with patrons striving for a drink. "Is that paint?" Sera studies the brick wall beside them.

"And graffiti. Chaotic isn't it?" She shoots Sera a wink. "Ben says this place is all the rage since it opened a few months ago."

"A few months ago," Sera repeats. "You would think they'd be able to afford a mop," she mutters, picking her heel up from the sticky floor a few times.

"You don't get out much, Ser-, just live in the moment tonight, promise?"

Her big brown eyes explore Sera's. "Promise," she finally answers. *Live in the moment.* That's Amanda's way of saying leave your panties at home. The song changes and Sera's eyes dart to the DJ booth on a raised platform protected by a wall covered in graffiti. By the time she turns around again, Amanda has snuck over to two stools by the bar as a couple escapes to the dance floor. Amanda pats the smaller stool beside her.

"Why do I get the small one?"

"Because these babies." She wiggles and her new push up bra is pushed to the brink, "are the only thing getting us drinks tonight."

"You are ridiculous." Sera hides a laugh and takes another glance around. Maybe it's her first time in the big city, but her anxiety has risen. Amanda has already turned her attention to that phone of hers. No doubt texting Hot Guy #150, if Sera wasn't 'living in the moment' she would shove that piece of plastic…

"Hey, Doll." Sera glances up to the bartender's green eyes gazing at her. The bar behind him is currently green, causing an eerie feeling to creep into her. "What can I get-cha, Doll?"

Amanda finally looks up." Two Redbull vodkas please."

"Redbull?" Sera interrupts.

"*Live in the moment,*" she taunts, eyes wide.

"Oh, double trouble. For a second there I thought this

siren was alone."

"She'll never be alone," Amanda informs him, reaching over to grab Sera's hand in hers.

"I see." He turns shooting Sera a sly smile before swinging around to reach for the cans of energy drink behind him.

"Are you trying to cramp my style?" Sera asks. Amanda knows very well Sera is hopeless at flirting.

"I'm saving you. Bartenders are players."

"You sound like you know from experience."

"Unfortunately." By the time the bartender turns back around, Amanda has her credit card out. "First round is on me, *Doll*."

She turns to scan the crowd and sip her drink. Sera does the same. With one last smile in her direction, the bartender turns to help someone else. The light from the strobe lights reflect off his eyes, and for a fleeting second, Sera thinks she saw his eye blink—sideways. She blinks, hard, a few times, but he has retreated to the other side of the bar. Curiosity causes her to study him for a few more seconds. He pulls out his phone from a back pocket. His fingers fly across the touch screen. Damn, he's a fast texter. In one swift motion, his phone is back in his pocket and two drinks are in his hand.

"Hey there, can I buy you a drink?" a brown-eyed stranger intersecting Sera's line of vision asks. His baby blue collared shirt is stark against his tanned skin.

Automatically, Sera turns to Amanda who is still typing away on her phone.

"Sorry, I have one." She lifts her cup to emphasis her point.

"What's your name?" he shouts into her ear. Sera flinches. She could have heard him from two feet away.

"Sera."

"Sarah?" He leans his ear closer to her mouth.

"No, Sera with an E!" she tries again.

"Yeah, Yeah, Sarah. I'm Jon. Nice to meet you." He extends his hand out to shake hers. As much as Sera hates it when people get her name wrong, she doesn't see the point in correcting him. Sera places her hand in his.

"Nice to meet you."

"Who is your friend, Sera?" Amanda becomes suddenly interested in the handsome guy next to her.

"This is Jon. Jon—this is Amanda." After introductions, he returns his attention to Sera, whispering more questions into her ear.

Amanda pats Sera on the back. They exchange a glance that tells her all she needs to know. Amanda scoots off the stool, heading for the door to meet someone. Sera watches her friend's retreating back reluctantly. There's nothing wrong with Jon, he's actually super cute, but flirting always makes her uncomfortable. He's asking her something else.

"What?"

"I said—"

Someone comes up on the other side, "Hey Angel." A blond haired, blue-eyed Adonis slips next to her. His arm wraps itself around her shoulders. Her eyes stare down at it before looking up to meet his cocky gaze, completely awed at his forwardness. Awe is probably the wrong term—she's more like disgusted.

From a small town, you don't tend to encounter these problems. A guy knows if you catch him acting inappropriately, everyone will know about it by breakfast the next day. Good luck to him getting a date ever again. Sera's definitely not used to this kind of attention.

"Hi." The rudeness is implied as she picks his hand up between two fingers and moves it off her.

"What are you drinking, Red? Let me get you a new one." His confidence never waivers. Who does this guy think he is? He waves and in one second, the green-eyed bartender stands in front our strange trio.

"I have a drink." Dismissively, Sera turns back to Jon. Jon's appears shocked as well. Apparently, even this is not a city thing.

The blond beside Sera takes the drink between her hands and throws it back with one gulp, slamming it down on the counter.

"Not anymore, Red." He smirks before turning to the bartender, "Two of the specials." The cocky stranger and the green-eyed bartender exchange a creepy laugh.

"What the—"

"Hey, bro, Sarah and I were talking here."

"So, Red, what brings you here?" His eyes focus on her, completely ignoring Jon like he's not even on his level.

"Stop calling me that."

His fingers twirl around the tips of Sera's red hair. "I mean, I'm not complaining, but you're a little far from home."

"How do you know?" He never responds. His head slides from side to side like a cobra ready to strike his prey. The green-eyed bartender places two strange fizzy drinks before them and shoots her that weird wink again.

Don't drink that.

A strange fizzy green drink? Sera wouldn't drink the concoction if you paid her. It doesn't take a rocket scientist to tell they are laced with something. "No thanks. I may be from far away, but I'm not an idiot," she responds, pushing the drink to the side.

Jon tenses beside her. Sera gets the feeling this obnoxious guy isn't a guy to mess with. From the blackness of his pupils, to the way his fists clench itching for a fight. She turns to say something to Jon, something to get him out of the line of fire.

"Sera here, was drinking with me." Jon is pushing between the blond and Sera—wrong move. Even she can see that.

"Not anymore, *bro*," the blond emphasizes the sarcasm, not yet losing his cool. He's creepily calculated, and she can't shake his eyes no matter where her eyes turn. When Jon dives in-between them, Sera takes advantage by sneaking away. She continues to press through the crowd trying to become anonymous with the random gyrating bodies. Her eyes scan the people she passes; Amanda isn't one of them. Fighting the burning curiosity, she weaves her way to the glowing sign for the restrooms.

A dark, creepy hallway opens up before her. For once, the girl's restroom doesn't have a line. Actually, the hall is completely void of people; even the music is a distant beat, almost like she has entered a bubble of some kind. Her hand reaches out and grabs hold of the restroom door. She begins to lower the handle when something pushes her against the door, forcing their way inside *with* her.

The door clicks shut behind her, and she whips around to see the aggressive blond leaning against the door.

Get out of there.

Her eyes are dark, nervously glancing around, inspecting her surroundings. No other doors, no window, in this three-stalled grey-tiled bathroom. His eyes finally meet hers, and she hides a gasp. They flash full of desire and determination.

"You left me with your boyfriend, Red." He sounds disappointed, like she had somehow let him down. He approaches her slowly, a lion stalking its prey.

"He's not my boyfriend."

As her anxiety rises, so does her lack of sense. Her stomach twists inside of her as he grows closer and closer.

"Oh good, then you won't mind that I bruised up his pretty face."

A slick smile spreads its way across his perfect face. Under the light, he's no longer as attractive as she had thought. It's almost as if he's wearing someone else's skin. His skin is taunt, pale, and wrinkled around his throat.

If this guy could beat up a grown man, what could he do

to her? With every approaching step he takes, Sera takes one step backward until finally she is out of room and is pressed up against the hard cold tiled wall.

"I don't know why I'm so attracted to you." He licks his lips as his neck does that cobra motion again. "There's something about you. I want to kiss you and kill you at the same time."

"I guess it's my *aura*." The sarcasm sneaks out of her before she can help it.

"Yes, your aura," he comments with another lick across his lips. Only then does she notice his tongue appears forked. His long, thin fingers reach for her. Sera flinches as he brushes her hair over her shoulder. Leaning in closer, he does something she doesn't expect—he smells her.

"You even smell delicious."

Completely freaked out, she finally has enough sense to push him off. "The feeling is *not* mutual." She only succeeds in pushing him a few centimeters, but she comes to realize it was a bad idea when his blue eyes begin to darken. The hairs on her arm stands at attention. His pupils expand—too much. Sera can swear his entire eye turns black and soulless before she forces herself to glance away. Over his shoulder, her eyes lock with her reflection in the mirror. Surprisingly, her mirror image doesn't look scared. Disgusted, but not afraid. That tells her all she needs to know.

"I will have you, Red, whether you like it or not." His eyes meet hers once again. They have returned to blue, almost like he had to collect himself. "But, I promise you'll like it." His smile is sly as he insinuates God-knows-what.

"See, aggressive guys aren't really my thing." She has to bite her lip to shut herself up.

"Well, Angels aren't really my thing, but I'm willing to try anything once." *What is with his nicknames?* His finger lightly traces a path down her shoulder. Sera's eyes fly immediately to his touch, something about it repulses her.

"No means NO, pal!" Her anger flares and she clenches her fists against his rock hard chest in an attempt to keep some space between them.

"I don't think you understand, Red, I'm no *Angel*, and I take what I want." He pushes her hard against the wall. His blue eyes meet hers once, and a toothy grin spreads across his lips before he leans in and starts kissing her neck. Those long fingers of his begin winding their way down her curves.

Sera squirms under his touch. "Stop!" she screams repeatedly, but he doesn't even acknowledge her. Her anger rises; frustration pushed to the maximum level as she struggles to hold back the rising tears. In a last ditch effort, she gathers all the strength that she can muster, and with one swift motion, she pushes him.

Sera blinks. She has to blink again to focus on the sight before her. The cocky blond stranger hangs unconscious, slumped over the sink which has broken in two at the impact. The mirror above shattered all over him and the floor. Water even seems to be spraying out from the broken pipes making its way to her patent leather boots. *Did I do that?* She stares at the crater his body has created in the cracked tile. Her cell phone chimes to life. Sera snaps back to reality realizing she is just standing there staring at the man's wide-mouthed. She needs to get out of here before he wakes up. She spins on her heels and dashes out of the room only to run smack into Jack.

"Sera!" Jack's happiness is evident all across his face. "I was looking all over for you. You weren't picking up your phone." He pulls the phone from his ear and puts it in his pocket.

"Sorry, I was in the bathroom." Her head nods behind her; Jack notices the tension around her as she tosses her weight from side to side glancing at everything and anything but Jack's curious eyes.

"Sera, are you okay?"

"Yea, I'm fine." Her eyes continue to avoid his. She needs to get him away from this door. She definitely doesn't want to be around when that guy wakes up.

"I don't believe you."

Damn it, Jack. He reaches around her and opens the bathroom door before she can stop him. "No, Jack!" Sera's hands reach for him, but he's already snuck inside. Her hands run through her hair searching for excuses, "I can explain…"

"There's nothing in here. I don't get it. You look like you saw a ghost or something."

Speechless and unbelieving, she pushes around him and peers behind the bathroom door. The blond creep has vanished. The sink and wall is completely untouched. The floor is spotless—well as spotless as a nightclub bathroom can get. What the hell is going on?

Sera wanders back out into the hallway and stares at the faces before her. The hallway is buzzing with activity, the music is blaring again. Her eyes scan the area around her, her body automatically on the defensive expecting retaliation.

"Sera?" Jack pops up in front of her, his face ruffled in concern and confusion.

"I need to find Amanda."

He nods, linking her hand in his before guiding her through the crowd to the glowing bar. As they continue forward, Sera can't help but study the faces of the people they pass. She has a feeling the blond isn't going to let her go that easy.

Amanda's slender back comes into view, sitting in front of the bar. Beside her sits a man with a baseball cap on. Her body relaxes, finally. Sera slips into the small stool beside her friend and Jack stands by her other side. For some reason, Sera feels safer with Jack beside her.

"Hey girl!" Amanda slurs smacking her on the back. "I was wondering where you went." Her eyes wander over to Jack. "Hey, sexy Jack," she says and grabs his hand.

"Hi Amanda." He hides a smile before slipping his hand out of hers and wrapping it around Sera's waist. "How are you?"

"Drunk!" she responds, giggling. "Where is your drink, Sera? You need to catch up!" she teases, tapping her finger against her empty glass. She could certainly go for a drink right about now. Jack leans forward and places an order with a bartender. Sera glances up and down the bar, the green-eyed bartender has disappeared. The new bartender places two drinks on the bar, and Jack leans over to hand her his credit card.

"Don't worry about it, I still owe you a dinner remember?"

With a smile, she sips her drink and tries to get her mind to relax. As the minutes pass by, she realizes she's getting more anxious—the opposite of what was supposed to happen.

Two hours later, she's still hasn't moved from the same stool. Amanda has left her to dirty dance on the floor with the baseball-cap hunk. Sera watches Amanda twirl around to face him and wrap her arms around his neck to pull him into a drunken kiss. The encounter makes her wonder why she isn't drunk at all.

"Want another one?" Jack asks her like he can read her thoughts. She meets his gaze; his eyes are slightly hazy. She has to be the only person not inebriated in his bar. Jack has been ordering shots and drinks for the past two hours. She's pretty sure they must have exceeded his credit card limit by now. So, she shakes her head in the negative. There's no point, apparently being immune to alcohol is another strange addition to the onslaught of other symptoms.

Jack is once again drunkenly talking about how pretty Sera looks tonight, but she allows her mind to wander. Her eyes gaze out across the club. Everything appears clear even with the lights dancing over people's faces. Every shape, every crease in their face, and even the sweat beading along their brow as they bump and grind on the dance floor is crystal clear. Through the sea of faces, something catches her eye. As the crowd parts, she can spot those piercing, blue eyes that make her knees weak every night. His chestnut hair glistens when the strobe lights hit his face. It's *him*! Sera stumbles to her feet. Her amazing eyesight can just barely make out that he's wearing all black making those eyes of his a major statement. She scrambles out of her stool and leaves a still blabbing Jack at the bar while she heads for the dance floor. If this is the man she's dreamed about for weeks, she has to meet him.

As she makes her way through the crowd, she loses sight of him. She ducks, pushes, and elbows her way to the center where she saw him last. Only when she gets there, she's standing there alone. Well, as alone as one could be in the center of a busy dance floor. She spins around trying to catch one last glimpse of him. Where had he gone? Did she imagine this, too? Sera suddenly wants to go home. This is no longer fun. *Maybe, it never was,* she can't help but think as she pries Amanda from the baseball cap stranger and heads out of the club.

Ten

Longest Night Ever

THEY STUMBLE OUT OF THE club arm in arm. Amanda leans over starting to tell her something before bursting into hysterical giggles.

"I guess I'm driving." That only starts another set of giggles. "That's a yes." Sera guides her over to where she could have sworn the car was. The street is completely vacant except for a few yellow taxis waiting out front. Her eyes scan the street again just in case.

Amanda laughs. "Where's my car?"

"I don't know," Sera mutters. "Stay here." She points to the sidewalk before unwrapping her arm from Amanda's and walking up to the bouncer gabbing into his cell phone.

"Do you know what happened to our car?"

"They must have towed it." He shrugs, making his muscles gyrate with the motion.

"Towed it?"

"There's no parking on this side."

"What? There's no sign here!"

"It's down there." He points to a rusted sign halfway down the block.

"Why didn't you warn us?"

He shrugs, returning to the conversation on his phone. *Jerk.* Sera turns, Amanda stands there in her tiny little dress shivering and wobbling in her heels. She has to keep it together to get them home.

"Sera? You're still here!" Jacks voice calls from behind her.

With a sigh, she spins back around, "Our car got towed."

"We can give you a ride!" he announces a little too happily.

"I don't—"

"Just trying to find the friend that drove us here." He keeps glancing around, "Short guy, dark hair, have you seen him?"

"No," she states with a shake of her head. A shiver rakes through her. Sera wraps her arms around herself.

"Crap."

"I guess we are in the same boat," she sighs, "Where do towed cars go?"

"I'm pretty sure the city has an impound lot."

"Great, let's get a cab." Sera wanders up to one of the yellow cabs sitting out front. Leaning in the open window she tells the driver they need a cab to the impound lot.

His dark eyes squint. "How many?"

"Three."

His eyes hold her gaze as he waves the trio inside. She shivers again.

"Amanda, come on. We are going to get your car."

"Okay." Amanda prances toward the cab on her tiptoes and slips around to the other door. Jack motions Sera to slide in first. Sandwiched between her two friends, the cab driver takes off through the city. The cab reeks of food and garbage. Sera has to hold back bile as she turns to Jack.

"Can we open a window?" she mutters leaning toward him.

"It's cold out there." He turns to face her now, his breath hot on her cheek.

"The smell doesn't bother you?" Her face scrunches with her words.

"What smell? That's just the city." Jack waves her off, returning his attention to the window. Sera returns her focus to the cab driver. He's wearing a hat which casts a shadow over his eyes. His gloved hands twist on the steering wheel.

Sera's eyes glance out the front window, the sights around her no longer vast and impressive, just unfamiliar, and a reminder that they are far from home. The cabbie turns around to strum up some conversation.

"Where are you guys from?"

"Outside the city," Sera mumbles.

"Angelica," Amanda answers like she's in school. Sera nudges her to shush.

"Angelica, huh?" His eyes meet Sera's in the rearview mirror. She gets a gut feeling that telling him was a bad idea. The car zooms around, weaving through traffic. The driver never seems to step on the brake. His head swivels toward the back seat. "What brings you into the city tonight?"

"A little *chaos*," Jack jokes, still staring out the window. Sera doesn't miss the color in his face fading.

"Yes, chaos." The driver smirks, returning his eyes forward. They flick once again to the mirror. Sera squirms in her seat, rubbing shoulders with both her friends. Those eyes... she needs to get out of this car.

The longer the car continues weaving in and out, the more her stomach fills with something other than queasiness—anticipation. She's getting that sixth sense that something is off.

The cab screeches to a halt outside the impound lot, finally.

"Thirty-six, fifty," The cab driver turns to announce.

"Thirty–six, fifty!" Sera gasps.

Amanda is the first out of the car. Jack lingers, tossing Sera a twenty-dollar bill, slipping out as well. Digging through her wristlet for some money, she pulls out another twenty before glancing up. When she looks up, his face is watching her intently.

"Here you go." She attempts to hand him the money— he doesn't take it. His eyes still study her. "Um..."

"You're a ways from home."

"Excuse me?"

RUN. The little voice inside her says.

The temperature in the car drops a few degrees; her skin prickles with electricity again. The driver opens his mouth to speak, but words never seem to come. Instead, Sera watches in horror as black and blue beetles cascade from his mouth. They fall into the seat in front of him. Their hard shells clack together. The driver's arm suddenly starts to wiggle, his gloves clench to a fist as it shapes itself into something—a tentacle. It extends for her as the beetles begin to topple over into the back seat. They climb over each other trying to get out the open door. Sera snaps to attention, slamming the door shut just as the tentacle lurches forward. The suction cups on the underside pressed hard against the window between them. She can faintly hear the popping sound as he pulls it off the glass.

Sera spins to run toward the gate when she spots a lone beetle trying to escape on the sidewalk. She stomps her heel through it, squishing it until blue goo oozes from its sides. When she looks up again, the cab is gone.

The tall entryway looms above them. Taller than all three of them combined with barbed wire wrapped on the top. Sera stands beside her two friends. Police officers run back and forth, while others sit in their parked cars ready for action. A night in New York City, one never knows what they are in for.

"Are you two just going to stand there all night or are we going in?" Amanda calls over her shoulder as she wobbles slightly on her heels heading through the open gate.

"Yeah, let's go." With one last glance at the street, Sera heads into the impound lot. Once through the gate, they veer toward the building marked Office. The line at this time of night is longer than she expected. Everyone before them is in various states of dress, most in heels and dresses, sparkles shimmer on the floor, and one guy looks to be in his pajamas. Then there are the tourists, no doubt trying to get their rental cars back.

"I'm going to sit." Amanda points to an open chair in the corner, leaving Jack and Sera alone, again.

She uneasily shifts her weight from foot to foot. She had just left Jack to peruse the dance floor for a figment of her imagination. He hasn't mentioned it making her feel even worse about it. She struggles to find the words to break the deafening silence, but nothing seems to come.

"Well, tonight was fun," Jack tries.

"Yeah, it was different. Not usually my scene though."

"Oh, thank God—mine either." He smiles, his eyes having a hard time focusing on her face.

"Really?" Jack is young, it just doesn't match his fun, easy going image. Sera finds it hard to believe he doesn't have a party side.

"Yeah." His hand does that adorable thing when he scratches the back of his head. "Places like that make me… uncomfortable."

"Oh."

"Plus, I usually have to open the shop at six in the morning it doesn't leave much time to socialize."

"I'm sorry, Jack, you have to be at work soon."

"Don't worry about it, I already made a call."

"Good, good. Wouldn't want to deprive people of their coffee—might start a revolution."

"Wow, your jokes just get worse and worse as the night goes on."

"Ouch! A little harsh there." She smacks his arm playfully. "In my defense, I'm a little sleep deprived." Starving also, but she'll raid the fridge when she gets home.

"I'm just kidding, Sera. I feel like I've known you forever. Is that weird?" His eyes get a second of clarity as they lock with hers before he hides a laugh. "I'm sorry, that was pretty—"

"No, it's okay, Jack."

"Next!" The cashier calls and Sera slowly realizes he means her. Wow, when did that happen? She and Jack make their way up to the counter. The beady eyed cashier eyes them wearily, must be a long night for him. He taps Amanda's license plate number into an ancient computer. We're talking old—before the computer mouse was invented. He hits the enter key a few times.

"That'll be five-hundred dollars, for the ticket and the tow."

"What?" Sera's mouth drops open.

"I have—"

"No, Jack, it's fine." Sera glances over at a sleeping Amanda in the corner. There's no way her best friend can afford this on top of her school tuition payment. "I'll take care of it."

Without further thought, she pulls out her credit card from her black clutch and hands it to the cashier. She winces as he swipes it, but she never tells him to stop. When it comes to the people she cares about, she's willing to do just about anything. Besides, Sera was only going to blow it on clothes anyway.

She gets handed a receipt and directed to line up outside. Jack has the honor of waking sleeping Amanda, who almost takes a swipe at him. Then they all file outside and wait.

A long golf cart appears with the police emblem scrawled on its side. Everyone in line seems to pile in quietly. The patrolman attempts to crack jokes that just go unappreciated at this hour. The entire cart looks like a bunch of zombies. Sera's tired head lolls onto Jack's shoulder. He welcomes it, placing his arm around her. She's too exhausted to care. Those hazel eyes of hers scan the lines of lines of parked cars they pass on their way through. There's so many. The cart stops to let off the Japanese couple. They retreat to their car and Sera hides a smile when she notices the rental logo on the back bumper.

In the corner of the lot, a street lamp flickers drawing her attention. The corner goes dark, and when it flickers on again, a familiar figure takes shape. For a millisecond, Sera can make out those eyes and his offensive stance. The blond man. Her heart pounds as she sits up from Jack. The light flickers on and off and he's gone. Her heart hammers against her ribs and her head swivels from side to side. *He's here.*

The entire time the cart winds its way around the lot, slowly losing a passenger or two at a time, until it is just the three of them left. The cart swivels to the side as Amanda's black coupe comes into view.

The lamppost hangs over her two-door car drenching it in light, almost protectively. Amanda is the first inside diving into the back seat and nestling herself across it. Sera thanks the poor patrolman stuck with the graveyard shift before following in her footsteps.

"Are you sure you're okay to drive?" Jack is suddenly at her side again.

"Yeah, I'm fine." It's the God's honest truth. She isn't impaired at all.

"Oh thank God," he lets out a breath, "Because I've been seeing two of you."

She stifles a giggle. "It's okay, Jack, climb in." They split going to their respective sides of the car. Opening the driver's door, she takes one last glance around before slipping inside.

The drive home was a chorus of snores and groans. Even with the serenity of the car, she couldn't stop her heart from racing. Her eyes find their way to the rearview mirror every few seconds. By the time Jack directs her to his apartment in a complex by the park, her eyes have begun their scanning again.

The complex is dark, even with the sky beginning to brighten with the coming day. The circular dead end is quiet, vacant. People tucked away in their beds like Sera should be.

"Thanks for the ride…" Without further warning; he

leans forward placing his lips to hers. This time, it was quick, fleeting, but it still left her surprised when he slipped out of the car, leaving her to stare after him. He stumbles once on the stairs before he fumbles with his keys in the door and lets himself inside. Sera shifts the car back into drive and spins back around leaving Jack's house far behind. It's been a while since she's shared a kiss with anyone else, but deep inside she knows she's supposed to feel... more. There's no butterflies, no excitement, when Jack kisses her she feels... nothing.

It only takes a few more minutes before she arrives at Amanda's brick apartment building. One peek in the back seat tells her she's going to be staying the night.

"Morning sunshine!" she calls, shaking her best friend.

"Mm," Amanda mumbles rolling over.

"Come on, we are home."

"I want cheese fries."

Sera has to admit that sounds pretty good about now, "How about some toast?"

"Okay," she grumbles scooting out from the back seat. "I love you Sera... you're always there for me."

"I know, babe. Come on, let's get you up these stairs."

"Race ya!" She giggles swinging open the vestibule door and running up the three flights of stairs.

"In these heels?" Sera calls after her, but there's no use. She makes it inside before having to peel out of her knee high boots and runs up the stairs after her friend. She finds Amanda on the third floor sitting against her front door.

"What happened?" Sera can't hide her laughter.

"I can't find the keys." Her hands slap against the floor.

"That's because I have them." Sera's hands dangle them for emphasis.

"Oh good. Let's go to bed."

Leaning over Amanda's slouched form, she gets the key in the door, and it swings open causing Amanda to fall inside. Both girls giggle uncontrollably.

"Come, time for bed." Sera hooks her arms under Amanda's and lifts her up with one motion. "Damn, you're super light. Have you been losing weight?"

"It must be from all my *extracurricula*r activities."

Sera's mouth quirks to the side, "It must be."

Amanda gets her feet under control, hobbles the rest of the way down the hallway, and falls face first into her bed.

"Goodnight, Sleeping Beauty!" Sera carefully places the garbage can by the side of the bed and twists her head to the side before closing the door behind her. Stealing a blanket from the linen closet, she makes herself at home on the pullout couch that is practically labeled as hers at this point. After the long night she's had, she's really looking forward to seeing that mystery man of her dreams. Within seconds, as hoped, she's transported from this world.

Eleven

Dreams become Reality

SERA'S ARMS ARE PUMPING. *Her heart racing as her legs struggle to get away. A small town is zipping past her, she glances around, nothing looks familiar. Her legs can't go fast enough, because she can feel it gaining on her. Something is chasing her, something big. A brick building labeled General Store with a large bush out front comes into view ahead of her. She whips behind it, hiding with her back against the brick wall. Her lungs struggle to catch her breath, but her fear is winning. A cold wind bristles through the bush causing her to take off into a run again. She's attempting to navigate through the narrow cobblestone streets of the strange town, but she can't seem to find a place to hide. It seems like no matter where she turns it knows. It's as if it could feel her. She can't explain it, but she knows it's going to catch her. No matter how fast she runs, the darkness seems to match her speed. Rounding another corner, her eyes* meet his. He stands there waiting for her, like he does every night in her dreams, his blue eyes gleaming at her approach. Sera opens her mouth to scream for him to move, but the words are stuck in her throat. He stands his ground, even when she begins to wave her arms. Instead, his hands outstretch for her pulling her to him.

Her arms reach for him, too. They extend trying to push him out of harm's way, but to her surprise, he pulls her into a warm embrace. His strong arms lift her swiftly and place her behind him.

She chances a peek around his back. The cloud of darkness quickly approaches creeping across the cobblestones like morning fog. He never falters, his feet planted firmly in the middle of the street. Sera stands there amazed. How could he be so confident? Can't he feel what's coming? The stranger's arms rise out forming the sign of the cross. He seems to be… glowing. A flutter of wind tickles her cheek. Surprised, she topples backward onto the cold stone street staring up at his back. It's unlike anything she could have ever imagined, before her stands the man of her dreams, and he has sprouted wings. Huge, white, glorious wings extending from the V of his shoulder blades past the tips of his fingers. Her fingertips extend, too, reaching out to them, when her attention is drawn elsewhere. The glow around him increases, slowly at first, but before long, it envelops him in light. The light being strongest at the palm of his hands, but it surrounds him like a bubble. All at once he draws back and pushes it forward. The bubble of light forms a shield of some kind gliding across the street, meeting the darkness creeping upon them. The darkness *retreats, shriveling behind the curtain of light until neither are seen again. The blue-eyed stranger turns to her, still lying on the ground, his wings retreating back into his torso. He extends his arms to help her up.*

Sera hesitates slightly, finally realizing the man that visits her in her dreams may not be a man at all. Regardless, he did protect her. She places her hands in his and he lifts her to her feet again. His eyes peer down into hers trying to communicate something with her or maybe he is trying to gage her reaction to the real him. Sera opens her mouth to ask him one of the million questions circulating in her mind when hands grab her from behind. Then something covers her eyes, there's a shout from a familiar voice, and everything turns black.

OPENING HER EYES, it takes Sera a few moments to realize where she is. The shape of Amanda's living room furniture comes into view. That's right. She slept at Amanda's place last night. Rolling onto her back, she gives herself a minute to reminisce about her dream. This mysterious dream-man grew wings, angel wings. He didn't have a halo or a huge valiant sword, but he glowed with a power she felt the entire Earth react to.

"Wow." Shaking her head, she moves to her feet, bracing herself for a monster headache. One second, two, three— still nothing.

"How the hell did I get away with that?" she mumbles, tiptoeing her way down the hall to Amanda's room. She knocks once to no answer. Creaking the door open she calls, "Amanda?"

Her best friend is still face down in a pool of her own drool fully dressed, heels still strapped to her ankles. *Why do I feel fine? We drank heavily for a Rolling Stone let alone twenty-four year old girls.* What was it that Amazing Anna had said? Don't internalize, live your life? She's paraphrasing of course, but this is what she had meant. Sera decides not to dwell on the fact that the amount of liquor used to sedate an entire fraternity has no effect on her and instead focus on something productive—like maybe some work. Amanda's homework emails to her have been piling up, and she's been a little distracted. She should really get going, but first, she wants to get cleaned up. With one last glance into Amanda's room, she borrows a towel from the linen closet and takes a quick shower.

Amanda still hasn't moved an inch since she left her when she walks back into her room, although her snoring has gone down an octave. Sera takes the time to peruse her open closet. Dresses and blouses scatter the floor in front of it from last night. A sweater catches her attention, blue like the sky and soft, too. She plucks it off the hanger and pulls it over her bra; it fits perfectly.

"That looks good on you." Amanda's voice is rough, like someone who had been screaming at the top of their lungs all night. Sera turns to see her friend wiping her mouth.

"You should keep it."

"No, I'll give it back." Her eyes glance down at it again; it's the perfect hue for her complexion and hair color.

"Don't worry about it, I owe you one. Maybe two." She mutters, rolling onto her back and rubbing her head. "Now, what the hell happened last night."

"You don't remember?" Sera sits on the edge of her bed.

"Just flashes of light and the guy with the hat, and… was Jack there?"

Sera laughs, "Yeah Jack was there. We drove him home."

"Oh, did you guys…"

"Um, no, but you practically did it with the hat-guy on the dance floor. Where did you find him, Rent-a-Tool.com? Like seriously."

"He was pretty cute, from what I remember." She hides a sly smile.

"Well, you don't remember much. Let me get you some water." Sera disappears, traipsing back down the hall to the kitchen and grabbing a water bottle from the fridge.

"Where are you going anyway?" Amanda calls out.

"I was just going to read through your homework at the coffee shop."

"Oh, the coffee shop, huh?" She takes the bottle from Sera's hand before winking at her.

"It's not going to work between me and Jack."

"Why?" Her swig cut short with disappointment.

"I don't know; it just doesn't feel… right."

"Sometimes you need a little wrong." Amanda gulps

down more water before propping herself onto the pillows.

"Nah, I've spent too much time with Mr. Wrong, I'm looking for Mr. Right." Sera turns to leave.

"Well, when you find him, tell him I'm looking for him, too."

Sera turns in the doorway. "You? Ms. Promiscuous."

"Hey, you wouldn't buy the car without a test drive," Amanda screams after her retreating figure.

Sera shakes her head and grabs her jeans from last night. Shimming into the jeans, she buttons them before her fingers reach for her neck to find her necklace isn't there. Reaching into her bag, she pulls it out and places it back around her neck. She releases a breath. She didn't realize how much she missed it was back where it belonged.

"Yeah, but you don't have to test drive every car in the lot!" Sera chimes back, stealing a pair of Amanda's tan boots from beside the couch.

"Prude," she calls back.

"Whore," Sera returns in jest before adding, "I'll talk to you later, sleep it off."

"Bye, love you."

"Bye."

PULLING INTO HER PARKING spot right out front of Jack's Coffee Bean, a sigh escapes her lips. With one swift motion, she swings out of the car and waltzes inside. Finding her favorite green chair in the corner available, she plops down and pulls out her laptop. Reaching for the charger, she plugs in before getting up to head for the counter.

As soon as she lifts her head up, her eyes meet Jack's. He's behind the counter, hands in his jean pockets. His curly golden hair is a little messy, and there are bags under his eyes. The long night is apparent on him, yet there's something about the look that works.

Sera wears an awkward smile and makes her way to the counter. In an attempt to look anywhere but in his eyes, her gaze falls on his arms. His biceps flex under his shirt, as she grows closer to him.

"Hey, Jack."

"Hey."

"Listen, about last night—"

"Thank you for driving me home last night, Sera, you were a life-saver."

"Oh, it was nothing, but what I wanted…"

"It was a crazy evening. I hope you had fun, despite it all."

"Um, yeah," she lies. Thoughts of the bathroom incident and the creepy cabdriver flood her mind, and she blurts out, "Did anything weird happen to you last night? Like I think I remember some weird things… and I wasn't drunk at all."

"You weren't drunk?" he laughs, covering his mouth. "Are you sure you weren't drunk?"

"Yeah."

"How can you be sure?" he tries again.

"I saw everything clearly, and I drove us home for Pete's sake."

"You know, Sera, people who are drunk never really think they are."

"True," she admits, knowing it doesn't make sense to normal people. Thing is, Sera knows the things that have been happening to her aren't normal. Nothing about last night is fuzzy or impaired. She remembers everything with vivid detail; including the eyes of the man from her dreams, which is why she nods, dropping the conversation.

"That's when I realized—"

"Jack," Sera butts in, ignoring the fact that he is still talking. "There's something else I want to talk to you about."

He blinks. "Go for it."

She glances around making sure that no one is listening. "I… I think we should just be *friends*."

He peels back; smile fading. Even his eyes lose some of their shine. "Oh."

"I just don't think I'm ready for a relationship." She stumbles through her words and continues, "I'm just going through a lot right now, and I don't want to get anyone else involved." She saves herself from giving away too much. "I'm sorry, I didn't think, I didn't mean…"

"It's okay," Jack finally says. His hand covers hers on the countertop comfortingly.

Saving her from further embarrassment, the door chimes with the entrance of a young couple. His entire appearance changes as the two patrons arrive at the counter.

His smile returns, but Sera can feel the fakeness. It's like an actor putting on a show. "So, Sera, the usual?"

"Yes, and extra whip cream please."

"Oh, it's an extra whip cream kind of day?" He winks before his back turns and expertly crafts her latte.

"You have no idea." They share a chuckle, dispelling some of the awkwardness between them. Once he turns back around, he hands her the steaming, caramel latte with extra whip cream, and she notices some of the warmth has returned to his eyes.

Thanking him, she returns to her spot and begins checking her emails. There are only five total. Plugging in her headphones, she gets lost in the music and dives into the onslaught of Amanda's nursing homework.

A half-hour later, Sera is so deep into correcting the jumbled mess of Amanda's homework, she barely notices someone standing over her. When she finally glances up, her heart stops suddenly in her chest. The eyes looking back at her are ones that she never thought she would see again, conscious at least. They are the ones that haunt her endless dreams. The mystery man she can picture with such vivid detail, is standing before her in an exact replica of the man that makes her weak in the knees. Every. Single. Night. His eyes are warm, blue, and limitless like the deep sea. His hair falls in wisps across his forehead until he slides his hand through it. Sera swallows. His lips are moving, but her mind can't seem to comprehend anything at this point. It's like the whole encounter is happening to a soundtrack of some kind, and she can't seem to get her ears or her mouth to work. The song stops. That's when she realizes her headphones are still in her ears. Embarrassment fills her and her cheeks redden as she pulls the ear buds out.

"What?" *Awesome, Sera, very graceful.*

He smiles, his teeth forming a perfect, slick smile across his lips. "I was just asking if this seat is taken." His voice is just as smooth as she'd always dreamed it would be.

"Oh, um…" She takes a look around the coffee house, which did seem to fill up while she was deep into Amanda's mountain of work. "No, go ahead."

The stranger takes a seat in the chair across from her; the proximity of him to her is doing something different to her insides. Her heart is beating like the drums in a rock song, a strange song that only her insides can relate to. Her pulse is racing to this song as well. Her mind can't focus on anything but the fact that he looks exactly like the man from her dreams. This man has stepped out of her mind and into reality like she had always wished for. What the hell is this supposed to mean?

He pulls out a book from somewhere behind him and leans back in the chair sipping a cup of coffee. Sera can't seem to take her eyes off him; maybe she's afraid that once she does, he might disappear like always. Hiding behind her laptop, she continues her assessment. The black shirt he's wearing is the same as what she thought she had seen him in last night. His eyes, the inhuman blue that ignites the fire inside her, are just as perfect in real life. His perfect strong jawline and shapely lips from her dreams are once again on hers.

He brushes his hand through his hair again taming an unruly stray. His hair is a dark chestnut brown that's long for a guy, but not long enough for him to put behind his ears. It keeps endearingly falling onto his face. It seems he's not quite used to it yet, his fingers reach for the strand every few minutes tucking it back, only for it to fall again. A smile plays across his lips. Can he feel her eyes on him? He never lifts his gaze from his book. The book with no cover, no title, and absolutely no indication into who this guy is, or what he's all about. There's something in the mystery of him that intrigues her. It gets her heart racing in a way that she thought would never ever happen.

Breaking her out of the trance, Jack places a cup down hard on the table between them.

"Hey, Sera, thought you might like a fresh one. You look busy there." He leans on the arm of her chair.

"Oh, thanks, Jack."

"What are you writing?"

"Oh, you know the usual Amanda jumble." She reaches into her purse to pay.

"Don't worry about it, *my* girl drinks for free."

Sera glares at him. Didn't they just have this conversation? It's almost like he's doing it on purpose. As the thought comes to her, does she notice his eyes lock on the mysterious stranger. He's trying to mark his territory. The stranger doesn't even give him the satisfaction of looking up.

A faint smirk plays on his lips, but his eyes remain on the pages of his nameless book.

"Thanks again, Jack." Her tone is dismissive as she turns back to her laptop. Her fingers deftly fly across the keys, but none of the words on the screen make any sense. Jack remains for a few seconds, then finally takes the hint and returns to the counter. Sera blinks, trying to re-read what she wrote, but it is just a mess of gibberish.

"Wow, they sure are friendly over here." His eyes never glance up, but she'd know that voice anywhere—as if it were tattooed on her heart.

"You have no idea," she mumbles under her breath, but he hears and laughs.

Finally, he lowers his book and peers over her way. Shyly her gaze returns to her computer screen.

"I'm Nate," he introduces. *Nate.*

"Sera," she murmurs as he reaches his hand out for hers. The moment their two hands connect, she feels a current of fire shoot straight up her arm and into her core. From her heart, the heat spreads its way slowly, out to the edges of her body. She quickly recovers, pulling her hand away and nods in the hope he didn't catch the way that touch affected her.

"Sarah, that's a really pretty—"

"No," she interrupts, "Sera with an E, short for Seraphina." You would think she'd be used to people getting her name wrong by now. It's only been twenty-four years, but to this day, it still bothers her.

"Oh." He looks taken back.

"Sorry," she apologizes, not meaning to come off rude. Without warning, a smile crosses his face, and he shakes his head to himself, allowing his stray hair to slip back over his eye. "What?" Sera asks, desperately wanting to be a part of this inside joke.

He looks up, "Oh, it's nothing. "It's a really pretty name. Where did your parent's get it from?"

"To be honest, I have no idea."

"Do you know the history behind it?"

"No, I can't say I do."

"Well, Seraphina comes from the term Seraphim, which are the highest-ranking Angels in God's court. They are said to be fierce and brave, characterized mostly by their fiery *red* wings."

"Angels?" she snickers, but he no longer looks amused. He's serious. "Um, no. I didn't know that. I, um… I don't really like my full name, that's why I go by Sera."

"It's a shame, Seraphina is a beautiful name. You should be proud of it."

She's full on blushing now. "Thank you," she finally gets out. Surprisingly, when it comes out of his mouth, she likes it, too. It rolls off his tongue like a Spanish accent rolls the R's. It's like a dialect she's unaware of.

"So is that your overprotective boyfriend over there?" he interrupts, stopping her from recounting his voice saying her name.

"Who?" she looks up, "Oh, Jack? No, we are just friends."

"Oh." He smiles. "Does he know that?" They both glance

over to notice Jack glaring at their interaction, while he pours someone's coffee.

"I thought so. We just talked about it less than an hour ago," she mentions, returning her gaze to Nate.

"Well then, Sera with an E, what are you tapping away at over there on your computer?"

"I'm just correcting a paper for my friend."

"Correcting? It sounds like you're writing it for her." He smirks.

"Well," she says, hiding a laugh, "It needs a lot of work."

"Your friend or the paper?" The smirk turns into a wide grin, like he knows something.

"Both." She returns his smile. "My friend, Amanda, has been trying to get through nursing school. It's been her passion for years. However, she's not a school person. So, I'm just helping her out."

"That's very nice of you. I admire that in a person."

"What exactly do you admire?"

"It's the culmination of everything, the loyalty/love/ friendship/encouragement/willingness to forgo your needs for theirs. They are all admirable traits."

"Wow, uh, thanks." Just when she thinks her cheeks couldn't get any redder, they do.

"Anytime, Sera." He keeps saying her name like he's trying to remember it. Maybe she was too harsh in correcting him.

"So, what about you? What brings you here?" She dives into questioning this mysterious man, desperate for more.

"I'm just catching up on some reading." He lifts his book

for emphasis.

"Are you from around here? I've never seen you before," she implores further.

"I've just moved here from up north." He smiles indicating his answer is another inside joke before sitting up in his chair and leaning closer toward her. "Your chest is—blinking."

"Wha—" Before the rest of the word has escaped her lips, she glances down to notice her vial-necklace nestled under her sweater slowly pulsing an eerie white color. "It's never done that before," she mutters, slipping it over her head and into the palm of her hand.

"What kind of necklace is that?" He hovers over the table to get a closer look. Sera glances up at him, his face is millimeters from hers. His scent lingers, reminding her of Christmas—pine, and maybe something else. His eyes return to hers when she allows the necklace between her fingers to slip into her bag. She becomes entranced by his blue eyes. She thought they were beautiful at night, but the way the afternoon sun currently glimmers off of them shows that they are breathtaking.

A phone begins to ring, breaking their eye contact. She blinks, and he leans back into his chair. "I think that's your phone." He points to her bag on the floor.

"Oh." Flustered, she pulls it out from the pockets of her purse. "Hello?" she answers.

"Sera, I'm dying." Amanda's hoarse voice on the other end informs her.

"No, you're not. Just drink the water I left you."

"I did. I tried to get up for more, but the room's spinning, and I almost puked."

"You might feel better if you do."

"How long are you going to be?" She coughs dramatically.

"Well, depends on how badly you need this homework." Hopefully, she needs it really bad, Sera would love an excuse to stay here just a little longer.

"Homework can wait, I need my friend." Amanda knows just what to say to get to her. "And I want a bacon, egg, and cheese."

Sera laughs, dispelling some nervous energy when she realizes Nate's blue eyes are still on her. "A bacon, egg and cheese? I thought you felt sick."

"Bacon cures everything."

Sera chuckles again. "Okay."

"You're the best, Sera."

"Yeah, yeah, I'll be right there." Sera clicks the phone off, placing it on the table and closes her laptop. "I have to go. My friend is sick."

"Sick?" His face calls my bluff.

"Okay, she's totally hung over, but I have to help her." Placing her laptop back in her oversized purse, she glances over at him one last time. *Damn you, Amanda.* She hoists her bag onto her shoulder and climbs to her feet. He hands her phone back.

"I took the liberty of entering my phone number."

"Oh, that was fast." She places the phone in her back

pocket and pauses, hesitant to actually leave. They stare at each other for a moment. His perfect blue eyes peering up at her willing her to stay longer. Is she seriously going to drop the mysterious guy she's been dreaming about for months to care for her friend? Of course she is, that's just what Sera does. "Okay, well—bye."

"I-will-call-you," he states. The sentence sounds rehearsed.

She smiles, the blush heating her cheeks. "Good bye." With that confirmation, she finally gets the courage to leave the man of her dreams in the coffee house. She glances back only once before opening the front door. His gorgeous eyes still follow her.

SERA WALKS INTO Amanda's apartment with a few bags, shuffling her way inside. "Sera! Is that you?" Amanda screams from down the hall.

"Yeah," she responds, wiggling around to shut the door behind her.

"I'm dying." The background noise sounded like she threw a pillow.

"You're so dramatic." She walks into the bedroom placing the bags on the floor. "Do you know I had to leave a very hot guy at the coffee house for you?"

"Jack?"

"Uh, no." Sera looks away.

"Oh?" Amanda looks intrigued now.

"I told Jack we are better off as friends."

"And you already met someone new? Do tell!"

She props a pillow up, leaning back, waiting. Sera pulls out a gigantic bottle of water and a bacon, egg, and cheese on a sesame seed bagel (her favorite).

Amanda's eyes go wide. "Oh my God! I love you!" She tears open the foil and has half of it in her mouth before Sera can begin.

"Well, some handsome stud sat across from me as I was doing your homework."

"Fixing," she butts in.

Sera raises an eyebrow, "Doing," she repeats. "Anyways, we just started talking and then exchanged numbers."

"No." Her mouth gapes open, showing half eaten egg.

Sera glances away. "Can you at least *try* to be a lady?"

"Okay." She snaps her mouth shut.

"So, yeah. He said he'd call me."

"Ah, my little Sera is all grown up getting digits and stuff. I have taught you well, my student." Amanda nods to Sera.

"I am older than you."

"You may be older, but I have more experience."

"Work experience?" Sera gets out between giggles.

A phone chimes, breaking them out of their laughter. Amanda immediately dives for her phone; lord only knows who may be calling her. With a roll of her eyes, Sera takes a bite of her bagel.

"Its not me." Amanda almost sounds disappointed.

"Hmm," Sera mumbles, pulls her phone out of her back pocket, and sits back down. The screen lights up with a text message. Her heart practically stops when she sees the caller ID. "TheGuyFromTheCoffeeHouse."

"Well, who is it Sera?" Amanda smirks, noticing the way Sera's eyes are wide.

"It's the guy from the coffee house." Sera half laughs.

"Ooo, isn't he desperate."

Ignoring Amanda, she unlocks the screen and opens the message:

Hey Sera with an E, it's Nate from the coffee house. I think you left your necklace here.

Sera blinks, reading the text over and over again. Her necklace? She thought she had put it away. She practically jumps up to snatch her purse and empties the contents all over Amanda's bed.

"What's going on? Sera?"

"Shh," Sera hushes her as her hands explore the folds and pockets—it's not there. Her fingers fumble over the keys as she texts him back. *Oh my, really? I must get it back!*

Her necklace has been a part of her since she was eighteen; she can't bear to part with it. She needs that necklace back.

I took it with me. We can arrange to meet up if you would like.

With a smile Sera replies. *Okay, sounds good.*

"You're killing me with suspense, what are you smiling

about?" Amanda brings her back into reality.

"Oh, it's the guy from the coffee house. I left my necklace, and he wants to meet up to return it."

"You left your necklace? Nice one, I have to give it to you, that was smooth."

"I didn't do it on purpose," Sera justifies and takes another bite of her bagel, she happened to be a little distracted.

"Sure." Amanda rolls over cuddled onto her side, shoving the last of the breakfast sandwich into her mouth. "Thanks for breakfast, it hit the spot."

"Anytime. Now get some sleep, we have work in the morning."

"Okay."

Twelve

The New Guy

THE DIRT CRUNCHES UNDER HER *feet deep in the folds of the jungle. The heat radiates down from above making it hard under the thick foliage to escape the singeing sun. Sweat pours down her forehead and into her eyes. She lifts a large green leaf out of her path and continues on her way. The sounds of the jungle around her are familiar, but the path she's taking is not. Actually, now that she glances downward, there doesn't seem to be a path. A jungle cat roars in the distance, the dangerously beautiful call to his prey as he no doubt pounces in for the kill. Sera ducks under a low hanging vine into a tiny clearing between four trees. Gently placed on a leaf before her is something that doesn't seem to belong; a radiant purple butterfly. It takes off into the air, wings alive with color as it soars between the circle of trees. After a few seconds, it finds its way to Sera, dancing in circles around her. Its wings tickle her ear and float across* her cheek before she realizes it's humming a tune. That's crazy, butterflies can't hum… and yet with every flap of its little wings, the melody escapes it. That melody, it's so familiar; a song that's always in the back of her mind. That song that sounds so familiar, but she doesn't know the words.

"What are you trying to tell me little guy?" She reaches her hand for it, and the butterfly spirals into a loop before spinning off through the woods. "Wait!" she calls, tumbling after it.

She follows it blindly through the dense forest, sometimes hopping over fallen trees, fighting with low hanging branches, and struggling to keep up with this stunning creature. A few times, she does lose it, but the humming always directs her back on track.

Without warning, the butterfly stops in a clearing of some kind. Sera peeks around, wincing at the blinding sun high in the sky. It appears as though she's entered an alternate universe. It's a meadow, no longer a dense jungle. It's brightly colored with flowers and thick moss.

"Oh, my," Sera whispers, eyes scanning their way over everything as she steps deeper and deeper. It's the most beautiful sight she's ever seen. The thick green moss cloaks large boulders around this meadow. To get a better view, she grabs onto the closest one and attempts to pull herself up. Her feet slip immediately. Kicking off her sneakers she tries again. This time her toes hook into little ridges of the rock allowing her to climb successfully to the top. Standing victorious atop the rock, she takes in the rest of the meadow. There are butterflies everywhere—all different colors of the rainbow and all vibrant as the sun above. They even seem to be humming the same song.

Sera draws deeper into this mysterious glorious meadow. Her bare feet hop from rock to rock trying not to disturb the flowers holding the butterflies. On her left, a pond comes into view. Lily pads litter the stagnant pond, which is host to some frogs. They croak in tune to the butterfly's hums.

This is a strange new world, she thinks as her purple butterfly comes flying up at her side once more. It swirls around her excitedly causing Sera to lift her arms before it skitters into a draping moss in front of her. Blinking a few times, she can make out that the moss is hiding something. It looks like... it's a cave. Suddenly, all the humming and croaking stops and the meadow grows eerily silent. Anticipation floods her veins; she glances around in alarm. What is going on?

From inside the cave, a snarl echoes out. The purple butterfly comes zooming out and takes refuge under the petals of a large sunflower. The ground beneath her rumbles causing her to slip to her knees. She can feel every step as whatever is in the cave is making its way out to her.

Climbing out of the cave in front of her very eyes is a huge golden dragon. She stares in shock, maybe even denial at the sight unfolding in front of her. Losing even more of her balance, she falls farther until the moss tickles her back. The dragon continues his approach roaring and snapping his jowls. Sera's eyes glance around for help, but now she is alone. All signs of the lively life have retreated. This was a trap. Gold wings extend from the dragon's back and with one final roar he jumps directly in front of her rock so that they are at the same eye level. All Sera can seem to focus on is those miraculously white teeth and how they can snap through her bones. He roars again tossing his head back, breaking Sera's intense glare. When he's facing her again, she meets his eyes. How can something so menacing have such calm, beautiful eyes?

Without thinking, her hand extends toward this creature. It's something behind his eyes, something misunderstood, and screaming for attention. Maybe if she shows him she means no harm, she can calm the beast, so to speak. The snapping of jowls stops, his roaring ceases as well, and if the meadow weren't growing silent, she never would have heard a tiny gasp—but there it was. Her purple butterfly friend peeks its head out from the yellow sunflower petal and starts to quietly hum.

Her body freezes in realization, that song wasn't meant for her. It's meant for the dragon. She faces the dragon again, now twisting his head to get a better look at her and she begins to hum the song. His neck croons closer to hear, and she clears her throat. He grows angry again before she begins, louder this time. At the sound of her full voice, the dragon calms, his wings, and teeth retract. His head shakes before he comes to a sitting position, his head the size of her body. Sera climbs to her feet continuing her magic melody. Regaining some confidence, she walks toward him with an outstretched hand. How many people can say they have touched a dragon? The way his leathery skin glistens under the intense sun attracts her. The dragon's eyes remain closed enjoying the song with delight.

She pauses millimeters from his snout; his breath hot on her palms. Eyes closed, she finally places her full palm on the side of his snout. He barely reacts until he begins to lean into her touch. Astounded, she continues to trace her hands all over his face. His skin isn't rough or hard like leather, its soft, and supple. It's golden like the sun, but when the sun's rays hit it, it glimmers. The monster allows her hands to explore him like he craves her touch. He never makes a noise, barely moves until her hand stops on the sides of his mouth. The dragon's eyes open. Blue and glistening under the sun as they peer back into hers.

Unexpectedly, the butterflies sneak out from their flowers and dance around the meadow again, their humming, a chorus with Sera's voice. This moment is something beautiful, she can't explain where the idea comes from, but she leans in and places her lips to the very tip of his nose. Another gasp echoes through the meadow. Surprised, Sera pulls back, wiping her mouth, slightly embarrassed and confused.

The butterflies take to the air around them swirling and twirling. The wind picks up her hair giving the illusion no gravity until they exclude Sera completely. Creating a tornado around the dragon, faster and faster they become a blur of colors. It grows smaller and smaller until they collapse on the ground in one lump. It's Sera's turn to release a gasp. She struggles to climb to the edge of the mossy rock to see below.

The butterflies have been reduced to nothing but faded confetti that litters the ground. In the center of the moss is the shape of a naked man. She leans closer balancing on her knees and cranes to look. The man moves. His back arches in an animalistic manner before he sits on his knees. He shakes his head from side to side and flecks of shimmering gold fall from his *dark hair. He glances behind him, their eyes meet. She knows those beautiful eyes anywhere. She gasps, losing her grip on the rock and falling face first over the rock. The one thought on her mind—Nate!*

Sera awakens with her torso on the floor and her legs still tangled in the sheets from her bed. Laying her head back against the carpet, she takes a minute to collect her thoughts. Her dreams have always been more than they appear, but, they are fantasy aren't they? Nate is not a dragon!

The alarm clock blares on, "Well, Diane, I guess we will never know." Reaching a hand under the bed, she tosses a shoe at the annoying clock. It crashes to the floor, the last thing it announces: "This week is going to be another one full of surprises."

Finding her way out of the jumbled chaos of her bed sheets, she slips out and into running clothes before making her way downstairs. She decides to stop for a bite to eat before heading out. She picks up an apple from the basket in the center of the granite island before tossing it into the air and catching it with her mouth while she stretches her quads.

"On another workout kick, I see." Her father is always one for teasing her. "I wonder how long your diet is going to last."

"Well, I have a feeling this one is going to stick." She speaks through another bite of fruit. "Plus, I'm no spring chicken anymore, I have to keep in shape." She lifts her right arm to humorously flex a muscle. Only as she does, she realizes her biceps have some definition and shape to them. Her father must notice as well because he leans in to squeeze it.

"Would you look at that, you work out one time, and get little muscles," he teases with a smile.

"Yeah, would you look at that." She smirks to hide the growing anxiety and makes a rapid escape. "Well, I'd better be off. See you later," she mutters halfway out the door.

Sera jumps down the four steps of her little blue farmhouse and lands on her feet. An owl hoots in the woods to her left. Instead of heading down the street to town, she heads left toward the wood. She hurtles over the guardrail and dashes into the heart of the trees. It's relatively quiet. Most of the animals are hibernating for the winter. All she can hear is the crunch of her footsteps in the undisturbed dirt and dried leaves under her feet. It calms her, allowing her mind to wander. Once again, questions envelope her mind dragging her deep into a vortex of unanswered anomalies. Until one singular anomaly comes to mind, *Nate*. What are the odds of dreaming about someone for months and actually running into them? This can't be a coincidence? She can't chalk this up to luck. She hides a smile and hurtles over a fallen tree. So deep in thought, she doesn't notice her phone chime to life until she spots the frightened deer hide behind a tree in front of her. Sera freezes. It doesn't run. The deer only peeks his head out, inspecting her. She refuses to even breathe because deer are so… jumpy. He's small, lightly colored, and curious.

"Hey, little guy." She tries reaching her hand out for the animal. "I won't hurt you," she adds and takes a step toward it. He doesn't move, only stares at her. "Come on." She tries again, and he seems to understand, taking a step toward her. "That's it, almost there." She watches in astonishment as the fawn makes his way to her. It's millimeters from her fingertips when her phone chimes once again. Without warning, the little deer spins and runs disappearing into the trees, never looking back.

"Damn," Sera mutters, pulling out her phone to not one, but two texts from Amanda. Apparently, there is a hot new guy starting work in their department today. She doesn't know why her friend feels the need to tell her these things. She knows Sera doesn't partake in the gossiping she and the other women insist on. With one last glance in the direction of the deer, Sera sighs and dashes back toward her house to get ready for the day.

SERA WALKS INTO WORK and finds the whole office abuzz. The elevator doors open, and she feels a dozen eyes on her. No one seems to be at their desks; they have flocked to the area between the cubicles and the elevator in little groups. When they notice it's only Sera, they continue whispering to each other.

Navigating her way through the dense crowd, she heads

for her desk. Amanda spins around in her chair, blowing on her nails. The air smells of freshly polished nails.

"Are you wearing lipstick?" Sera drops her purse down on the desk.

"Maybe." Amanda pops up a shoulder and slips her red nail polish into her purse.

"And... eyeliner?" Amanda's eyes are vibrant against her olive complexion.

"Cindy says—"

"Oh, Lord. Not this again."

"You'll be eating your words, Seraphina Cross."

"I doubt it." Sera sighs, "So, my whole speech on inter-work-relations went in one ear and out the other?"

The elevator chimes with another delivery. The third floor grows silent around her. So quiet she can make out the clank of the elevator locking into position and the swish of the doors as they open. A singular figure walks out from the elevator. He stands a head above all the ladies that have begun to crowd him. All Sera can make out is his dark features, hiding under a thick perfectly trimmed beard. He shuffles like he has something in his arms as Mrs. Valentine, our manager, greets him. This poor guy doesn't stand a chance.

"I'm going to go introduce myself." Amanda adjusts her bags and pulls her hair from behind her ears.

"I don't know why I bother," Sera mumbles, collapsing into her chair. Her desk has a cloud of spicy smelling perfume and residual nail polish remover lingering from Amanda as she heads toward the flock of women. The only men we get up here on the third floor are maintenance men to repair the ancient copier or a florescent light bulb. To have one working with us every day will be... different. Sera's checking her email when she hears Amanda's flirty tone.

"You must be Gabe, I'm Amanda. I'm in billing, so I'm sure you and I will be working pretty closely. My desk is right here, so if you ever need anything, you know exactly where to find me."

Sera peeks around the cubicle wall and struggles not to roll her eyes. Amanda stands before him, looking up with her puppy dog eyes. Sera's seen that move a thousand times. Men fall at her feet, usually. This guy only shoots her a nod. He then steps around her and continues on his way. Sera's mouth drops open while she lowers herself back into her chair. The new guy passes by her cubicle, and she gets a better look. Cindy from H.R. is right; this guy is a total hunk, but something about him makes her insides twist. Her heart rate elevates. If she had to guess, he's full-blooded Greek or Italian with his dark hair and dark eyes paired with that tan skin; too tan for New York in the middle of December. His cologne is strong and spikes her heart rate even further. In his hands, he's carrying folders, many folders. He gets a few steps past her when he pauses, sniffing the air. Maybe, he smells the nail polish remover.

Curiously, she watches as his head slowly turns back toward her desk. When their eyes meet, she can swear his pupils dilate slightly. She blinks, and he's at the entrance to her cubicle.

"Hi, my name is Gabe." Slowly, a smile spreads across his face. It looks strange on him, almost like he's not used to smiling. It's awkward.

"Uh, hi—I'm Sera."

"Se-ra," he repeats. Her name sounds weird coming from him. The fact that he got it correctly on the first try makes her slightly uneasy.

"Would you be able to show me to my desk?"

"Um," she looks around for help, but Amanda and the other women look on curiously from behind the other cubicles. "Sure, why not."

His smile deepens showing teeth, even more awkward. She climbs to her feet, wobbling slightly on nervous legs before facing him. He stands there, dark eyes studying her, before she points down the hall.

"It's this way."

He finally steps aside allowing her a millimeter of space to slip past him. Sera's shoulder brushes his chest as she does so. "It's this last cubicle in the corner." She continues down the corridor, more than happy to put some space between them. He follows her, closely. "Here it is."

Silently, he walks around her and places the files down on the empty desk. "What do you do here, Sera?" His voice is deep, calm, and calculated.

"Billing, aged accounts, insurance follow-up, appeals, that sort of thing."

"I'm in *collections*."

"I'm aware." She glances back, feeling eyes still on her.

"I'm sure we will be working pretty closely on the same cases."

"No, not necessarily," she deflects, maintaining a hint of friendliness but trying to be firm.

"You don't seem like the rest of the women here." His statement is a surprise and she takes a few seconds to respond.

"If by that you mean, am I going to fawn over you, favor you, and drool every time you walk by, the answer is no. I am not like that."

"Too bad." He winks at her—he actually has the audacity to wink at her.

"Well, I'll leave you to get settled."

"You don't have to—"

With that, she turns to leave. The office women drop their heads back down to their desks when she faces their direction. So nosey. For years she's tried not to become the subject of gossip—now she has the feeling that's not going to be the case anymore.

Sera makes it back to her desk to find Amanda once again swirling in her chair. "Soooo, what happened?" Amanda leans in.

Sera sits on the edge of the desk trying to figure out exactly that. "I have no idea."

"What did he say?" she presses.

"He came up to me and asked me to take him to his desk."

"And…"

"And I did."

"That's it, that's all you're giving me? Your closest friend? Really?"

"Amanda, there was nothing said except..."

"Except?"

"He said I wasn't like the rest of the women here."

"What's that supposed to mean?"

"I don't know. Maybe because I wasn't hobbling over everyone else to get to him."

"I wasn't hobbling." Suddenly, her nails become interesting as she avoids Sera's gaze.

"He gives me the creeps," Sera mentions.

"Good." Amanda's on her feet. "More for me." With that, she leaves Sera rubbing the goose bumps off her arm.

Throughout the day, Sera finds herself on the top of her game. It's like the first time she tried Jack's coffee. Her veins are strumming with energy and this time, her mind is so much clearer and focused. Work seems to breeze by. After her lunch break, she's even finished "correcting" Amanda's paper and emailed it back to her. She's about to head to Mrs. Valentine for more work when Gabe approaches her desk.

"Hey, Sera. Since I'm just getting the hang of things around here, is there a good place to eat?" he asks, folding his big, strong arms over her cubicle and resting his chin on top of them.

She leans back in her chair to get away from his stark cologne. "Well, there's the cafeteria on the first floor, but I wouldn't eat there unless you're really desperate." His dark eyes gleam at me as I continue, "There's a good deli down the street, or you could have pizza and Chinese delivered, but you might want to meet them in the lobby. Food has a way of disappearing around here."

He nods. "Would you like to come with me to the deli? You know, so I don't get lost."

His proximity is doing something weird to her insides again. It's a strange sensation she's never felt before, like the anticipation from a big rollercoaster drop.

"Sorry, I just got back from lunch, you can ask Amanda, I don't think she went yet. Her desk is—"

"No." he states a little too loudly, "I'm sure I will find it okay. Maybe tomorrow then?" He doesn't wait for a response before stalking off toward the elevator. Sera leans over, watching as he leaves and tries to figure this guy out. He turns around inside the elevator meeting her gaze, and without missing a beat, he winks at her. The doors close breaking her spell. This guy—whoever he is—is someone she doesn't want to mess with. She shakes her head before turning, meeting the curious eyes of Nosey Nancy. With a roll of her eyes, she leans back in her chair to stare at the list of emails coming in for the day. She skips past the three from Nancy and continues on to her past due claims and picks up the phone receiver to get started once again.

Sera is still on the phone when Amanda strolls up to her desk with her purse over her shoulder at about quarter to five in the afternoon. She waits as patiently as Amanda can by going through everything in Sera's purse, trying on her perfume, reading through her notebook, and popping the top on her lip gloss all before Sera finally places the phone on the receiver.

"Are you done going through my stuff?" Sera asks tossing her things back into her bag.

"So, Sera… I hear New-Guy-Gabe has been asking around about you." Amanda raises her eyebrows in unison a few times.

"I don't date people from work."

"But," she mutters, "I don't get it, he's such a stud. How can you resist?" she leans back trying to see him from Sera's desk.

"There's something fishy about him, and he looks like a player—you should stay away." Sera points an accusatory finger at her.

"Don't hate the playa, hate the game," Amanda announces.

"He doesn't have a chance in hell at playing games with me."

"How can you have such will power Sera? I mean he's totally gorg. How do you not swoon every time he glances in your direction?"

Sera rolls her eyes, "I don't swoon."

"You don't say. Well, I look forward to the day when Seraphina Cross finally meets her match."

"You and I both," Sera mutters.

Her best friend laughs, "Come on let's get out of here." Amanda attempts to pull her chair out for her.

"Hold on, I just need to finish this…"

"What are you? Competing for employee of the month? I think Gabe's got that covered, let's go." Amanda finally succeeds in prying Sera out of her chair. Sera turns her computer off before grabbing her purse and jacket out of the bottom drawer of her desk. She glances back at the cubicles. The top of Gabe's head can be seen over the top of his. He stirs in his seat.

"Let's get out of here," Sera announces. The two girls walk over to the elevator before the rush of the rest of the office.

"What do you think of this lipstick?" Amanda randomly asks pursing her lips.

"It's a little ridiculous for work."

"I meant the color."

"It's nice."

"It's called 'The Mistress.'"

"Oh, well then it's totally appropriate for you," Sera teases, playfully smacking her arm.

They share a good laugh before the elevator doors open. Climbing inside, Sera closes her eyes as the pulleys start to lower them. Amanda is blabbing on, knowing she needs a distraction. Amanda's chatter is background noise to Sera attempting to control her breathing—in and out, in and out, until finally the elevator clangs to the bottom. The doors open and they weave their way through the maze of patients in the lobby.

Walking down the oval driveway to their cars, Amanda

is telling Sera all about the guy from the bar and how things just aren't working out.

"Hey, Sera!" The girls both turn to see Gabe running down the driveway toward them. How did he make it down so fast?

Amanda elbows her in the ribs and she whispers, "I'll catch up with you later." Reluctantly, she lets Amanda slip her arm from hers and head to her car as Gabe approaches. His cologne hits her first, and she chokes trying to breathe through her mouth.

"Hey, would you like to grab something to eat?" he asks pointing over his shoulder to his huge truck. *Wow, this guy is persistent.*

"I kind of have plans, I'm sorry."

"Oh, okay," the disappointment on his face is apparent with his every word, "How about lunch tomorrow?"

"Uh, yeah, we'll see." She shrugs turning toward her car, "I'll see you tomorrow." Her eyes lock with Amanda's across the way. There is no doubt that she has been watching the entire interaction. Sera sees her friend mouth 'Oh my God' and Sera rolls her eyes before collapsing into her car. She starts it up and shoots her a little wave before pulling out of the spot and heading for home.

Thirteen

Accidents Happen

RIVING DOWN THE DESERTED, dark parkway toward home, it begins to rain, and she allows her mind to wander to the events of the past couple of days. Up until now, she's been trying to suppress the thoughts, but being alone once again, they creep back up on her. Her mind immediately returns to the accident and waking up the next day. The way she woke up feeling strange and lively, she doesn't fail to notice all these weird things began happening after that day. Something happened that night. Something she doesn't remember, and she's determined to figure out what it was.

Although, she can't say that she hates these new changes. She's never felt more... alive.

Only, she can't help but wonder *why*.

If her dreams have taught her anything, it's that

everything is related. Every action has a reaction, and Sera can't help but wonder what the possible repercussions of these actions could possibly be.

Her mind swirling with questions unanswered and feelings that are indescribable. However, no matter how hard she tries, the tears will not come. She wants to. She craves that feeling after a good cry when all is content and her mind can be right again, but something inside of her is preventing the tears from coming this time.

The rain pours down against the road with an anger that echoes her internal pain. The sound thrums against the car roof calming her slightly. She has to get her mind right.

Sera is so caught up in her head, she doesn't notice the rare black deer that wanders onto the road, until it's too late. Her hands struggle to whip the wheel back, to try to avoid it. Only, the deer takes a step forward. It's hit full force. The impact causes the top of Sera's head to hit the steering wheel, that's when things get blurry.

After a few minutes, she rubs her head having recovered slightly. Her chest aches from the seatbelt that kept her from flying through the windshield, and she pictures the hideous bruise she'll have tomorrow. As her mind comes back together, she realizes the air bags never deployed. Maybe she didn't hit the animal as hard as she had thought.

The rain has stopped. The ground appears dry. Slowly, she climbs out of the car. Mentally preparing herself for what she'll find, she wanders around to the front of the vehicle. As the front of the smashed in sedan comes into view she notices the deer is *gone*. There is nothing there. No animal, no blood, nothing.

Her eyes glance toward the side of the parkway. Her feet follow. There are no hoof prints in the soil. No trees with which to hide. The only solitary thing she can see is a fence separating the road from residences. She begins to get that weird feeling in the pit of her stomach again.

Something is wrong.

All the hairs on the back of her neck are standing at attention now. She can sense it, smell it in the air around her—something isn't right. She walks back to the front of her little vehicle inspecting it to make sure it's okay to drive. The air around her thickens, it becomes hard to breathe, and with a spilt second decision, she decides to haul ass out of there.

Sera is whipping around the front of the car now heading for her driver's seat when she feels as though there are eyes on her. Increasing her pace now, she has to get out of here, even if she has to push this damn car.

That's when she sees it. The growing headlights from a car flying down the parkway. There's no time to move, think, or do anything but wait for the inevitable impact. For the second time, she braces herself. Only this time... her body seems to be reacting differently. Her mind and body seem to pulse with this energy she has never felt before; an entire range of emotions surge through her. This strange sensation courses its way through her every vein, spreading its way through to her hands.

Her hands that were protectively covering her face move. They pulse harder now, like they have their own heartbeat.

Behind the pulse comes a glow much like the vial on her necklace did. It is soft at first, but then as the energy behind them increases, so does the brightness. It's bubbling up inside her ready to burst. The car is millimeters from her at this point when her hands instinctively turn outward and a power explodes out of her. Just as fast as it had appeared, it releases itself from her body.

Sera watches in awe as time seems to slow around her. The black suburban has frozen inches from her protective stance. Her senses are hypersensitive as she clearly deciphers the young driver texting on his cell phone, those brown eyes squinting and glazed over. She can smell the alcohol on his breath as if she were in the car right there with him. She can make out every inch of his skinny face and angular nose with insane precision. She wonders if she will remember this face as the man who kills her. As time continues to warp around her, she doesn't seem to comprehend that she's causing all of this. Her hands still glow with a power she has never known before. It's bursting from her glowing hands forming a shield of some sort around her. It's protecting her. She can feel that. It's just like Nate had done in her dream.

Just as suddenly as time froze it speeds up again. The truck in front of her veers around like she wasn't even there. It swerves into the left lane and zooms off down the parkway leaving Sera to stare after it. Stunned, and frankly a little exhausted, she glances back down to her illuminated hands. She stares at them until the soft glow fades back to normal.

Fourteen

The Unexpected Date

S HE COULDN'T TELL YOU HOW long she stood there in the middle of the road, or how long until she realized she was mumbling, "It was me. It was me."

Her phone chimes from inside the car, bringing her back to reality. Slipping inside, she unlocks the screen to read: *I'll be at this location tonight. Feel free to come by whenever for that necklace.*

An address is written beneath that. Sera debates going after all the strange things that have happened. Maybe she should go home and rest. She's obviously hit her head.

Instead, she climbs back into the car and straps her seat belt on before deciding against heading home. The truth is, she needs a distraction. Some freaky encounter with the deer isn't going to ruin her life. Especially not with a mysterious stranger that seemed to appear from out of her dreams.

So instead she replies: *On my way.*

Sera clicks the address underlined on her phone. The GPS blares to life computing directions already. "In three miles take Exit Thirteen."

With one last deep breath, Sera shifts the car into gear and glances in her rearview mirror before merging back onto the highway.

The anxiety in her quickly transforms into nervous excitement as the journey toward Nate continues. As if there weren't enough questions swirling around in her mind, Sera now has even more questions about the mysterious Nate. Despite it all, Sera can't help but find it all just a bit gosh darn exciting. Her foot presses harder on the gas, eager to settle the butterflies inside of her.

"Take Exit Thirteen." The GPS shrills again. Her hands twitch and she turns the wheel to take the exit. A few houses pass by her window, but she continues keeping her eyes on the road ahead. She continues for another couple miles before things start getting dark. There's no more street lamps lining the way, houses are farther and farther apart, and then she can no longer make them out. Trees. Lines and lines of trees are all she can see as the road winds.

"Turn left ahead." Sera almost misses the turn because it is so dark and overgrown with foliage. Not to mention the lack of a road sign makes it a little hard to distinguish. Her white sedan jostles her back and forth, and she pulls off the asphalt road and onto a dirt one.

"Continue two miles, the destination is on your left."

"What the —" Sera continues her trek through the dirt road. "Where the hell is this guy meeting me?"

A few times she debates turning around. After the creepy encounter with the blond in the club, she finds herself a little hesitant to meet this guy so far from home. Her hand reaches for her missing pendant before returning to the steering wheel. "I need to do this, everything is going to be fine," she attempts to convince herself. The road winds even farther before the GPS blares back to life causing Sera to jump.

"You have arrived at your destination."

"But nothing's—" Before she can finish her sentence, the trees part and a field opens up before her. A picturesque log cabin sits quaintly on the center of the clearing. The house illuminates from within. A high-pitched roof with triangular glass panels, make it clear that no one is expecting any privacy. Her car bumps under her again when she hits the gravel, causing her to close her mouth when she pulls up beside a black car parked right out front.

Sera slips out of the car and then tugs on the edges of her blouse. Only now is she suddenly self-conscious of her work clothes. Closing the car door, she climbs the three steps of the porch eyeing the wooden Adirondack chairs on either side. Automatically, her hand finds its way to her chest again only to find it bare. With renewed motivation for being at a stranger's house in the woods after dark, she reaches out to press the doorbell. The chime echoes through the whole house.

Soundlessly, the oversize front door opens. That beautiful scent of Christmas hits her again. Nate is standing in the center of the foyer as if he were waiting for her. Dressed in a white collared shirt and slacks, he peers over at her. Again, Sera finds herself tugging on her blouse. His blue eyes illuminate when they meet hers.

"Please, come in." Even his voice is smooth and velvety.

Carefully, Sera takes a step inside the threshold of this grand foyer. Above her dangles a huge glass chandelier with crystals hanging from it, reaching down to her like fingers. She takes in the expertly crafted wooden floors, walls, and a high vaulted ceiling. On the right, a spiraling staircase wraps alongside the wall and up to a second level.

"I have your necklace right here." She didn't even notice that he wasn't beside her any longer. She follows him to a room on the left. The smoky scent of a fire meets her when she enters. Before her is a cozy room. Covering the walls are floor to ceiling bookshelves. The center hosts a large brick fireplace situated around it sits a plush green couch and two chairs that look an awful lot like the one at Jack's shop.

"It's right here." He picks it up from the chain off the coffee table; extending his arm toward her.

It's like she's back in that dream again, her feet take her around the couch to him. Her vial dangles from his fingers. Her eyes flick from his back down to the vial. It does have a glimmer to it that it didn't before, but it's not glowing as it had earlier. She finally takes it.

"Thank you. I would be lost without this."

"Can I ask where you got something like that?" He settles into the couch.

She hesitates. "It was a gift," she answers before sitting on the couch beside him. Not too close, but not too far away either. The scent of the fire isn't the only thing she can smell. His scent lingers around her as well. She can't really put a finger on the scent, no matter how hard she tries.

"A gift from whom?" His tone strains, but his eyes are still warm.

"It's been so long I can't seem to remember." With all the craziness of the past few days, she hasn't exactly had the time to hunt down the origin of her favorite necklace. Apprehensively, she glances around the cozy room. "Uh, well, I should be going." Sera gets up and walks around the couch back toward the foyer.

"Wait." Nate follows her. "You must be starving coming from work, I was just about to have dinner if you'd like to join me."

With a shake of her head, she replies, "I couldn't possibly—" Her words pause on her lips as her eyes follow his outstretched finger. The entire back wall of his house is all glass. His dining room table is lit only with the moon and the glimmering stars above.

Like a moth drawn to a flame, she's enraptured by the moon, causing her to walk mindlessly deeper into his house. The back of his house overlooks a cliff. She can just make out the endless forest and winding river below.

"Do you like it?" he asks from beside her.

"Are you kidding, it's gorgeous." Her eyes never leave the vast sight ahead.

He pulls out a chair, and she sits at the small two-person table. The moon filters light down onto them like a spotlight. He carefully seats himself across from Sera as he takes the liberty to run his fingers through his hair. A silence falls over them for a second as Sera takes in the table setting before her. Candles, wine, a table set for two.

She shakes her head, "Did you do all this for me?"

This mysterious dream-man meets her eyes. They widen with surprise at first then they appear to soften. "Yeah, *all* for you."

"Thank you," she murmurs. She didn't plan on this becoming a date… and yet, it still blew Jack's attempt out of the water. She allows Nate to pour her a glass of wine and serve her his homemade food.

Throughout dinner, she can't help but glance out the window every so often. Something about this place is so… magical. While they eat, she tries prying him for more information. She must find out who this mysterious guy is and why exactly she dreams of him every night. The more questions she asks, the more vague he gets, instead, deflecting the questions back toward her. It's crazy, but if she didn't know any better, it would appear that he knew her answers already.

"So what do you do for work?" Sera tries again.

"Security," he replies, with one of his classic one-word answers. "You look like you work in the medical field, am I correct?"

Her brows scrunch, "Yes, how did you know?"

"You just look like you care a lot about people."

"Um, who do you protect to afford a home like this? Madonna? The President?"

"Oh, the house? I built it myself." He shrugs.

She shakes her head, "You mean you designed it yourself?"

"No, I built it with my own two hands." He wiggles his fingers for emphasis.

"No way." She breathes glancing around the high ceilings.

"What can I say, I had a little time on my hands between *assignments*." He responds. He's hiding something she can tell.

"Who do you work for now?"

"I'm freelance at the moment, so I take assignments on a case by case basis." Those blue eyes of his are almost smiling at her. They seem to laugh at a joke she knows nothing about. They stay suspended like that for a few seconds. The long white candlesticks between them cast a light glow over everything. The moon spotlights his chestnut hair and that smile of his temporarily dazes Sera.

Something inside of her gets a funny feeling. Different from butterflies and totally opposite of what she felt earlier with the deer. It was almost like a tug, a pull.

When she finishes eating, she quickly excuses herself to use the restroom, desperate to get her mind right before continuing this charade. Entering the bathroom, her eyes widen.

Even this room is beautiful, she thinks tapping her finger on the white marble countertop on the vanity. Like the rest of the house, the room is made from wood panels, the toilet and claw tub are all spotless white porcelain. Underneath the marble sink is intricate cabinetry and above the sink is a large oval mirror encased in a plain white frame. She had planned on texting Amanda while in here, but as she holds the phone between her hands, she can't decide how to even explain this... yeah maybe it's best she doesn't open that can of worms right now. Instead, she fixes herself in the mirror and after three deep breaths, she returns to the dining room.

Coming back to the table, she stops short. The moon casts its spotlight now on an empty table. *How long was I gone?* She slips across the dining room to the kitchen. Peeking up the three steps to the loft style kitchen, she's again met with nothing but empty counter space. Nothing in the sink and strangely, the appliances look like they've never been used.

To call her confused would be the understatement of the year. As it turns out, this isn't the weirdest thing that has happened to her this week.

A shuffle coming from the front of the house draws her attention. Sera walks back toward the foyer. Nate is in that cozy living room getting the fireplace started. He looks up as she enters and even shoots her a smile as he motions her to sit on the lush green couches. Making her way through the living room, she takes the time to admire this mysterious man. His back is broad and strong as he stokes the fire.

Her mind wanders while she continues to wait. She happens to notice the lack of modern electronics. Not a television or a computer. No radio, stereo, iPod—*what a weirdo!* Who has just has a bunch of books in their living room?

When he gets the fire blazing, he climbs to his feet, "Would you like some wine?" his finger points to a wine decanter on the little table beside her.

"Sure."

She watches as he pours two glasses with one hand as he turns to her, "So, how was work?"

He hands her a glass "Work, um…" Sera stutters over her words as the ride home from the office re-enters her mind. The hands in her lap have started to shake slightly. She takes a sip of wine. It tastes… different. Sweeter almost, but strong. The fruit seems to explode on her taste buds.

He takes a seat beside her, "Are you okay?" his hand hovers over her knee for a second before he places it gently on the couch beside her. His eyes shine with concern as they meet her eyes again. The blueness of them glimmer back at her. She finds it… intoxicating.

Sera shakes her head. She's starting to grow lightheaded, "I don't know."

"You don't know if you're okay?" he asks again, his eyes a little more concerned this time.

"No, I'm fine." Sera corrects, "Just some personal things going on."

"Personal?"

"It's hard to explain." She takes another sip from her glass. She can't seem to stop.

There's that secret smile again, "Try me."

Shyly she glances away, "I've just been going through some things these past few days. It's nothing, really."

"Sera…" The way he says her name makes her shiver. "I can tell when you are lying."

"I'm not lying." Her eyes meet his again—big mistake, still gorgeous.

"You have a face that can't lie."

"How can you tell all that? I barely know you."

He breathes, "I have a confession to make."

I knew this had to be too good to be true. Her heart begins to race, "A confession?"

"I like you." Her eyes widen. Not what she was expecting. "I wanted this to be a spontaneous date. I haven't dated in… a while. I'm a little out of practice. Could you possibly forgive me and consider giving me another chance?"

A sigh of relief, "I haven't dated in a while either."

"And why is that?" She shies away from his question, but his gaze lingers.

"It's hard to explain," she breathes. "It's almost like dating is different. I don't like the changes."

He's amused, "Different? In what way?"

"There's no romance anymore. There's apps and booty calls, everything is so accessible at the tap of a finger. Guys don't even *try* anymore. No one opens car doors anymore, or throws rocks at girls' windows. They don't even walk to the door and ring the doorbell they text you when they're outside. Maybe I'm an old soul, but I just don't have the energy to entertain that garbage."

He nods, "I can understand that."

"Can you?" Even as the words escape her lips, she regrets them. Of course he does. She can sense he has an old soul as well, from the way his phone is still sitting on the table before them. He's never even looked at it once. Also, it's the way there's no electronics in this place and the romance of that candle-lit dinner under the stars. This Nate, he's *different*.

"I can," he responds, his arm finding its way to the back of the couch behind her. The closer he gets, the faster her heart thrums in her chest. Her palm is sticking to the stem of the wine glass, as it grows sweaty. She takes another sip to distract herself from his beautiful eyes.

"Well, um, that's—"

"Sera, you know you can trust me right?" he asks, "You can tell me anything."

She meets his eyes; somehow, she feels the urge to respond honestly. "That's what I'm afraid of."

"You're afraid of me?"

"Kind of." The words slip from her mouth before she can stop them.

"Why?" She doesn't miss him moving back a centimeter.

"Odd things have been happening to me lately, I don't want *you* to be one of them." The truth is, she doesn't want to wake up, and find out this is all just another dream. But, why is she telling this stranger all this?

"Odd things? Like what?"

"Just weird things, you wouldn't get it." *Stop talking Sera! Geez.*

"You'd be surprised by what I can comprehend."

"I doubt anything would surprise me anymore."

"Oh, I wouldn't say that." There's that secret smirk again.

"Do you ever feel like everyone is in on a secret, but you?" His smile falters as she continues. "That's what it feels like. I just feel like things are different, and I can't for the life of me figure out why."

"Like what?"

She finally falters, she barely knows this guy, why is she divulging so much about herself? It's like she can't stop it. "I'm stronger, smarter, and immune to alcohol apparently." She places the wine glass on the table in front of them, although, as she says it, the room sways slightly.

"I see," is all the mysterious Nate replies.

"That's not all." It's like she's opened up a floodgate and can't stop mid way, "I think I'm seeing things." She gasps. Her hands cover her mouth. *Shut up Sera, shut up!* She wills herself. "What was in that wine?" He blinks, his face alone screams with guilt, "Was there something in that wine?" she whispers afraid of the answer.

Nate ignores her question, "Do you feel as though you are in danger?"

"Yes," she blurts out again before re-covering her mouth.

He stands immediately pacing the living room floor, "Why?" his voice is commanding. Something within Sera is once again compelled to answer.

"I had a car accident today," she responds through clenched fingers, "And I feel as though someone is watching me all the time."

His fists clench at his sides as he leans against the mantle. "I knew it."

"What the hell is going on Nate? Do you know something I don't?"

"I know just as much as you."

"I find that hard to believe." Sera climbs to her feet to meet him at the fireplace. "Do you know more than what you are telling me?"

He turns to face her now, his mouth contorting, trying to withhold the truth. It looks like he had some of the wine too, "Yes."

She takes a step back. This was a mistake. She should never have come. "I… I have to go."

"Sera wait! Sera, I can explain." He reaches for her. She escapes him by swinging around the couch and into the foyer. "Sera! It's not what you think."

She swings open the door and holds it for a second, "Nothing is what I thought it was. Nothing will ever be the same again."

She slams the door behind her and dashes down the steps to her car. She pauses when her white sedan comes into view. Her breath hitches in her throat.

The door behind her opens, and she can feel Nate standing there. She slips around the completely repaired fender and climbs into the car. Turning the car in reverse, she peels away from the house and swings the car around to face forward again only to zoom off down the dirt road away from him. Why does he seem so concerned for her and then would slip her some weird truth-telling wine? Just when she thinks she has things under control, more things come out of the woodwork to toss her for a loop all over again. She was right about one thing. Nothing is what she believes it to be.

SERA COMES STORMING through the front door. Her mother sits in the recliner. Barely looking up from her Kindle, she greets her daughter, "I was wondering where you were."

Sera takes a step into the house, "Uh, yeah I just came back from… well, I think it was a date."

"Another date?" That grabs her attention, "with the guy from the other night?"

"Uh," Sera shifts uncomfortably on her feet, "No, it was a different guy."

"Oh my. Who would have thought, my little Sera."

"Who indeed," Sera deflects with humor. "So many gentleman callers, so little time," she mutters with a southern accent and begins ascending the stairs.

"Well, I hope you had fun sweetie. Just remember, I want to be a mother-in-law before I'm a grandmother."

"Mom!" Sera gasps dashing up the rest of the stairs.

Fifteen

The Mall

SERA FINDS HERSELF SITTING at her desk the next day, staring blankly ahead at her computer screen. Emails keep popping along the right hand side of her screen. She ignores them. Everything that is happening is finally catching up to her. Worst of all, last night was the first night in almost six years that she hadn't dreamt at all. Not one snippet. She doesn't even feel like herself anymore. Even going for a run this morning, didn't snap her out of this daze.

Mostly, she keeps thinking about Nate. God what is it about that mysterious man that she can't seem to get off her mind. Isn't it strange he knew all about her—and what was with that wine? Amanda comes skipping down the hall, breaking up her thoughts.

She props up onto her usual spot on the corner of Sera's desk. Popping her leg over the other, she cracks her gum and asks, "What's up hot stuff?"

At those words, Sera unleashes. It only takes a few moments to tell Amanda everything, but to her, it feels like she talks forever. Unloading to her best friend about the necklace and the oddly gorgeous dinner with one-sided conversation. When at last she looked up to her best friend's awed brown eyes, her mouth droops open slightly.

"Who are you?" she asks Sera. "Let me get this straight. You met a sexy guy at the coffee house, got his number, had a gorgeous romantic date, and you are mad that he wants to know all about you? I mean I knew you were out of the loop when it comes to dating, but come on!" She grows dramatic tossing her arms in the air a few times.

"So, it was a date?" Sera finally realizes the truth.

"Duh."

"And this is normal?"

"Well, I wouldn't say normal," Amanda twists on the desk causing Sera to fidget, "I'd say this guy is some kind of saint and you should marry him!"

Sera laughs.

"I mean who are you, getting guy's numbers at coffee houses? You're a little ginger fox, you know that?"

Somehow hearing those words from Amanda was all Sera needed to calm down. She's right. He seemed concerned for her safety, that's a good thing right? She'll never forget the fire in his eyes when she told him she felt someone watching her. He flinched like he had been physically hit. Maybe, things are simpler than they appear.

"Oh my, Sera, your boobs!" Amanda shrieks.

"Thanks, it's my new bra…"

"No, they're glowing. Your boobs are glowing."

"What?" Sera glances down to see the vial casting her cleavage in a ghastly glow. "Oh, it's just my necklace." She pulls it from her shirt. It blinks slowly with that light it has.

"Oh." Amanda giggles. "That's new."

"It's been doing this lately. The last time it glowed…" The pieces slowing begin to pull themselves together. *Nate!*

She slips away from Amanda and walks out into the row of cubicles. It pulses faster as she walks toward the elevator—faster and faster until the entire thing is lit up. Someone stands before her. Her eyes take in the dark slacks, the white collar shirt with a few buttons strategically forgotten. It allows a few tufts of hair to peek out from underneath his collared shirt. Her face finally meeting his.

"Gabe," she breathes disappointment.

"Where are you headed little lady?"

Her hand wraps around the necklace, "Just headed to the bathroom, excuse me." She slips around him and heads toward the bathroom in the front.

She quickly slides into the unisex bathroom and secures the lock into place. Her eyes glance around uneasily. Public bathrooms make her nervous, ever since…

Bracing her hands on the edge of the sink, she stares into her reflection.

"Get it together, Seraphina." Even she has to admit there are strange things going on around here. From the necklace, to the two new guys in town, to the trip to NYC, and she doesn't even want to begin to rationalize what happened with the deer.

It causes her heart to race, her palms grow sweaty, and she's constantly scared as hell. Then why is it that she's never felt more alive?

When she finally heads back to her desk, Amanda blocks her path this time. She had rolled her chair into the hall using her legs as a barrier.

"What's the password?"

"Turtle?"

"Turtle?" Amanda bursts into laughter. "Seriously?"

"What? It's the first thing that came to mind."

"I'm sure it was." In between remaining giggles she gets out, "Do you want to come to the mall with me at lunch?"

Amanda gives her those puppy dog eyes of hers that she knows Sera can never say no to. "Yeah, sure," Sera concedes, mainly because she doesn't want to be here alone with creepy Gabe.

"Good! While we are there we can get you some 'date clothes.'" She raises her voice a little to insinuate something Sera doesn't quite catch on to.

"You don't like my wardrobe?"

"Let's just say petticoats and bloomers have long since gone out of style." She jokes with a southern accent and wheels her chair back into her cubicle.

Walking through the vast mall during lunch, Sera follows her best friend into almost every store that sells clothes.

Don't get her wrong she enjoys shopping, but she usually has a game plan going in. She knows what she needs, she finds it, and she buys it. Amanda is the complete opposite. She is a compulsive, I-need-want-everything buyer. Happy for a break from reality, she follows her friend from store to store, watching her refresh her winter wardrobe.

"Sera, oh my God! This color would look so good with your eyes. You absolutely have to try it on." She tosses her a green blouse. With a roll of her eyes, she walks to the back of the store and disappears into the dressing room just to appease her friend. Sera locks the stall behind her and takes a seat on the ledge releasing a breath.

"Here, Sera. Try these, too." Amanda tosses some clothes over the top of the door. "Don't forget to come out and show me, I want to see them."

Realizing she's not going to get away without trying them on, Sera reluctantly begins changing. She steps out in the green blouse.

Amanda seems to like it. "Oh my God, Sera, that's gorgeous. I love it!"

"Really?"

"It's fabulous. You should totally buy that."

"You don't think it's too… green?"

"No it's perfect."

With a shrug, Sera slips back into the dressing room. She pauses before the mirror. This shirt is definitely too green. Maybe if it were in red, it would look better. Sera shoots a longing glance at the back of the door. Stepping back outside is probably not the best idea. Amanda would no doubt toss a million other things at her.

"Sera?" Speak of the devil. "I want you to try on that white polka dot dress next. I think it would look so cute with those black pumps we saw at the other store."

To amuse her, Sera picks up the polka dot dress from the pile. The thing looks tiny. She pulls on it between her hands. "This thing is like skin tight." She whispers to herself. Maybe, going to the mall was a bad idea.

"Sera?" Amanda tries again.

"Okay, okay," she yells back before turning to unbutton the blouse. Glancing down to release the button through the eyehole, she notices the shirt she is wearing is no longer the bright green it once was… it is *red*. Not just regular red, the exact shade she was imagining in her head only moments before.

Hastily, she unbuttons it, needing to get the freaky shirt off her. As soon as it's over her head, she throws it across the tiny dressing room.

Oh my God, what is happening to me? She sits down on the ledge of the changing room with her head in her hands.

It takes a few calming breaths before she can rise to her feet. Cautiously, she walks over to the red shirt prepared for it to attack her at any moment. She picks it up between her two fingers and twirls it around examining it. No doubt, it is a different color. She reaches for the tag. Mindlessly, she reads it aloud a few times reminding herself, "Green."

Sera exits the dressing room in a blur, Amanda is talking

to her. She can't seem to comprehend anything she is telling her. She can feel the color drain from her face as she walks to the register. She has to buy the shirt, it's the least she can do since she may have ruined it.

Once they leave the store, she can slowly get her breathing back under control. After a few more minutes, she makes it to the end of the corridor. Amanda turns to her almost inspecting her.

"What was *that*, Sera?" Amanda asks, arm gesturing behind them.

"What?" she says wondering if Amanda caught the new color of the shirt.

"You completely freaked in there, what happened?" Amanda stops in her tracks grabbing hold of Sera's arm.

"I… I don't know." She bites her lip. How can she even begin to explain this to Amanda? She's been wondering the same thing herself. She glances up to Amanda to read her face, but what catches her eye is the figure near the emergency exit. He's standing down the hallway from them. His blue eyes meet hers, and her stomach churns with nervous anxiety. He's dressed in a weird black outfit that screams undercover special ops or something of that nature and that face of his screams revenge. Probably because the last time she saw him, she had pushed him through a bathroom wall. Her body seems to go on the defensive as soon as she sees him, the aggressive blond from the club. How did he find me?

"We have to get out of here," Sera whispers, but her eyes

never leave the back corner.

"What? Why?" Amanda responds. She attempts to gesture with her hands, but the shopping bags seem to weigh them down.

"Amanda, now!" She gives her a glare that means business and Amanda follows her in the direction of the elevator. They speed walk down the hallway, glancing back every so often to see the man, but she can't seem to lay eyes on him anymore. Somehow, she knows he's not going to let her out of his sight. She finds herself running the last few steps to press the button for the elevator.

"Come on, come on," Sera mumbles under her breath.

"Sera, what is going on?" Amanda must sense her nervous energy because she glances around trying to figure out what Sera keeps looking at.

"I just have to get out of here. I think I'm having a panic attack," she breathlessly states the first excuse that pops into her head.

Finally, the elevator doors ding open. Sera dashes inside, pressing the 'P2' button before hitting the 'Close Doors' button multiple times.

The doors close, and it begins to lower them down. Sera leans an arm against the wall. Taking a deep breath, she finally turns to Amanda. "I'm sorry I freaked. I just haven't been myself."

Sera is still unable to make eye contact with her best friend. Her eyes dart around the small elevator. Never did she think she would actually feel slightly comforted by an elevator. She closes her eyes when the walls of the elevator begin closing in only a few more minutes.

"You think?" Amanda responds sarcastically.

Suddenly, there is a loud bang on top of the elevator and it jerks a little harder than usual as it reaches the level. Sera reflexively studies the ceiling. Above her head are two dents the size of feet. She grabs Amanda's arm and quickly bursts out of the elevator. Occasionally, her eyes zip behind them for any sign they are being followed. Sera's feet push her faster until she is pretty much dragging Amanda to her little sedan.

Her hands are shaky at the wheel, but that doesn't stop her from zooming out of the parking garage. She's putting plenty of distance between them and the mall, but that doesn't prevent her from glancing in the rearview mirror every few seconds.

Her car is speeding past intersections as she heads back to the office. Her eyes continue to scan the road when her eye catches on the half-moon image, and she whips the car to a screeching halt on the side of the road. She jumps out immediately, after placing the car in park and completely ignoring the words Amanda is spewing at her.

Sera finds herself running into Amazing Anna's shop. She stumbles slightly on the sidewalk before making it inside. The door chimes as she enters. Her eyes lock with Anna's. Anna is sitting in a high-backed white chair in the center of the shop. If that wasn't freaky enough, she doesn't at all look surprised to see Sera filled with terror.

"Anna, what is happening to me?" She gets out sucking back the tears.

Anna's face fills with something similar to pity, "You will figure it all out in due time. You are just going through some changes right now, but this is the 'new chapter', we were talking about."

"You knew?" Sera breathes. "You knew this would happen? Why didn't you warn me?" *Why is everyone around her keeping secrets?*

"I couldn't tell you. I was told not to."

"By who?" She yells her hands flying up at her sides.

"I can't say." Her eyes fall from Sera's face.

"Oh, that's convenient," Sera's voice is getting more animated. Her restless legs begin to pace back and forth in the small lobby.

"Seraphina." The way Anna states her name calms her slightly. She comes to stand before her, placing her delicate hands on Sera's shoulders. "This is your calling. This is what you have been waiting for. It's your time to shine. Don't be afraid of it, embrace it," she cryptically tells Sera.

"So things will get better?" she asks as a sole tear chases its way down her cheek.

"*You* will be better, *you* will adapt." Anna pauses before adding, "The struggle however, is just beginning."

"You sound like a fortune cookie, why can't you give me a straight answer?"

"I've been bound not to... you have been given an incredible gift Seraphina, what you choose to do with it will define who you are and ultimately who you were meant to be."

"How will I know what the right decision is?"

"I know you will make the right decision, it will be black and white, as easy as good vs. evil," she responds with a wink.

She takes some comfort in this knowledge. She's still a little scared at what the future holds, but Anna's faith in her is what inspires the faith in herself. She reluctantly says goodbye and makes her way back to her car. She is preparing herself for the explanation she has to give Amanda. Only when she gets there her friend never says a word, she places her hand on her knee for a moment before she turns back to the road, starts the car, and heads back to the office.

Sixteen

Possessions & Confessions

A FEW HOURS AND AN OUTFIT change later, she finds herself walking through the front doors of the coffee house. Her stomach twists and tugs at her, and she turns to see Nate sitting there in the same spot as the other day, complete with nameless book. As soon as she enters he looks up, their eyes meet. His eyes once again entice her and pull her toward him. Even with all the strange things going on around her, Nate has always been the one constant in her life—at least subconsciously. Just like in her dreams, she's drawn to him.

That tugging in her stomach leads her to that green chair she loves so much. He rises to his feet to meet her. Their eyes remain locked and she pauses before him, "Hey."

"Hey," he mutters in response. They stand like that for a second, staring at each other until he coughs, "I think we got off to the wrong start."

"I'm sorry I left like that last night."

"It's my fault, I came on too… strong."

"It's not you, it's me—"

"Yeah, that's what they all say," he interrupts.

She smirks not having a smart remark for that one. She glances down to the table. Two cups sit upon it; he was expecting her.

He motions for her to sit, "I took the liberty of ordering your drink."

She slips into the comfy chair like she usually does, only this time she feels Nate's eyes on her. She's secretly happy she stopped home to change into that red blouse she had purchased. It pairs perfectly with the pencil skirt she wore to work.

"My drink? How did you know?"

"The gentleman behind the counter was more than helpful on the matter."

Sera glances over to see that Jack is studying their interaction from his spot behind the bar. "Oh," her mind only temporarily at ease.

It seems Nate's appearance was also part of the strange things occurring to her. It's almost… could she still be sleeping? What if she is dreaming right now? She pinches herself just in case. "Ouch."

"What was that for?" His lip quirks up like he's holding back a laugh.

"Nothing," embarrassed she hides the redness in her

cheeks by digging around for her laptop within the folds of her purse. Opening it up, she begins typing up some paperwork for the office. It was hard not to be slightly distracted when she returned from lunch.

Nate begins reading from his nameless book and Sera pecks away at her computer keys. That was the way an outsider would see it. Sera gets the feeling more is going on. She could feel his eyes on her, and every once and awhile when his eyes returned to his book, she would steal a glance as well. She could feel every breath he took, her cheeks warmed at the thought of him watching her.

It continues like that until Sera's stomach growls embarrassingly loud. Nate glances up right away, "Are you hungry?"

"Um," her cheeks redden even more, "I guess so."

"Why didn't you say so, let's go."

"Okay, let me just—"

Nate is on his feet heading for the door as Sera is still packing up her stuff. She hadn't heard him approach, but Jack is upon her when she glances up.

"Sera, can I talk to you for a second?"

"Uh," one glance over at Nate and she responds, "Sure, what's up?"

"Are you sure about this guy?" he nudges his head toward Nate's figure by the door. Nate looks pained, almost like he wants to rescue Sera from the encounter.

"Yeah, why?" she whispers.

"I don't know exactly, there's just something about him.

I don't trust him."

Before she has time to answer, she can feel a body behind her. The flipping in her stomach is out of control and the heat radiating off his body is driving her slightly insane.

Nate's deep voice responds, "That's funny because I have the same feelings about you."

The tone is different from the one he uses with Sera. It's threatening.

Jack seems taken back by Nate's approach. "Uh, excuse me?"

"I believe you heard me." Nate gestures with his hand for the door. They walk for a few steps when Jack responds.

"No, I meant excuse me, as in who do you think you are talking to?" Sera stops in her tracks, Jack's tone is darker than she's ever heard him. Nate continues toward the door, his hand reaching out for the handle when Jack responds, "And if you think I'm going to let you leave here with *my* girl, you've got another thing coming."

Immediately, Sera is struck with something. Her entire mind goes blank. Words escape her as a strange sensation spreads through her entire body. Her vision is black and her body cold as ice. She can't feel her limbs, but somehow she knows that she is moving. She is moving toward Jack. There's a commotion around her. Everything inside her is trying to make out what is going on. All she can seem to make out is a muffled argument.

"Let her go!"

"Leave… alone."

"Know... what you... are."

"Nothing... wouldn't do for her!"

"Release her!"

The voices stop. There's shuffling on the floor, grunts, and thumps. There must be a scuffle going on. Something is happening outside. Where is she again? Who is she with? Why are they fighting? Her mind is a jumbled mess. She can't seem to get her mind to focus. Until one word shakes her.

Seraphina.

A thought comes to her mind. It's not a complete thought, only a word—a name. It's on the tip of her tongue. Its... N... N...Nate. Nate!

Suddenly, Sera remembers... Nate. She's here with Nate. Jack. A scuffle. *Oh no!* Slowly, her mind begins to return, but her body still feels submerged in ice water. She fights the force taking control of her body. With all the strength she can muster, she clenches her fists. One finger at a time it seems to take an eternity as they slowly lower into place. Once she can feel her fingernails digging into her palms, she turns her attention to her feet. Stomp your feet, she thinks repeatedly; willing her body to react. Again, just as slowly as her hands, her feet being to tingle like pins and needles.

She places her feet firmly on the ground, and clenches her fists harder, forcing the blackness out of her mind.

She has control again. She has won the fight over her own body. When she opens her eyes, it is to a scene unlike any other. Her coffee is in a puddle at her feet. All the lights are out in the coffee house and there's a layer of black smoke creeping along the floor. Jack was just tossed across the room, banging into the tables and chairs by the window. He flew like he weighed nothing less than a feather. Jack jumps back to his feet like a ninja before running back at Nate and their arms lock in a struggle. Sera still stands there feet apart, fists clenched, and picks her head up. Her eyes lock with both of them. They look up mid-fight, arms still entangled and pause to stare at her.

Their arms drop immediately and both walk over to her. There's that strange feeling in her stomach again—the bad one. All her hairs on the back of her neck stand at attention. Something is wrong here.

"Sera, are you okay?" Nate speaks first. He bends over inspecting her face.

"Yes." She turns to Jack now. He looks different. Besides the bloody lip and torn clothes. "Jack?" she whispers. Nate's body reacts, his fists drop to his sides and clench a few times. Jack makes his way around Nate, closer to her. His face brightens slightly as he forces a smile through his cracked lip.

"Yes, Sera, what is it?" He comes closer; Nate can only tense.

"Jack," she repeats returning her gaze to Nate. "I need to get out of here. I'm leaving… with Nate." With those final words, she leaves the coffee house, knowing from his eyes Nate would follow.

Once outside, she can finally breathe again. Nate guides

her over to his car and opens the door for her. Walking around to the driver's side, he gets in without a word and speeds out of the parking lot. After a few minutes of silence, Sera starts to feel normal again.

Nate is the one to break the silence first, "Are you feeling okay?" His eyes never leave the road. His fists appear white as he grips the steering wheel.

"Yes." She rubs her hands; they are still cold. Maybe it was all a dream? Maybe she will wake up in a few minutes. Without another word, Nate spins the car into a parking spot right in front of her favorite pizza place in town. He's out of the car in seconds, and after another second, her door opens. They walk inside without a word, and he motions for her to grab a seat.

Mindlessly, Sera slips into a booth in the empty pizza shop and glances out the window. Her mind attempts to process what she just experienced; she's trying to make sense of something she doesn't have all the answers to. What could be going on with her?

Before she knows it, Nate places a pepperoni pizza between them. He's looking at her differently. Almost like, he's *inspecting* her. She stares back at him. So many questions plague her mind. However, the only thing she can focus on is how out of place he looks here at the pizza shop. It's his aura. The shop itself is gaudy red, white, and green all around. The ceiling has the "Birth of Venus" painted upon it. Nate with his straight back and his inhumanly blue eyes just seems above it all.

"Sera…" he starts, but it seems he can't find the words.

"Nate, what is it you really want to say?" Her voice surprisingly comes out soft, even after all that has happened.

"Are you… freaked out?" his voice replicates her softness.

She picks up a slice of pizza, taking the time to savor the bite and process her answer. Is it crazy that she isn't exactly 'freaked out'? She would just like some answers. Her silence must have been too much.

"I knew it. I was trying not to get too worked up again, but I can't help it." His breathing increases as he continues, "I still feel the need to protect you." For the first time she's not worried. The warmth in his deep blue eyes tells her all she needs to know. "Just tell me how you did it."

"Did what?" She takes another bite.

"How did you break… Jack's hold on you?"

"That was Jack? In my mind?" the pizza drops to the plate in front of her. "How?"

He glances away, "I…"

"Nate, I need to understand what is going on. I feel like everyone is in on a secret except me."

"To explain, I would have to start at the beginning. Are you sure you want to hear it all?" his voice is hesitant, his eyes still warm.

"Nate, please tell me what is going on here. I'm starting to think I'm going crazy."

Reluctantly, he nods. "Not here though, let's go home."

"My car… it's still at the coffee house." A shiver shakes through her at the thought of returning there.

"Okay, to your car then."

They finish the pizza and drive back to the coffee shop in silence. He pulls the car into a spot. With a deep breath, he turns to her. "I want to make sure you keep an open mind before I tell you all of this."

"Nate, please just tell me what is going on around here." Her voice comes out quiet as the tears well up behind her eyes. She has wanted answers for days now. Finally, she might get them.

He takes another deep breath before giving into her pleading face. "Okay, I guess the best place is to start at the beginning." He glances away from her, afraid her eyes would be too much for him. "I don't know how to say this, so I'm just going to put it all out there and hope for the best." There's another deep breath.

Geez, what could he possibly say? Sera squirms in her seat preparing herself.

"I was an Angel," he blurs out. "A real life, work for the big guy above, Angel." She can feel her eyes widen as he continues, "I had been appointed as your Guardian Angel. During that time, I got to know the real you. The behind closed doors you, that no one else can see. Due to some *unforeseen* circumstances, I wasn't there to protect you the night of your accident. I just felt like there was more to this, that it wouldn't be your ending. It couldn't be. I couldn't let you pass on. That's when I saw my finger was bleeding. I didn't even think twice. I let you ingest some, knowing it would let you heal yourself. I wasn't thinking about the repercussions of those actions, I reacted purely on instinct. But, everything that you are experiencing right now, is because of my blood—in your human system."

"I... I..." She can hear herself mumbling but can't seem to control it.

"I know it sounds far-fetched, but it's the God's honest truth. I refuse to lie to you anymore. I have a feeling there's more going on here than meets the eye."

Her mind is still a jumbled mess trying to process this. Her first thought, he must be kidding. This is a twisted joke. It must be. She meets his eyes, concern and sincerity greet her. Could he possibly be serious? This must be a dream. She slyly pinches her outer thigh. Pain. It's not a dream. What was she expecting? Honestly, radioactive spiders seem more realistic at this point.

"Sera, you need to trust me, especially now."

That seems a little backward. She needs to respond. She can feel the silence between them choking her. She jumps on the first emotion that hops into her head. Anger. "I need to trust you?" she repeats with a laugh under her breath. "Trust you? You've been nothing but secretive around me, even giving me the truth-spilling wine and lying directly to my face when I asked about your past, your job."

He stares at her, blinking blankly as she continues. "You did all this to me and just dropped me off at home like everything was the same. I woke up alone, thinking that I was losing my mind. You invaded my dreams for months then just show up here like we can be chummy friends." She can't seem to stop the words as they escape her mouth. "Is this all a game to you? How could I possibly trust you when all you've done was keep me in the dark?"

Without another word, she turns and lets herself out of the car leaving him staring after her. She walks around the car heading for the front of the coffee house where her car sits. Nate cuts her off before she is even halfway there.

"What do you mean invade your dreams? I can't do that." His eyes explore hers, concern plastered all over them.

Her anger only increases, "And I'm supposed to believe you now? Is that how you do it?"

"Do what?"

"Invade human women's dreams and trick them into following you around like a lost puppy dog, is that how you get all your *dates*?"

He winces. "Sera, I'm telling you, I don't have the power of mind control. That wasn't me. I only tried to help you," his blue eyes plead with her as they scan her face.

"Help me? You made me a freak!" She shrieks. That did it. He takes a step away from her. She blows past him, with stubborn purpose walking to her car and whipping the driver's side door open.

Getting home seemed to take forever as she navigates the roads through her steady stream of tears. She can't help but feel so... betrayed. How could he have done this to her? What is she now? She pulls her car across the street from her house. Slipping out of the car, she freezes. There's that feeling again—the feeling of being watched. She spins around, eyes scanning the dead-end street before running the rest of the way inside and locking the door behind her. She dashes up the stairs two at a time, whips open her bedroom door, and closes it behind her before collapsing face first onto her bed.

Whether she believes Nate or not, it doesn't excuse the fact that he kept something from her. That and he has seen her in the most intimate of ways. Was the date the other night all for show? Is this all a game?

She thinks of all that has transpired, she comes up with a question she can't figure out the answer to. Why couldn't she see him when he was her Guardian Angel, and now she can? It's the thought that haunts her into her sleep, only to force her to see his beautiful face once again.

Seventeen

Gabe-teraction

DIRT EXPLODES TO HER RIGHT and sends her flying into the nearest ditch. She's struggling to climb to her knees and catch her breath all while calming the butterflies that are exploding inside of her. They are outnumbered now; her comrades are all but lying dead around her. It was a war they were convinced they would win, but once they got there, it was like the Natives with sticks fending off the English settlers with guns. Out manned and out powered, they fell, one by one. Sera is one of the few that remain. She has more pride than to just give up. She pumps her gun and takes a deep breath before peeking her head up over the mound of soil. She fires off a few rounds to approaching soldiers before she falls back down to reload her magazine.

Reaching into her pocket, she finds she only has a few more shells left. She shakes her head in frustration and peeks again to see soldiers rapidly approaching. Quickly, she fumbles to pull the shells out of her pocket and place them into the shotgun. Her hands are shaking with nervous energy. One of her last shells falls to the dirt in her rush. Suddenly, she feels hands pulling her up by the collar of her uniform. She struggles against it. Her fingers continue trying to cock her gun. The hands find their way to her throat. She flips the gun up, hears it click into place, and attempts to aim over her shoulder. Unexpectedly, she feels something jerk the enemy forward, the hands around her neck loosen, and she whips around to find the soldier's body falling limp onto the ground. She glances up; her eyes meet bright blue ones. His eyes are all she can see as his black mask is hiding his identity. He must be a sniper or assassin because his black uniform isn't one she recognizes. She takes a step back cautiously and finds herself sliding back into the ditch. She turns to dash away toward homebase when she feels hands on her shoulder. Reflexively, she whips around and punches him across the face, breaking free from his hold.

"Sera!" he screams after her. She freezes, taken completely off-guard that he knows her name. She turns to face the strange blue-eyed man. He slowly approaches her, slipping off his mask and shaking his chestnut hair free. Sera recognizes Nate's handsome face immediately. How could she not recognize those impossible eyes?

"Sera, I'm on your side." He lifts his hands indicating he means no harm. She inhales a deep breath as he reaches into his pockets to pull two extra 9mm's and hands them to her. She smiles up at him and throws her arms around his neck.

"You're a life saver Nate! Let's go kick some ass." As a soldier comes charging over the ditch, she whips around and shoots him straight through the chest. They charge up and over the mound to kill some enemies together.

She and Nate are fighting side by side making good progress through the hundreds of soldiers left. Against impossible odds, they are prevailing and making a huge dent in their numbers. She turns around to make sure Nate is still with her. He comes into view ahead of her after the body of a dead soldier drops at his feet. He glances up and winks. Even now, she still can't help the smile that crosses her face as she begins to walk toward him. He's all she can seem to see. The gunshots and explosions are going off all around. She's almost to him when she feels something jab her between the shoulder blades. It pierces straight through her. She glances down to see the tip of the instrument protruding through her chest; stabbed in the back, literally. What a coward!

She looks up to see Nate running toward her. She collapses into his arms when her knees go weak underneath her. She can vaguely hear him screaming, "No!" as he shoots the enemy behind her that is causing her premature death. Nate is telling her something, but she can't seem to focus. The pain is too much. Instead, she just stares back at his blue eyes. If she dies, she wants them to be the last image she will ever have...

Her eyes flutter open as the blankets around her throat are beginning to cut off her supply of oxygen. She rips them off and just lies there staring at the window in contemplation. The sun is just beginning to stream through her blinds. She doesn't seem to need an alarm clock anymore. It could quite possibly be this new energy level; it won't even allow her to sleep. Even at six thirty in the morning, she can jump out of bed and head out for a run, no coffee needed, and that's just what she does.

Running through the old familiar streets of her small town, she seems to have more energy than usual. She finds herself pushing to limits she couldn't have even dreamed about before. Closing her eyes, she lets her feet guide and propel her forward. She loves this feeling of the outdoors. The smell and ambiance of nature makes her feel so free. Feeling the wind in her hair, the beating of her heart matching her footsteps, she thinks about how she's never felt so... alive.

Whatever Nate had done, it does make her feel... good. The thought of Nate makes her stop in her tracks. She remembers the hurt in his eyes last night; she can almost still feel the knife in her chest from her dream.

She had caused that look. Perhaps, she over reacted. She processes this and takes a seat on the stone wall alongside the entrance to the town's cemetery. Didn't he save her life? She has to be at least mildly grateful for that, doesn't she? Staring out over the tombstones of various people that at one time walked this Earth. The gray stones stand out prominently against the frost on the grass below them. It's eerily silent, and she can feel the cold slowly start to creep into her, realizing her feet are taking her through the cemetery.

She's not sure if it's the weather or where she is, but the cold seems to seep into her bones. Mindlessly, she continues to walk for a few more minutes until she stops. Before her looms her grandfather's grave. The large marble stone foundation with the large angel standing above it reads, 'CROSS.' The angel is looking down at her, wings drooping at its sides with a serene face that almost looks like pity. The angel's hands clasp in front, poised to hold something. Looking down at the Earth that holds the remains of her grandfather, a thought crosses her mind—it could have been *her* in here.

It finally dawns on her as the memory of the large pool of blood she left on the street springs to her mind. In that moment of clarity, she concludes she owes Nate an apology. Moreover, she has more questions about what she is and what exactly she can do now. Nate is the only one who can answer these questions. She kneels in front of her grandfather's stone and whispers a silent prayer for strength and guidance before taking a deep breath and climbing to her feet again. She'll text Nate as soon as she returns home.

SERA IS AT HER DESK when Amanda pops her head in to check on her. The concern shows all over her face. Suddenly, it dawns on her. The last time she saw her best friend she had freaked out at the mall. Amanda slips around the cubicle wall, propping herself onto Sera's desk, a position she has taken a million times before. Only somehow, this time is different. *She* is different.

"What's up hot stuff?" It's Amanda that breaks the tension first.

"Nothing, just trying to get these claims out." Sera returns to her computer screen. Great. Denial. It's been working for her so far.

"How are things with the sexy blue-eyed stranger?" In typical Amanda fashion, she pries further.

"Good, that reminds me, I have to text him." Sera leans over, digging through the drawers of her desk.

"Well, I just want you to know things with me and the orthopedist didn't work out." She informs. Sera hides a roll of her eyes at the dramatics, but she had already expected this.

"Why, what happened?" she asks only to appease her.

"Turns out he's engaged! Can you believe that? He was totally flirting with me and the next day everyone is congratulating him on his engagement."

"That pig," she exclaims pulling her phone out of the pockets of her purse.

Amanda is still venting on about the sexy doctor that broke her heart, but Sera's mind is a little distracted by a new text she has waiting for her.

I'm sorry about last night, can we talk about it? Sera finds herself reading and re-reading the text from Jack. She's almost scared to reply. It's not like she can ignore all the weird things that have been happening to her, but maybe she shouldn't exactly go alone to see him.

Amanda breaks her train of thought, "Right, Sera?"

"Huh? Oh, right."

"Is there something you want to talk about?" she places her hand over Sera's phone.

Looking up to her friend's big brown eyes, she wants to tell her the truth. She wants to spill her guts and tell her all the weird things that have been happening to her this past week, but something in her is holding back. Part of her is afraid that Amanda *will* believe her and their relationship will change forever.

"No, I'm just swamped with work and stuff." She lies to her best friend's face for the very first time and forces a fake smile to accompany that lie.

"Okay Sera, I'm here when you are ready." Amanda makes a face knowing something is amiss. She scoots off Sera's desk and heads back toward her own, leaving Sera to glance back to her phone.

Can I stop by after work? Sera finally texts back. There is something in her that doesn't want to believe that Jack would hurt her. He has had her alone hundreds of times before and he never once laid a finger on her. Her phone vibrates with an incoming message; she glances down to see his reply.

Of course! See you later.

There's that hint of anticipation again. She really doesn't know what Jack could possibly say after Nate's confession last night. Then it dawns on her, didn't Nate tell her Jack was the one with the hold on her mind last night. He didn't exactly get a chance to explain what exactly that meant before she flipped out and left him in a cloud of dust. She might be regretting that a little. The hurt in his eyes was sincere. Even stone faced Sera can admit she overreacted a little bit.

A few hours later, Sera's stomach begins growling uncontrollably. With all her running, she must be burning major energy because she is constantly starving. Her hand slips into her bottom drawer to pull out her emergency stash of Easy Mac and heads toward the elevator. As she passes Amanda's desk, she can only shoot her a wave because Amanda has the phone receiver to her ear talking to a patient while scrolling through her Facebook timeline on the computer.

"Hold on one second Mrs. Alto." She puts the call on hold to call out to Sera, "Where do you think you're going?"

"Break room." She takes a few steps back toward Amanda's cubicle, "You look like your busy."

Amanda rolls her eyes, "She can wait on hold."

"Amanda, I'll be back in…" Sera glances at the directions on the side of the container, "Two minutes."

"Fine, let me get back to Mrs. I-don't-see-why-my-insurance-doesn't-cover-my-boob-job."

"Good luck," Sera calls over her shoulder and continues to the elevator. That is exactly why she keeps refusing Mrs. Valentine's offers of a promotion to Accounts Receivable/Collections. She doesn't want to be the bringer of bad news. She takes pride in resolving billing issues, not pestering people that got caught in the system. In her eyes, that wouldn't be a promotion, no matter how much money they offer her. Money doesn't matter when you lose your soul.

The elevator doors close behind her. Her eyes dance around the enclosed space around her. Even years after the tree incident, it still haunts her. After what felt like an eternity of deep breaths, the door finally opens to the main floor. Opens to chaos as always: doctors walk by in lab coats, nurses whisper to each other, and patients pause while glancing at the numbers on the office suites. She navigates her way through them all to a door on her right and keys the code into the pin pad. The door beeps that it's open and she swings her way inside. It clicks closed behind her before she heads for the microwave.

A minute feels like forever when you're starving, so she passed the time by flipping through a gossip magazine someone has left on the counter. It seems like the world has become obsessed with the 'American Dream.' However, Sera has a feeling they are only distractions. The world is fighting wars that no one hears about, the world is bigger than who's had plastic surgery and whose husband cheated on whom. The door beeps that it's opening. She turns to meet the employee entering, but no one ever does. A shadow crosses over her, she glances up, but nothing is there. The room grows silent, the sounds of the hustle outside no longer audible. The beep from the microwave makes her jump slightly.

"You're losing it, Sera," she mutters to herself as she opens the microwave and stirs her mac and cheese. The smell wafts up to her, and she's spooning a mouthful in when she turns and freezes. Almost choking on cheesy noodles she comes face to face with a defined chest in her face. She coughs a few times as her eyes slide up to face the new guy, Gabe.

"Gabe, you scared the crap out of me." She places the container on the counter and wipes her mouth. He silently takes a step toward her; his eyes are weird... "Gabe? Uh, are you okay?"

A scratching noise fills her ears, the sound of something dragging against the floor behind him. Fear begins to flood her veins. Something is telling her to run, but her curiosity is making her stay. He reaches his hand for her.

Suddenly, the door beeps open and Amanda comes traipsing in. "There you are!"

"Amanda!" she's never been so happy to see her best friend in her life. She turns to say something about Gabe being weird, but as she turns, she sees that he is no longer beside her. She almost thought she imagined it, but isn't that his stark cologne tickling her nose?

"What's up? You look like you've seen a ghost." Amanda jokes closing the fridge behind her and opening a container labeled "Dana."

"I just... I thought I saw... never mind." She realizes how crazy she would sound. Anna told her not to get Amanda involved, maybe Sera should listen to her. She did predict the 'changes' maybe Anna knows more than she's let on. To change the subject she adds: "Why are you eating someone else's food?"

"Whaaa?" she mutters with a mouth full of food. She

swallows, "Oh don't give me that look. It's only tuna, I'm doing the girl a favor."

Sera rolls her eyes. "You're ridiculous."

"Why are you so hungry all of a sudden? Are you on that low carb diet again?"

"No," Sera defends. She has always had a thicker figure than her stick skinny parents. She has tried every diet possible, read every health book she could get her hands on, yet her body never seemed to change. "And, noodles are a carb." She lifts the cup for emphasis.

"A good carb though, right?" Amanda asks, her face full of pure ignorance. Amanda was born hitting the good gene jackpot. Her mother was a runway model, her father some prominent gentleman in London when her mother was overseas. To this day, she knows nothing about him, and her mother is a vault that will probably never utter a word. She has never known the pain of being on a diet or having to work out. She has never had a bad haircut because her oval face can make anything work. Even those bangs she's sporting nowadays. Amanda was probably born walking in heels and dresses, she doesn't look like a bumbling baby deer on stilts like Sera does when she attempts. Amanda has a grace and a confidence that Sera desperately envies, although she did seem to make it through an entire night in the city in boots… baby steps.

"No, not a good carb."

"What about whole wheat pasta?"

"Cardboard." Sera calls over her shoulder and sneaks out

the door before the diet interrogation continues. Amanda was out for answers. Answers, to questions that would quickly turn toward Sera. At this moment, Sera didn't have answers to any of them. So instead, she runs.

Eighteen

Divulgence

LATER THAT NIGHT, SERA FINDS her parking spot in the front of Jack's Coffee Bean is occupied. She reluctantly parks in the back parking lot. With a deep breath to calm her nerves, she exits the car. She's walking toward the front door when an icy cold breeze filters through her jacket. There's that feeling of being watched again. She lowers her head and quickens her pace until she finally reaches the entrance. She almost tumbles inside as she trips over her own two feet coming through the door. It takes some of the anxiety out of her, replacing it with slight embarrassment.

She has to take a few steps inside before Jack pops up from behind the bar.

"Hey, Sera," he calls over his shoulder as he packs the shelves with coffee grinds. "Take a seat. I'm just closing up."

She nods in response heading over to her favorite chair

in the corner. Her eyes peer out the window scanning the parking lot looking for anything out of the ordinary. When she can't seem to find anything, she takes her jacket off and watches Jack as he closes up shop.

He finally walks over to the door and flips the sign to 'Closed.' The backs of his shoulders rise and fall before he turns around finally walking over to her chair. Sera keeps switching positions to ease her nerves, secretly glad she stopped home to change into jeans before she arrived.

Jack sits down across from her after she has settled into a position with her legs folded across each other. She's trying to appear casual, meanwhile inside she is nervous for what he's about to reveal.

"Sera," he starts hesitantly, "I want you to know, I'm really sorry for last night. I didn't mean for anything to happen to you, but sometimes I can't control things." He confesses never meeting her gaze.

"Jack, I have no idea what you are talking about." He finally lifts his blue-green eyes to meet hers before continuing. She uncrosses her legs placing them firmly on the ground now.

"I don't even know where to start…" Why does that sound so familiar? "I've never told anyone my secret, but I owe you an explanation. I hope you can forgive me."

"Ugh, still no clue what's going on?"

He looks down again before beginning, "It all started when I was about seventeen. I started hearing voices. My rich parents, of course, took me to shrink after shrink; I was put through test after test. They inspected, prodded, probed, and studied. But, they couldn't find anything wrong with me. It wasn't until my sixth doctor that I began hearing the voice of a woman during my session. The encounter was different; I could actually see the shadow of her beside me. She was almost translucent like a ghost, but her features looked as though she were real. The woman told me she was my therapist's grandmother, even though she didn't look a day over twenty. Her deep, calm, wise voice made me believe her and told me she was older than she appeared. The lady continued to tell me that she had passed without telling anyone of her Will kept in a secret deposit box under her maiden name. I remember the interaction to this day. I kept fighting her, because I thought my parents would have me committed.

"The woman argued with me, pleaded, until I finally spoke. I told the therapist everything. Even down to what her grandmother was wearing. I'll never forget her face. The therapist was so calm and collected. One of those stiff as a board people, once the news hit her she turned to sobs right in front of my eyes. She informed me the family was involved in a huge legal battle over her grandmother's estate. Finding this Will would settle everything once and for all, and get her family back.

"She looked up at me from her tear-strewn face. Reading my mind, she told me that I wasn't crazy. She told me I had an incredible gift."

He lifts his face up to Sera's to gauge her reaction before

continuing, "My parents didn't seem to think so, they pretty much disowned me, and I've been on my own ever since."

Sera closes the gap between them, placing her hand over his. "Sera, a lot has happened since then." He starts playing with her fingers, "Something led me here. I came into some money from a happy customer, and I had this overwhelming urge to start a business. Next thing I knew, I saw a sign on a coffee shop window a few towns away that there was a business for sale in a small town called Angelica. Something in me told me that this was it." His other hand reaches for his heart, "So, I bought the shop, fixed it up, and on my very first day, *you* come wandering through those doors. I will never forget it because you were wearing that polka-dot dress of yours. Your hair was pulled back into a bun and your smile brightened up this whole place. I just knew I had made the right decision."

"Oh Jack."

"But, then strange things started happening."

"Strange?"

"Yeah, I've been getting a lot more spirits as the days go on and my sight—as they call it—has gotten stronger. They aren't just voices anymore, I can *see* things. I've also developed weird senses and other inexplicable 'things' that some can call intuition, but everything I see seems to come true. I think it's much more than that."

"Okay, but what happened to me last night?"

"Well," he gets flustered now, his hands grow sweaty inside mine, "The spirits, they like you, too."

"They like me?"

"Yeah, they flock to you for some reason." He confesses, "There are so many around here, it's getting hard to control them. They seem to know what I want, and I'm the only one that can get them what they want… so they *do* things for me. I didn't ask them to, but last night one of them…" he pauses.

"Jack! What is it?" Sera pulls her hand from his.

"They possessed you." His voice comes out softer than a whisper.

Sera's mouth drops.

"I'm so sorry, Sera. I never meant for that to happen. I would have tried to stop them but that guy, Nate, started with me and things got heated and…"

"You let them *possess* me?" She hisses, shivering at the memory.

"I didn't let them, they do it on their own. I can't control them anymore. Something is coming, or happening and they are all riled up." His hands reach for Sera again desperately. She slips from his grasp, up on her feet before he can grab hold of her.

"Jack. What about the kiss the other night? I wasn't in control then either."

"You weren't?" The hurt shows on his face.

"No," she admits softening her tone.

Shaking his head, those curly blond ringlets bounce. "Sera, I need to tell you, I've never seen anyone push a spirit out of themselves before. It was amazing."

"What do you mean?"

"When a person is possessed, they are under the control of the spirit, you have no choice in the matter. But, somehow you took control back and pushed them out of you."

"Hmm, how did I do that?" She wonders rhetorically.

"That's what I was hoping you could tell me." He takes a step forward closing the gap between them.

"I really don't know. I just kind of ... fought for my mind back."

"That's incredible. I have a feeling you're stronger than you think," he whispers. His hand reaching for Sera's cheek, she shies away taking a step backward.

"Sera, what's wrong?" She hadn't realized she was shaking her head until his words.

"I just don't know how I'm supposed to take all of this." She takes another step back. "Everything is happening too fast. First Nate's confession, and now you are... what? Some kind of medium?" he shrugs with a nod, "It's like I'm getting a crash course in a world I didn't know even existed."

"What did Nate tell you *he* is?"

"I don't want to get into it, Jack. I just don't know what to believe anymore. It's as if anything is possible."

Jack leans in a little closer, "Can I tell you something?"

Sera meets his eyes. "Yes."

"Ever since I met you, I've been feeling the exact same way."

Too many confessions for one day. Sera finds herself staring into those blue-green eyes she has seen every day for the past few months. Only they're looking back at her with a look she's never seen from him before. A look she knows she can probably never replicate, so she glances away. With so many questions and thoughts swirling around in her head, she doesn't want to add love triangle to it as well. On top of that, she gets the feeling Jack's still holding something back from her.

"Jack, I think I'm going to go. I have an early day tomorrow."

"Really?" he looks down, disappointed, "Okay, but are we okay?"

Sera pauses, maybe the possession wasn't his fault, but keeping secrets from her is. There's definitely more to this story than meets the eye. She can't exactly figure out if she has to start avoiding him. Plus, where would she get her coffee if that does occur? "Yeah, just don't let it happen again."

She turns to leave when he grabs her arm and spins her pulling her firmly into his rock hard chest. *Damn, who knew pouring coffee could make one so... buff?*

His voice is warm in her ear, "I promise I'll do anything in my power to protect you from this world, but I have a feeling you're already involved in it somehow."

He pulls away maintaining eye contact. Those blue-green eyes call to her, Sera almost divulges every secret she's ever had to him before the lights flicker and his hold is seemingly broken. There's something about Jack, she still doesn't trust.

Sera walks out of the coffee house alone, heading around back toward her car. The night is colder than she remembers only an hour or so earlier. Pulling her jacket closer, she picks up her pace. The parking lot is darker than it was before too, it seems all the street lamps have gone out. That's odd—too odd. Chills start to rack her body. Someone's watching her. The hair on the back of her neck stands at attention. All her senses seem to be on high alert, some internal alarm has just gone off. Something here is wrong… all wrong. She can sense something evil afoot.

Her feet pound the pavement. Only a few more steps and her car is right there. The door handle is centimeters from her now, her fingers reach out to grab it.

Something jerks her back. Arms wrap around her tight, too tight. They enclose around her in a death grip. The bicep at her throat tightens.

"Hey there, Red." He breathes into her ear. Sera thrashes against him. "I told you I'd find you." The more she struggles, the tighter he holds her, "I'm not letting you out of my sight again. Didn't I tell you I get what I want, *Angel*."

She coughs; the agony in her lungs is like fire as they search for air. He sniffs the air. Reaffirming it is still the creepiest thing she has ever experienced. His grip tightens and her head lightens as the world around her goes hazy at the edges.

Something twinkles against the night sky like a star. Slowly, at first and then brighter, and brighter. It's the only thing keeping her mind from falling into the darkness. It can't be a star; it's glowing brighter… brighter. It's coming from… her necklace.

The realization brings with it the brightest pulse yet. The man behind her shrieks and the arm at her throat releases her. She crumples to the ground gasping and rubbing her throat. Sera turns just in time to see the blond from the club walking back and forth shrieking in pain. She blinks and almost misses it. His eyes turn red as his entire body shakes and turns black before it poofs into ash that falls to the ground.

Sera stays bent over on the concrete holding her throat and staring in disbelief until Nate comes jumping over the bushes from behind.

"What happened? Sera are you okay?"

She blinks, "How—" She coughs, "What are you doing here?"

"I came to protect you... but I see you can handle yourself. What happened?" he walks to her helping her to her feet again.

"My necklace." Her hands slip from her throat to that vial she can't seem to part with. "It saved me."

"The necklace...?"

"Nate what just happened? Where did his body go?"

"Demons," he shrugs his shoulders, "they return to the ground once killed." He calmly states.

"Demons... wait... what?" She paces frantically now, "Why are Demons trying to kill me?"

"That's exactly what I'm trying to figure out, Sera. I know you are confused, but I am not the enemy."

"How do I know that? How do I know you are not a

Demon?"

He looks offended, but he replies, "Your necklace... it only pulses when I am around, it doesn't remain lit."

"Is that what it means?"

"I have a feeling it's more than that," he mutters under his breath.

"How?"

"It's not something I can explain. Many things in my world are just felt."

"Surprisingly, I can understand that."

A calm silence settles over them. Nate is the one that breaks it, "What were you doing here?" his fingers run through his hair.

"Getting coffee," she mumbles switching the weight from one foot to another.

"You came to talk to Jack didn't you?" *So totally caught. Can I not keep a secret from this guy?*

"Yes." She admits. "And how did you get here so fast?"

He pauses, "Don't get mad..."

"Whenever, someone starts a sentence with 'don't get mad,' the conversation will most likely end with someone getting mad." She glares at him expectantly.

He laughs nervously, "I was following you."

"Okay. Nate, I have to admit, I'm a little mad."

"Hear me out," he places his hands out as he continues, "You feel as though someone is watching you and then the accident—I think you may be in danger."

"What do you mean in danger?" but, as he says the words

aloud, she knows them to be true.

"I'm not exactly sure," he admits. His eyes follow her back and forth as she paces in front of him, "but I know I was right." He points to the pile of ash beside them.

Sera swallows hard. "So the deer, it might have been demonic because it disappeared?"

He nods, "Now you're thinking, is there anything else you can remember that felt... off?"

"Uh, Nate." She begins hesitantly, "That's not the first time I've seen this guy." She points to the ash pile.

His face grows serious, his jaw clenches and only one word escapes his lips, "Where?"

"Saturday, Amanda and I went into the city."

"The club?" he asks with a closed mouth.

"So that *was* you?"

"Tell me what happened?"

"Why did you leave when I was heading toward you?" The hurt must show in her eyes because he changes his tone.

"I didn't want our first encounter to be in a grimy city bar." He glances down toward his toes. "Now, what happened when you saw him?"

"He was at the bar, and he followed me into the bathroom. He sniffed me and he tried to *attack* me."

"How did you get away? Was it the necklace?"

"Um, no. I had left that at home. It was me, I didn't exactly know my strength at the time." Nate must have caught her drift because a sly smile crosses his face.

"Okay," he nods, "I have just one more question."

"Which is?"

"Just now, why didn't you fight back?"

"Oh, uh. I don't know it all kind of happened so fast… it's kind of hard to think when someone is constricting your air supply."

"I guess it might be." He smirks. "Let me follow you home."

"You were going to do that anyway, weren't you?"

"Yes. Only now, you know about it."

"How many other times have you followed me?"

"All the time, it was my job."

"Was?"

"Come, let's get you home." He deflects opening her car door. Sera sits in the driver's seat glancing up at him. His gorgeous blue eyes focus on her face, her heart starts beating fast in tune with the necklace at her throat. There's something about this mysterious man that she seems to find so irresistible, yet there are still so many unanswered questions floating about.

"Just answer me one question." He nods her to continue. "Have you seen me naked?"

"*That* is your one question?" he hides a laugh. "It's not like that, Guardians are only there to protect. Half the time they don't even notice such irrelevant stuff as that. They would only move in when the subject was in danger."

Sera glances sideways at him, "Okay."

With those last words, Nate closes the door and protectively watches her pull away and out into the street.

Pulling up to her house, she doesn't notice Nate's car, but she can feel that he is there. She crosses the street and walks up the front steps of her old farmhouse. One last glance up and down the street still shows all is silent.

Nineteen

Mom-tervention

SERA IS FRESH OUT OF the shower and getting ready for bed when her necklace pulses at her throat again. Her heart begins beating wildly; her fingers reach for her phone.

The bedroom door unexpectedly opens. Slowly at first, skeptically slow. Sera jumps. Ready to defend herself at any cost, she crouches on the bed against the wall prepared to pounce. The door continues to open until…

Bianca Cross walks into the room. One look from her mother is all she needed to see that she overreacted. Then she caught sight of her reflection in the mirror: Her hair quaffed in a fallen bun, her mascara still slightly smudged from the shower, and the crazed look in her eyes finally causes her to soften.

"Oh, Sera," are the only words her mother mutters

before she pulls her into her arms and strokes her hair like she used to do when she was a child.

They sat like that for almost an hour while Sera mentally put her life together again. "I'm sorry Mom." Sera wipes away a remaining tear with her finger.

"It's okay, I am first and foremost your mother." She sighs—a sigh that tells her there is more, "To be honest, we expected this break down. We just expected it to come a while ago with that break-up of yours. Only, it never came. You dove into work, you spent nights correcting papers with me in the living room. To be perfectly frank, this melt down is a long time coming. Just... don't let it define you. Get it out and move on."

"What if it's not something you can move on from?"

She gives Sera a stern look like she's trying to read her mind, "Then you adapt, don't let things get to you. Especially if you have no control over them."

Sera wants to ask her a million more questions, she wants to spill her guts, but the words Psychic Anna told her still resonate, *If you love her, keep her out of this.*

She can't involve her mother. She will do what she was instructed. She will adapt. She will get better. Things will change. "Okay, no more mopey-Sera."

"Don't get me wrong, the running is paying off dear, but coming home at all hours of the night and eating all the food in the house is starting to make me think your taking *drugs*."

Sera laughs, Bianca shoots her that look that warns her she sees nothing funny with this matter.

"You think I'm doing drugs?" Again, she can't control the giggles.

"Are you high right now?" Her mother's eyes tear into her.

"What? No!"

"Well, Hun, the appetite, the weight loss, the paranoia—your father and I are just... worried."

Sera covers her face with her arm, "Dad thinks this, too?"

"There was a conversation. We weren't judging you, we are just worried."

"Mom, I'm not on drugs," she announces, but what else would becoming half-Angel compare to? Nothing Sera could ever put into words. She's not proud of it, but she even debated letting them think that she was on drugs for a second. In the end, she decides against it. Sera refuses to have her parent's view of her tarnished.

"Is there anything you want to talk about?" Her motherly instinct is on overdrive today.

"No. It's nothing to worry about Mom." She hoped that was the truth, but something deep inside knew it was a lie.

Bianca pauses for a second, waiting for Sera to reconsider. "Okay then, get some sleep dear."

"Goodnight Mom."

The door closes softly behind her, and she listens to the footsteps on the wood floor trace their way down the hallway. Her parents are getting too close to this. They are starting to suspect things. For the first time since returning home from college, Sera debates moving out. Maybe she could move in with Amanda or maybe she's better off alone? The truth is, she's scared—scared of being alone. What if someone attacks her again? Who would be there to scream for?

After her little intervention with her mother, Sera is more than ready to close her eyes on this day. She's tucked into her covers and watching some bad reality television when she hears something strange. She reaches for the remote and hits mute.

Again, it comes, a tiny noise dinging against her window. Sera tosses off her covers and slips out of bed. Her breath is trying to quiet the incessant beating of her heart. Then just as she takes another step toward the window, something comes crashing through.

When Sera looks up she realizes she's crouched on the floor in an attack position, but the only thing she see's is a rock on the floor of her bedroom. Curious, she slowly walks toward the window. There's a thump outside. Her heart beating wild, her hair blowing behind her as the wind echoes through her open window. She finds the courage to peek outside.

The pull of the string causes the blinds to retract. Nate's soft face peers back at her from the other side of the pane. He raps once more mildly sarcastic as he maintains a crouched position on the slightly slanted roof he's perched on. Relieved, she flips the lock and swings the window open.

"Nate?" Glass crunches when she lifts up the broken window. "What are you doing here?"

"You said no one throws rocks at girls' windows anymore. So, I did."

She stifles a giggle. "It's supposed to be a small rock, just enough to clink the window and let her know you're outside."

"Oh." His hand shuffles his hair out of his eyes as his cheeks redden.

"But, we have another human expression..." His eyes glance up expectantly, so she continues. "It's the thought that counts."

"What does that mean? To humans?"

"It means that you tried. That's what really matters, in the end."

"Maybe."

He still looks upset so Sera continues, "Are you checking on me?"

"Your light was on."

"Why were you outside my house?"

"I was just making sure you were okay."

"I'm okay. Just a simple case of insomnia."

He's quiet for a few seconds, "I can't seem to get used to sleeping either."

"Can't get used to sleep? Sleep is the best. I would sleep all day if I could and even better, no one tries to kill me in my sleep. Well, most times, anyway."

"The truth is, the only time my mind can relax is when I watch you sleep."

"That's not creepy at all."

His eyes inspect her room. "Is that secular humor?" he

responds.

"Did you really watch me sleep?" Sera's suddenly self-conscious of her old striped pajamas.

He nods, "It was my job."

She processes this slowly, "Do I snore?"

"Only when you're sick." He adds peeking into her closet; his fingers graze her hangers causing them to jingle.

"Oh, I'm embarrassed now." Her hand flies to her forehead.

"I found it endearing." He wanders about the room touching her picture frames. It's almost like he's trying to memorize everything.

"You couldn't touch these things before, could you?"

"No." He turns with a sigh, "I couldn't use anything secular in the battle against the supernatural."

"What about me? Could you touch me?"

He comes to sit in the chair at her desk kicking his feet up on the pile of papers – he looks comfortable, like he's done this before. She can practically picture him there propped up on her desk with his hands behind his head. He breaks her out of her daydream.

"I don't know if you could call it *touching*. When touching, both people can feel it—it's shared. I reached out, but you never felt me. All the times I prevented you from tripping down the stairs or missing a curb, spilling coffee on yourself, you've never felt any of those things." He sighs before a slick smile shines across his face. "Which reminds me, you're very clumsy. Definitely not the easiest person to protect, you know." Sera hides a smile and turns to sit on the edge of her bed facing Nate in the chair.

"Imagine wanting to fly but only having wheels. I was preparing for a world with wings, but I never got off the ground."

"A world with wings isn't careless," he says.

"I wasn't careless, I was lost in my own head daydreaming about a world I couldn't have ever imagined." He nods in understanding. "Do you know why I felt that way?"

"No, there are things I still need to figure out."

Sera doesn't have a response so she stares at the small nail polish stain on the oak floor. The silence grows. Her thoughts are contemplative, until she finally glances up to meet his gaze. His azure eyes are on her with a raw openness she's never seen before, even in her dreams.

"I want you to touch me." Sera states.

His perfect eyes go wide, "What?"

"I want you to touch me for the first time."

He pauses nervously for a second until he's on his feet. The footsteps toward the bed seem to take forever. Once he stands before her, his hands remain at his sides. Sera reaches out, entwining his hand in hers. A soft gasp escapes his lips, and he only watches her turn it around inside both her hands. Her fingers dance over his palm. His fingers twitch in response. They are soft. Instead of callouses, there are only tiny white scars scattered in the palm and one across his thumb.

Gently, she pulls his arm to her face. He cups her cheek

in the palm of his hand. Her eyes close savoring his touch. It feels familiar, yet strange. His hands are suddenly warm, not sweaty, but warm like he had been holding a hot cup of coffee. They smell slightly of pine and saw dust. When she opens her eyes again, his eyes are staring intently at their hands connected at the side of her cheek.

His mouth had fallen open while her eyes were closed, and she struggles to hide a giggle. That draws his eyes to hers. He swallows, now able to keep his mouth closed.

"How was that?" Sera whispers.

"Everything I imagined and more." He breathes, reluctant to pull his hand back.

Eventually, Sera softly pulls his hand from her face. They remain clasped between hers. He's standing in front of her. The height of her bed brings her to only his chest as she remains sitting. Sera's eyes dart up his broad chest. His eyes are on their hands until he feels her eyes on him. When he meets them, things are different between them. There's a feeling of intimacy, openness. She's never had with anyone before, and she has that feeling, deep inside (the one that is never wrong) that tells her she never will again. This man—Angel, whatever he is—has changed her whole life. Even with all that has gone on, one look in his serene blue eyes is all she needs to realize she can never go back to the way things used to be. She's not even sure she would want them to.

Twenty

Fess up Sera

SERA'S WASHING HER FACE IN the river. She needs to get this dirt off her hands and cheeks. From what, she can't recall. She dries her dripping face with her shirt before getting up and turning to face the forest once more. Once she's inside the canopy of the treetops, she can't seem to see the sun anymore. It's growing dimmer as she continues deeper inside its depths. Her fingers graze the trunks of the trees, she's checking them for some kind of marking, but she can't seem to find it. So she trudges along, checking another tree, and then another before she changes direction and starts heading left. It isn't until she sees the purple flutter of wings that she stops in her tracks.

Sitting on a flower in a bush is that purple butterfly again. It takes flight, circling around her a few times before heading off and directing her path. She giggles and then follows the frisky insect. She follows over trees and under branches holding onto the thought that she will see Nate soon. It's the only thing keeping her going. It's getting even darker and becoming harder to see, but it isn't until she starts to hear weird noises that she really starts to get scared. All she can seem to think about is that Nate is out here alone, too. She's so lost in her daydreaming about Nate that she barely notices when the butterfly lands on a branch in front of her. Cautiously, she approaches the branch. The butterfly takes flight, soaring up, up, and away from her before disappearing in the night sky.

She releases a sigh, slowly turning to the branch. Pushing it aside, she wanders through to the clearing in the other side, only to find, Nate isn't here.

Instead, she finds an army of statue like warriors standing at attention. Some are carrying torches, others ornate knives and swords, and they are all dressed in weird body armor. She gasps aloud as they all turn in unison—their all-black eyes gleaming in the moonlight. They all take a step forward as a unit. Her eyes scan the strange faces until she recognizes one. Gabe. He seems to be leading the pack. His strong arms and tan skin glisten under the firelight from the torches. It appears as though all the soldiers are built in a similar manner. Big arms and broad shoulders, look like they lift cars for breakfast, and she begins to wonder what they could possibly do to a small girl like her.

Gabe yells something loudly, in a strange language. The soldiers respond in unison before beginning to approach her. She turns and runs back into the forest. She zips past trees and hurtles over rocks, but she can still hear them behind her. They are taunting her now.

"Come here, Angel."

"I like a woman that plays hard to get."

Those are just the few phrases she can catch. Their catcalls and excited screams echo around her in the dense forest. All is dark. She can't seem to find her way. The moon itself is hiding. They are catching up. Her nerves begin to get the better of her. She doesn't seem to notice the low hanging branch until it clotheslines her. She's falling, falling to the floor as footsteps are becoming louder and louder in her ear...

On her now daily run, Sera finds herself contemplating her future. She doesn't need to run; her body is becoming more defined by the day. She seems to have a ton of pent up energy and running helps her release it. Mainly, she does it because she actually likes it. It gives her such a freeing feeling. In a world in which she can't control, her breathing and pumping of her arms is something she can. The sun on her face and the wind in her hair is just a great way to start her insane days.

Above all else, this is the only time she has to herself to think. Once again, she begins to wonder where her life is going. For once, it's different from her usual thoughts. She has something she didn't have before... *hope*. Even though her world is crazy, to her it somehow finally makes sense. She has always had a sense of waiting she could never explain. It feels as though everyone in her life was moving on and she was stuck standing still.

Now that she's started this next chapter in her life, she finds herself worrying what will happen to her old life. What would she do if anything were to happen to her friends or family? How could she even begin to explain things to them? Amanda would understand. She always seems to know Sera better than she knows herself. She would have to answer a slew of questions—most of which she probably didn't have the answers to herself, but deep down she knows she needs to tell someone she can trust. Somehow, she understands she's going to need someone she can lean on in the coming weeks.

Sera arrives at work early to stop by Amanda's desk only to find that she's not there, once again. She immediately heads back down the elevator to check the break room. The elevator clangs to the first floor, and she releases a breath as she exits. Briskly, she walks out and to the left hand side. Keying in her password for the break room, it beeps and she opens it to find Amanda shoveling a bacon, egg, and cheese in her mouth, gossiping alongside a few nurses. Catching sight of Sera, as she no doubt dramatically opened the door, she mouths something to the effect of 'what's wrong' through a mouth full of breakfast sandwich.

"I need to talk to you." Sera says.

Amanda rises to her feet, tosses the rest of her sandwich in the garbage, and follows Sera outside. The automatic double doors take them out to the front and the fresh scent of pine from the trees hits the two girls.

Her best friend starts right in, "So, are you finally ready to tell me what's been going on?"

Sera can hear her attitude, but she only responds, "Yes.

I need to talk to someone before I go absolutely insane." She feels as though she has been holding this secret for months and not days. Keeping things from her best friend isn't possible despite what Anna warns. Now, the secret has become a poison eating away at her insides.

They come to sit on the picnic benches out in the courtyard. Sera takes a deep breath. "I just want you to know beforehand, it's kind of hard to process. It took me a while to truly swallow it myself."

"Okay." She pauses, "Give it to me straight." Amanda sits down on the bench beside her, bracing her hands on her knees.

Sera looks out at the pine trees ahead of them and starts from the beginning. She told her about her dreams and Nate, the accident, and by the time she ended with I'm part Angel now and I've developed... *gifts*. Amanda's mouth starts to gape open slightly. She allows Sera to finish without rebuttal and stays staring at her for a few more minutes than actually necessary before finally breaking the silence.

"Wow," Amanda sighs. "I knew you were a goody-two-shoes, but an *Angel*. God damn Sera, can you give a girl a shot?" she jokes and Sera finally laughs.

Laughing feels good, for some reason, she was surprisingly nervous to tell her closest friend about the events of the past few days. Honestly, she was scared Amanda would think she was a freak, but she should have known better. Sera pulls Amanda into a big hug as her eyes begin to tear. It's in this moment, on the picnic table, outside of their office, that makes her realize Amanda will always be there for her, no matter what happens.

"So, tell me more about this Angel-hunk. Is he hot? I want to meet him. Can we get some of his sexy Angel fellas to double date?"

Sera wipes a stray tear from her cheek, "I don't think that's going to work, but yeah he's totally gorgeous."

"Dish. I want all the steamy details!" Amanda commands playfully smacking her knee.

As Sera tells her friend all about the angelically handsome man that has been haunting her dreams and mysteriously popping up in her life, she can't help the huge smile plastered all over her face.

They are still talking about Nate as they walk into the office to get their workday started. They stopped off at Amanda's cubicle first, but before Sera continues toward her own, she spins back to her.

"Don't freak out, but I may be in a little danger. So if I'm MIA for a little bit, it's just because I'm trying to figure things out. I don't want to put anyone in harm's way, okay?"

"Danger?" she leans closer, "Danger from what exactly?"

"I don't really know." Amanda's thoughts bring up Sera's own questions. "You know what, never mind, it's probably nothing to worry about." Sera shakes her head dismissively, waving her hand as she wanders back toward her desk.

Twenty-one

Workplace Drama

ATER THAT DAY, SERA IS FINISHING extra work when a little email pops up on the corner of her screen that a meeting is scheduled. Not just any meeting, a meeting with her boss, Mrs. Valentine.

She hasn't had an individual meeting with her boss since… well, her interview. Something must be amiss. The rest of the hour went by slower than her college graduation ceremony. It ticked on and on. Sera couldn't focus on work and her phone didn't ring once. By the time the big hand landed on the hour, she was out of her seat and wandering down the hall. She circled around the bend and noticed New-Guy-Gabe was not at his desk, his computer still off, and a pile of work sitting beside it.

She continues to the back corner where Mrs. Valentine's office sits. With a deep breath, she knocks on the door.

"Come in," a deep voice responds.

Another deep breath and her hand falls to the pendant on her neck. It's slightly warm. She glances down. It's doing that pulsing thing again. Hesitantly, she opens the door.

The room is slightly darker than usual. Mrs. Valentine's high backed chair is facing the opposite way as Sera makes her way inside. The overhead light is off, but there's a desk lamp on behind her. The high chair casts a large shadow over the room and throws Sera into darkness.

She seats herself in one of the chairs opposite her boss's huge intimidating mahogany desk. Once seated, Mrs. Valentine immediately spins around. Her face is now shadowed in the wake of the big chair.

"Ms. Cross, it has come to my attention that you have been engaging in… let's call it *inappropriate* conduct with someone within the office."

"Inappropriate conduct?" she gasps.

"I really expected more from one of our top billers." Just as she finishes her sentence, the door opens behind her and in walks Gabe. "Oh good, Gabe, you made it."

He brings with him a whiff of something. It's strange like garbage or rot.

"Gabe? What does he have—"

Her boss interrupts her, "Gabe, here has informed me that you two have been *indecent*." She can't seem to say the words aloud. Sera looks back and forth between the two.

"Indecent? Is this a joke?" Sera turns to Gabe. He looks taller from this angle. His tan deeper, his eyes… darker. He has this weird look on his face, almost like he's pleased with creating lies that will ruin Sera's career is a game to him. Then he does something she wasn't expecting… he winks at her.

"Interpersonal relations are no joke here, Ms. Cross." Every time she says her name, it sounds condescending. Sera's fists begin to clench at her sides. *Could this really be happening?*

"What is this? Is this because I wouldn't go to lunch with you?" Sera has blocked out Mrs. Valentine completely now.

Gabe leans on the desk, gradually drawing closer to her. "No Angel, this is a lot more than that."

Sera's necklace is glowing brighter in the darkened room. It casts an eerie glow across their faces. The closer Gabe gets the stranger she begins to feel. His gorgeous features suddenly begin to change. His green eyes darken until they are a solid black mass. Those alluring facial features grow longer until they substitute evil grotesque ones in its place. He smiles down at Sera like he's finally happy to be out of the character he's been playing.

Disgusted, she turns to Mrs. Valentine, could she be one of *them* too? The pulsing light at her throat illuminates the dark room enough so that Mrs. Valentine's eyes glimmer against it. They are not as she remembers; they are crimson.

This is wrong all wrong. "What are you?" she whispers. Gabe jolts forward, Sera immediately jumps to her feet causing the chair to smash in front of her. Gabe lunges for her again, but she slips out into the hall and slams the door behind her.

Sera begins speed walking down the hall, trying not to alarm anyone. Maybe she is seeing things again. She zips past a few cubicles until she can feel her necklace thumping against her bare chest. Pausing, she turns around. Mrs. Valentine's door is still closed. Although, there's a distinct smell to the air around her now. She can feel heaviness, like something is weighing her down. The hairs on the back of her neck are at attention once again, a sign that something is wrong. Her eyes dart around the cubicles around her.

It doesn't happen right away, but as she continues to survey the office, Nosey-Nancy pops her head up from her cubicle. It's not the fact that it happened. Nancy always had a manner of being the first to pop her head into everything. It's her eyes. They shine crimson and they stare directly at Sera like laser beams. Her head bobs uneasily above the edge of the cubicle, like a head bobbing above the water.

Get out of there.

Like some creepy game of Jack-in-the-box, her other coworker's heads begin to pop up in the same manner. Their eyes are all gleaming blood red. Their heads twisting to the side like curious puppies. All of them seem to be staring *through* her as though she would easily become their next meal.

Before she realizes it, she's running—running for the elevator, running for safety, and running for her life. She can feel their eyes tearing into her back, more and more people she called friends are peeking their red eyes over at her. *There it is! The elevator. Only a few more steps, only a few more…*

Gabe steps into the center of the hall, blocking her from her only way of escape. The sheer size of him blocks the entire opening, one bicep on each side of the cubicle. She glances behind her. *How did he get around her?*

"Where do you think you're going Angel-face?"

"I'm seriously getting sick of these nicknames."

He looks like he's about to laugh. His elongated head leans back, his black eyes close, but the sound that comes out of his mouth is deeper. It's an impossibly deep rumble that shakes the very ground she stands on.

Get out of there NOW!

Her internal voice calls her body into action. As Gabe is weaving back and forth across the space between them, stalking her like a lion would stalk its prey. His feet spaced apart, his arms bulging at his sides now, she needs to get out of here.

The weight she feels is increasing so fast around her, she can barely breathe. She attempts to process her next steps, and her body jumps into action. Sera squats low, shifting her weight from side to side until Gabe makes his first move.

It's only a matter of time, she knows as they watch each other for a couple seconds. Proving her right, he lunges for her slightly to her right. Her legs leap to the left. Kicking off the cubicle wall, she flips around him and lands in a crouched position. Gabe eats carpet. She breaks into a run toward the elevator whose doors have just opened.

It feels as though it all happens in slow motion. Sera's

feet pound toward the elevator. Her heart beating so loudly she can hear it in her own mind, her arms pumping at her sides until finally, she lunges into the elevator.

She feels claws scratching into her shoulder as the doors close behind her. She whips her head back to see a black hand wrapped around her bicep with hideous dark nails puncturing her skin. Instead of opening back up, as the sensors should have, the elevator doors continue to close until she hears the crack of bone breaking inside of the arm, and it finally loosens its grip on her. Breaking free, she rolls over onto her back and slides herself against the back wall trying to get as far away from the door as possible.

Once the elevator begins to move, the grotesque arm slides to the top until the weight of the elevator finally breaks it off from its body, and it falls to the floor of the elevator in front of her.

She winces at the sight of the blackened hand with witch-like fingers and long black nails on the floor in front of her feet. What's interesting is there is no blood, it isn't until it starts twitching and evaporates into the floor that she realizes what it is. But ... that would mean Gabe is...

Strangely, she has never felt so safe in an elevator before. When the elevator dings that it has reached the bottom floor, she jumps to her feet and dashes out of the elevator as soon as the doors open. The automatic double doors on the front of the building open for her and she continues to sprint down the driveway, past the line of trees, and toward the parking lot.

Clicking her alarm off, she swings open the car door and plops inside before closing the door and locking it five times. She takes several deep breaths as her grip on the steering wheel causes the metal to whine in complaint. Her grip loosens, her head falls down onto them, and she allows herself to cry. What just happened? Was Gabe a Demon this whole time? What about her co-workers? The look of their red eyes causes a shiver to wiggle through her.

A sob escapes her lips when another thought dawns on her; no one called the elevator, yet it was there. That sensor should have reopened the door, yet it crushed the arm instead. She didn't even have to press the button for down, the elevator just *knew*. Those gut feelings she gets are now telling her something else—someone, somewhere is looking out for her.

Twenty-two

Sera Comes Clean

ONCE SERA GETS HER emotions in check, she places a call to Amanda who thankfully happened to be on lunch at the time the drama at work occurred. She told Sera everything seemed to be back to normal when she got back. All her co-workers were back to their annoying nosey selves asking her where Sera had run off. All was business as usual, except Gabe—no one seems to have seen him at all today.

Sera's fists clench against the steering wheel again, why her? Why is all of this happening to her? As her anger increases, her hands on the steering wheel begin to glow slightly. The power seemingly drawing from her increased feelings of frustration grows brighter.

Amanda is still babbling into the phone, Sera interrupts, "Uh, Amanda."

She grows quiet, "Yeah?"

"I can't come back to work."

"What? Why?"

"I'm a ticking time bomb. I don't know what I am capable of, I don't know how to control it."

"We can get through this together Sera, don't leave me."

"I'm not leaving you, I just can't work there anymore. Maybe I can find a position billing from home or something."

"Sera…"

"I know, I know, but, things are coming after me too. Wherever I am, no one is safe."

Amanda breathes heavily into the phone, "I just don't want to lose you."

"You will never lose me."

"Promise?"

"Promise." Sera breathes a sigh of relief.

One solution down, only a million more to go.

Sera starts her car and drives off toward home. Somehow, on her way there, she takes a detour. She can't seem to find the energy to explain her early appearance to her mother. She's debating on whether to call Nate when she is passes Jack's Coffee Bean. Something inside her is begging her to stop. She obeys, pulling into the parking spot right in front and heading inside.

Walking through the door, the aroma of coffee wafts toward her, and it seems to calm her nerves. Maybe it's Jack's psychic voodoo, that makes this place feel like home. Jack doesn't seem to be behind the bar today and surprisingly, she's disappointed. She had a feeling he had more to tell her.

He had the answers she so desperately seeks.

She places her order with the skinny blonde with pink highlights before taking her spot in the green chair in the corner. Curled up in her chair with her latte in her hand, she stares out the window as her mind attempts to wrap itself around the day she's just had.

"Sera?" Jack calls from the hallway to his office.

With a forced smile, she replies, "Hey Jack." He takes a seat across from her and she can feel his eyes study her.

"Are you okay?"

"Yes." She lies. It must not have been that convincing because Jack is on his feet with his hand out for hers.

"Come, let's go to my office to talk." She allows him to take her hand and follows him down the hallway to the back. The nervous feeling she had around Jack has diminished. He would never hurt her on purpose. He welcomes her into his office. It's surprisingly modern. She's never been in here before; it just doesn't seem like Jack.

It's modern, sleek, glass bookshelves have shelves alternating randomly across the width of it. His desk is large and glass sits on curved, sleek, gunmetal posts. Also, it's neat. For some reason, Jack's Californian appearance made her think he should be more carefree and disorganized. Behind his desk sits a few filing cabinets and next to her is a black leather couch. Jack takes a seat on the couch and motions for her to have a seat next to him. She does so, but for some reason avoids eye contact by keeping her eyes on her hands in front of her.

"Sera, you are definitely not okay."

"I am okay now, but I had to quit my job."

"Why? What happened?"

Something urges her to respond, honestly. "Something happened at work." He looks at her through blond ringlets that have fallen into his face as he waits for her to continue. With a deep breath she does, "My boss called me into the office today with these strange accusations. But, then I noticed something weird about her eyes…"

"Were they red?" he interrupts.

"Uh, yeah, bright red. How did you know?"

"Red eyes are a sign of possession." He motions her to continue.

"Will they be like when I was *possessed*," she whispers the word as it still haunts her. "That I didn't know what was going on?"

"Yes, they have no memory of what happens while under the influence of a spirit."

"It was the creepiest thing I've ever seen." Her arms wrap around herself, "But

what do all black eyes mean?"

"Why?" he gulps, "Did you see black eyes?"

"One of my coworkers, his eyes turned all black like an alien or something, and he attacked me."

"He attacked you? You were attacked by a *Demon* and you survived? How?"

"A Demon?" She repeats as Jack continues to hound her with concerned questions. On some level, she knew this.

"How did you get away, Sera?"

"I just ran."

"Sera…" his face grows serious now, his eyes fall to the floor.

"What is it?"

"There's something else I need to tell you." He twists now, pulling her hands into his.

"No more secrets Jack."

"Right, no secrets." He breathes deeply. "Well, remember I told you the spirits like you? And the entire spiritual world is just becoming more and more open to me?"

"Yes."

"Well, in the spirit of transparency, I feel I need to tell you. I was contacted by someone so purely evil, I will have a nasty taste in my mouth forever."

"Who?"

"Lucifer," he whispers his name insinuating just the mention of it could cause him to appear. "He reached out to me the other night. It was through a spirit."

"What?" She is on her feet in seconds pacing back and forth.

"Sera, please sit back down."

"I can't. I just need to release some nervous energy. Just tell me what happened." Her pacing continues.

"He asked me to use my relationship with you to get you to join us."

"Join us? *Us?*" My mind caught that before anything else.

He glances toward the ground again, "Yes, he informed

me my gifts are not by accident. He had given them to me. This was all some kind of sick plan of his."

Sera's feet stop in front of Jack. He glances up to her face. The look must not have been too pleasing. "Sera, my powers may be evil, but I am not."

"How is this even possible?" She rambles.

Not able to take it any longer, Jack jumps to his feet grabbing the sides of her arms to keep Sera still.

"Sera, I would *never* hurt you. I *love* you," he admits as his sea green eyes explore hers.

"Did you just say what I think you said?" She blinks.

"I'm sorry, I'm sorry I brought all this on you, but," he breathes, "I can only be so sorry because it brought me here… it brought me to *you*."

"Jack…" Sera whispers, before collapsing to her knees in front of him. He mirrors her, dropping to his knees as well. "There is something I need to tell you as well."

He places his hands on her face bringing her eyes up to meet his, "What do you mean?"

"I don't really know how to tell you this, but you didn't bring this all upon me." She continues to tell him about Nate and the accident and something to the effect of her being half Angel and how she seems to attract evil now. When she finishes, his hands have dropped from her face, and he is sitting a little farther back than before.

"Sera, what is Nate to you?" his eyes full of pain as he expects her answer.

"I…" She blinks. "Um, I don't exactly know."

"But, it's serious?"

"His-blood-runs-in-my-veins, serious."

Jack leaps to his feet like she had just scalded him with hot water. Resting his lean frame against the glass bookshelves, he folds his arms in front of him.

"Jack…" her voice trails off slightly. What could she possibly say? The hurt in his eyes is more than she can bear. "I had no idea you felt so strongly. I didn't plan for any of this to happen. I never wanted you to be in the middle of this."

Her eyes begin to fill with tears as the words slip from her mouth. He caves, coming back to kneel in front of her. "It's not your fault." He reaches his hands out helping her to her feet once again, "Actually, it sort of all makes sense now."

"What do you mean?" she asks keeping her eyes on their clasped hands.

He chuckles a little as he explains, "Well, now I know why the spiritual world is all worked up about you. I know why I find you so irresistible."

Sera coughs uncomfortably, "And why exactly is that?"

"Because you're half human, half Angel. You are a beautifully, powerful anomaly."

"What makes that special?"

"You are the only one of your kind."

"Really?"

He continues, "You can make your own rules, you are human you can walk the Earth and communicate with other humans. You are your own *race*."

"Why are you looking at me like that?" his gaze makes

her shift in the chair uneasily.

"I was right, Sera, there is something about you," he laughs. "I've been reading up on what I thought was mythology lately."

"Cut to the point."

"Well, Angels don't bleed. Angels don't hunger, want, thirst, or do anything besides the work of God. The fact that Nate felt the way he did about you, the fact that when he cut himself, he actually *bled*, goes against everything I've ever read about Angels."

"So, what does this mean?" her head is shaking from side to side now.

"It means you, Sera, are a once in a lifetime anomaly. Someone up there," he points to the ceiling, "really went through a lot of trouble to make you who you are today."

Without a word, Sera plops down on the leather couch. Jack again finds his way next to her.

"I don't know what to say…" She whispers trying to put all the pieces of this puzzle together.

"You don't have to say anything Sera. Just take it all in." Jack whispers back into her ear as he places his arm around her on the couch, pulling her closer.

"Jack, can I ask you a question?" she peeks up at him.

"Ask away."

"When I was possessed you were fighting Nate, how were you able to keep up with him?"

His mouth scrunches up as he contemplates this, "I don't know. That was right after I was *contacted*. Maybe, he's trying to even the side by expanding my gifts."

"Okay," she nods, "I have another question: If you are 'evil' then how come I feel so safe with you?" She makes sure to make quotation hand signal as she says evil.

He smiles for the first time since she mentioned Nate. "Because you know I'd never hurt you."

"Not like that." She rolls her eyes, "I meant when we were at the club, I could feel danger, but when I was with you they didn't bother me again."

"Again? So, something did happen in that bathroom."

"Yes."

"Was it Demonic? I smelled evil around."

"He had black eyes, yes."

"Where is he? I'm going to kill him." His fists clench at his sides.

"He's dead. Well, as dead as Demons can get." He looks at me expecting more. "We killed him yesterday."

"Yesterday? Then, how did you get away at the bar? You looked so freaked out."

"He approached me at the bar. I snuck away from him, but he followed me into the bathroom. He kept calling me Angel. I didn't know what he meant at the time." She pauses before adding, "He tried to *touch* me."

Jack's body stiffens, "I wish I had killed him myself."

"I got away. I ran into you and things were fine from then on."

"How exactly did you escape a *Demon?*" he catches her gaze.

She can't stop the smile that crosses her face when she remembers the cocky blond propped up on the wall of the bathroom with broken shards of mirror around him and the sink spurting water all over his face. "I pushed him through a wall."

"You pushed a full grown Demon?" He sounds suspicious.

"Yeah."

"Wow, I wish I could have seen that."

"That's another thing I don't understand, why couldn't you? He was just there when I left and gone as soon as you opened the door."

"I'm not exactly sure. That, unfortunately, sounds like a question for Nate." The way he mentions his name makes it sound foul. "I just know that for me, no one can see what I see. So maybe you are in the same boat, now we can see things on a spiritual level that others can't."

"Are there two different levels of spirits? Because I can't see yours?"

"Maybe it's because we are meant to be on different sides." He admits the connection Sera was trying so hard not to make.

They sit in silence for the next few minutes both continuing to process. Eventually, Sera has a question first. "Jack, what do your spirits want from me?"

His curls bounce slightly as he turns his head back to meet her.

"What do you mean?"

"You said they were all worked up about me. Well, what do they want from me?"

"Uh, I don't exactly know." He looks uncomfortable. "They haven't exactly asked me anything, I just see more and more around. I feel a… disturbance. He stands looking away at his loss for words, "It's hard to explain."

"It's okay Jack," she shrugs. "I was just wondering."

They sit on the couch for a few more minutes in silent contemplation until Sera decides she should get going. Jack walks her down the hallway and across the shop to the front door. The shop has closed since they had gone into the back. The lights are dimmed and he reaches into his pocket to take out the keys to let them both out.

His hand pauses before the lock, and he turns back to her. "Sera, I want you to know. I'm not going to do it."

"Do what?"

"Help him. I refuse to harm you. I will do anything in my power to help you Sera, do you understand?" His blue-green eyes glimmer in the dim lighting. Her gut feeling is picking up something else now… love. Sera glances away, embarrassed.

"Thank you Jack," she smiles up at him, "I'm sorry to put you in this position."

Why does everyone seem to be in danger because of her?

"This isn't your fault. None of this is. Don't ever feel like you are a mistake, you are just the opposite."

"Thanks," she meekly states before he pulls her into a hug. His strong arms wrap around her protectively. Part of her wishes she could reciprocate the feelings he has. On the other hand, a small part of her has always belonged to Nate. It's hard to put into words, but heck so is the rest of her life now. They say their goodbyes, and he protectively watches her walk to her car and head off for home.

Twenty-three

Hostility

AFTER WHAT CAN ONLY BE described as a long day, Sera is finally heading home. She feels as though she could cry again. She always knew there was something different about her; she always knew she was waiting for something. Only, what she wasn't expecting was the fact that her presence alone could put the people she loves at risk. Risk for possession, risk for harm, and even risk for death. She doesn't even want to imagine her parents with red eyes; she shivers at the unwelcomed thought.

Finally pulling up to the little blue farmhouse, she steps out of the car. As soon as she closes the door behind her, she's hit with that gut feeling again. The bad one—the one that screams trouble. Her necklace is no longer pulsing at her throat, it's maintaining its solid glow. All the hairs on her neck are standing at full attention. She tosses her purse onto the hood of her car, and her body immediately taking a defensive stance. A cool breeze filters through her sweater as the naked branches of the trees surrounding her sway like creepy fingers against the dark night sky. Another cold breeze hits, and it carries with it that putrid smell of garbage… and something else. The smell is so strong, she can taste it in her mouth. Gagging, she scans the deserted street.

The houses that line the left side of the street have all gone dark, not a single light to be found. The night around her is silent. Not a cricket or owl in the trees, it's a haunting silence that envelopes everything around her. It's like the street is stuck in a bubble.

Sera finds herself squinting toward the dead end of her street, the shadows from the dense woods hiding all their secrets. *Something* is there.

Her instincts take over, closing her eyes; she attempts to clear her mind. Blacking out her feelings is what makes her take focus. There's something else in the smell. It smells like sulfur and rotting garbage. Almost like that time she burned her hand on her curling iron. Her entire room had this gross smell to it. It reeked of… burned flesh.

She gasps her eyes fluttering open. Her feet take a step toward the dead end. She stares at the shadows ahead of her, willing them to show her what they hide. Slowly, as she focuses, a dark figure appears in the wood. It appears to be getting… bigger. It's coming *closer*.

Get out of there.

The internal voice is screaming at her. Every fiber of her

being is telling her to run, but the closer the figure gets the more it appears *human*. Human, only it's approaching on all fours like an animal. Sera's heart is racing inside her chest. Especially, when the smell only gets stronger, more agonizing. She also begins to pick up a clicking noise echoing from the approaching shadow.

Seraphina, get out of there!

No. She has spent her entire life in hiding. Whatever it is that is happening to her or coming for her, it's going to come to a head tonight. This is going to stop here, one way, or another. She'd rather die taking a stand than cowering in fear for the rest of her life.

The closer the figure gets, the more repulsed Sera begins to feel. It's not just about the smell any longer. The thing has set off some internal alarm in her brain. The night grows colder and colder, her heart increases, her palms grow sweaty from clamping them so hard. Her breath increases causing little puffs to appear in front of her. What is this thing?

Her feet feel like they are stuck in cement. Maybe, she should have run. That voice has never been wrong before. Even if she wanted to, her body doesn't seem to cooperate. This must be what shock feels like. The clicking is growing louder with each step. It isn't until the figure finally leaps over the guardrail and into a spotlight of moonlight on the street that she can finally see what it is. It is a *she*.

She is human, or at least she was. It's a young woman still dressed in a long blue nightgown. Her long, dark hair is all disheveled and her nightgown is covered in soot giving the illusion that she had crawled for miles.

The woman looks up from her crouched position on all fours and Sera can see her glowing red eyes. Her cheeks are sunk in, she appears to be only skin and bones. She doesn't recognize the face. The woman opens her mouth to speak and a chill runs down Sera's spine at her words. It isn't what she is saying; it's the woman's voice. It's not her own. It's deep, too deep, and too… *evil*. She remembered what Jack told her earlier; this woman is possessed.

"Surrender yourself to the dark one," the woman's deep voice states. Her neck twists grotesquely to the side.

Sera doesn't know what to do. She just stands there in disbelief. What did she think she could do? She can't harm a human. The woman will wake up and remember nothing of this. She shivers.

"Surrender… Surrender… Surrender." The woman repeats and continues her spider-like approach. Sometimes her legs come over her arms as she crawls forward. Sera comes to the realization the crackling sound is coming from this ladies' *bones*. Completely freaked out now, Sera takes a step backward. Big mistake. The woman leaps onto her eerily fast. She's on her chest knocking Sera flat on her back against the concrete road. She crouches on top of her with her dirty hands reaching for Sera. She rips the pendant from her neck and wraps her hands around her throat.

No, my pendant! It lands on the curb in front of her house before the glow fades and the vial falls dark. Her hand reaches for it, uselessly.

"Surrender or die!" The woman is yelling now; the hands at her throat, growing tighter and tighter. Sera stares up at this skeleton woman with her eyes wide. She can only watch the woman cut off her air supply.

In the last moments of her life, something bright and hot comes from behind her. The woman falls off her chest. Sera turns to see the woman land on her front lawn with a tumble before returning to her feet with cat like reflexes. The woman lets out a sound that can only be described as a growl of some sort. A man walks up from down the street. He's tall and broad, dressed in all black complete with ski mask hiding his identity. The possessed woman approaches again low like a predator stalking prey. She's about to pounce on the person that saved Sera's life.

Sera rolls onto her stomach, watching as the man throws another ball of fire from his hands as if it were a simple baseball. He misses, and her father's truck in the driveway is now a piece of burning scrap metal.

He pulls out a silver blade from a loop in his pants that seems to be glowing white, and he dives for the woman. She narrowly misses it scrambling up into a tree. She climbs like a spider all the way up and across a branch, upside down. When she stops about halfway across, she twists her head all the way around at an unnatural angle.

"Join us or be destroyed." Her horribly deep voice chills Sera's blood all the way to her core. Never taking her gaze from Sera, she lands on the stranger's chest knocking him onto his back. She begins to scratch at his face like a tiger.

Her movements are so fast her eyes can barely keep up.

Her little internal voice must have finally noticed she needed encouragement, it finally responds.

You are stronger than you think.

Stronger. Isn't that what Jack had said to her as well? She *is* strong. She's contemplating her next action when the woman slashes the mask off the stranger's face. His face twists away from another slash. Chestnut hair comes tumbling out. Gorgeous blue eyes meet hers only a moment before he bends to escape another blow. *Nate!*

A floodgate opens; the next moves Sera makes are all instinctual. She jumps to her feet. Her body takes it from there. Her eyes close her emotions surging around her like a tornado. She can feel as it pulls from the very tip of her toes to every strand of her hair. She controls them, bringing the power of it all to her core. It becomes too strong, and she falls to her knees, fists clenched at her sides. Biting her lip, she somehow maintains her hold. Her fists are clenching so hard she can feel her nails digging into the palms of her hands. She can't stop. Vaguely, she can hear Nate's voice outside of her little bubble.

"Run, Sera, run!"

When she opens her eyes, she brings her fists in front of her, and they are glowing. Suddenly, it all becomes clear. She stands to her feet, all her senses have returned. Nate is screaming at her to run. Instead, she feels her power making her stronger, more confident. She takes a step closer to the woman. Whoever sent her made a mistake coming here.

Her power comes to a head, and she extends her hands toward the woman. Then Sera allows the power to release itself from her center through her hands. Pure white power surges from Sera's outstretched palms. It smacks into the woman on top of Nate's broad chest as if she hit her with a baseball bat. Falling onto her back on Sera's front lawn, the woman immediately begins convulsing like she's having a seizure before lying still and evaporating into the ground.

Fully exhausted, Sera falls to her knees. Nate stumbles to his feet and runs for her. He pulls Sera's weak body into his arms.

"Sera, are you okay?"

"What happened... the woman... red eyes, but she evaporated?"

He nods in understanding, "It was too late. There was nothing good left in her." his hands explore her face, her body, "Sera, Sera stay with me."

"I just feel so... tired."

"What did you do?" his voice shrieks. She's never heard Nate so out of control before, even in her dreams. His eyes are glancing this way and that, like he was looking for something.

"I did what you showed me in my dream." Sera gets out between yawns.

"You dreamed of *this*?"

"I dreamed of *you*," she whispers before falling into a dreamless sleep in his arms.

Twenty-four

The Proposal

THE SOUND OF A CRACKLING fire breaks through the darkness. Sera awakens from the deepest, dreamless sleep of her life in an unfamiliar bedroom. Her hand flies immediately to her chest. Her pendant has returned to its rightful spot.

Confused, she takes a glance around. She's lying in a huge four-poster mahogany bed. White linens drape across the top. Directly across from her is a fireplace with a huge stone mantle. Situated above the mantle is a three-pronged sword of some kind. It shines as the flicker of the fire reaches it. Beside the fire is a wall of bookshelves and another chair like the one in Jack's coffee shop. Next to the bed, Sera finds her reflection in the mirror of a vanity desk. Geez, she looks… exhausted. From the wood exposed interior and the poignant smell of pine. She can only be in one place—Nate's house.

As if reading her mind, the door opens. In walks Nate, shirtless, tall, perfect. He's very well built—to put it mildly. His jeans hang low, exposing the curve of his hipbone. The image makes her bite her bottom lip. She barely notices the steaming cup of something between his hands because of his half-naked distraction. Then she notices that on his shoulder he has a bandage.

She sits up against the headboard, "You're hurt."

"I'm the one that should be asking if you're okay."

Sera rubs her forehead, "Yeah, what happened?"

"I was hoping you could tell me." He takes a seat on the edge of the bed and hands her the cup.

"I don't know," she states taking the cup from him. "My body just reacted."

Nate turns serious, "I've never seen someone use so much… power."

"Never? But, I saw it in my dream."

"What *exactly* do you dream about, Sera?"

"Just dream stuff. You're there, usually."

"I need specifics. Do you dream about Angels and Demons?"

"Yes, sometimes."

"And what you did, you saw *that* in your dreams as well?"

"Yes. Nate, I think my dreams are more than they seem."

"I was thinking the exact same thing." His hand reaches for her open one. It's still warm from the cup he was just holding. The touch warms Sera from the inside out. "Will you tell me about them?"

I nod, "Every night, since I was about eighteen, I've been having these vivid dreams. *You* have become like a reoccurring character in all of them." Sera begins to blush as she tells him, "It came to the point where I would just begin to search the dream for you. At some point, I would always find you."

That brings a smile to his face as well, "And, there were Demons?"

"Sometimes. In one they chased me, in others it was you with... wings."

He flinches almost like she touched upon a subject she wasn't supposed to. "I have something to tell you, Sera."

"Wait, I'm not finished."

He nods for her to continue. "These dreams showed me how to use that power. What can that mean?"

"The dreams showed you what to do?"

"Yes, only it was you glowing—not me."

"I have to tell you," he glances down at our hands, "I've never seen anyone in Heaven or Earth, do what you just did."

"Seriously?" Sera pulls her hands back, alarmed.

"Yes." His eyes are kind, allowing for her to pry farther.

"Could that be why Demons are attacking me?"

"Maybe, but I don't see how they could know you even carried such powers when you didn't know yourself."

"True, only... that's not the first time I've done something like that."

"What do you mean?" His tone grows more serious.

"The night I came here, I told you I had an accident. It was more than that." Her face shies away from his gaze, "I saw a deer, blacker than night and eyes redder than my hair. When I got out to check on it, it disappeared into thin air." She lowers her eyes to the cup in her hand when his serious face becomes too much, "I was getting ready to leave when there was a car coming down the road, my body just reacted. I shielded myself from it, somehow."

"And someone saw you do this?"

"I can't say for sure, but I feel like people are watching me all the time."

Nate turns toward the fire. "Sera, you need to trust your instincts. They are more advanced now. It may mean life or death."

He takes a deep breath, "I have something to tell you now," he begins hesitantly. "Since we are in the spirit of transparency, I feel like I have to tell you what has been going on with *me* this past week or so." Sera's breath catches in her throat as he continues. "Sera, I had been guarding you for months before. I would watch as you tossed and turned in your sleep. I would see things that you couldn't. I knew there was something about you. I knew there was so much more to you. Only, I couldn't put my finger on it. Angels, we aren't used to feelings. I don't know if being on Earth for so long made me more susceptible, but I started having *romantic* feelings for you."

Sera loses all feeling in her fingers. *Holy crap*. She places the coffee cup on the nightstand beside her before she does something embarrassing.

"I didn't know what it was at first. Seeing you with that Jack guy, it just made me feel *angry*," Nate admits, glancing down for a millisecond before his eyes meet hers—bright blue and deeper than she's ever seen them. "I've never felt so many emotions before, conflicted, jealous, angry, confused, guilty. Angels don't feel any of these. I had no idea how to handle them all. I needed some space to get my thoughts in order when you were involved in that accident. You were lying there in a pool of blood, and I just didn't know what to do. When I saw my finger was bleeding, I just reacted. I wasn't thinking about the repercussions." He's on his feet now pacing back and forth as he recites the rest.

"After I tucked you into bed, I was summoned to the Throne Room. You see, it's against the law what I did. I went too far in trying to save you. I didn't even know it was possible for Angels to bleed. But, it happened, and I had to accept the consequences."

He's struggling for words now, his pace staggering, "Um, well. What I wanted you to know is… Well, the reason you can see me now is…" his fingers glide through his hair. "I was excused from Heaven. I… I'm considered one of the Fallen now. That's why you can suddenly see me. That's why I decided to come back here. I was just trying to make sure you were okay. I couldn't leave you like that. And in the sake of full honestly, I wanted to see if I stood a chance with you." Once he finishes, he comes to sit back beside her on the bed.

Sera sits there staring at the flames of the fire before her.

Of all the things she pictured in her head, how was this not one of them?

"I feel guilty." She finally says.

"Don't," he responds. "I don't want you to feel that way, that's not why I told you. You want answers, and I want to give them to you. No more secrets."

"No more secrets," she reiterates. "I get it now. I get why you did what you did." It seems like a lifetime ago when she was actually mad at him for keeping secrets.

"I know this must sound crazy to you because to you, we just met, but, I have known everything about you for months now, and I just couldn't bear to watch you deteriorate in my arms like that. I… I love you Seraphina. I would do anything to protect you."

He takes her hand in his once more. Bringing it to his lips, he kisses the top of her hand.

It's her turn to reach for him; her fingers graze his jawline. Those blue eyes of his close, relishing her touch. She has known him for months now too, hasn't she? Her instinct takes over once more. The breath she was about to take gets caught in her throat when leans forward.

Her lips touch his. His eyes open surprised, but Nate doesn't dare move. Sera slips her hand from his to bring it to the other side of his face pulling him closer.

The vial at her throat pulses again filling the room with its light. Oh no—not this again.

Only when she opens her eyes again Nate's lips are still pressed firmly against hers. He pulls away softly. His eyes widen further as he takes in the vial shimmering down to a slight glow.

"I don't understand," Sera mutters, shaking her head. Her fingers cup the vial around her throat instinctively.

"I… I know what it is. I know what's in that vial." A soft smile is spreading across his face as he points to her chest.

"What?"

"Of course. It all makes sense… but how?" his hand filters through his dark hair again.

"I'm lost. You have to fill me in here, Nate. Why didn't it harm you?"

"Because it can see I meant you no harm."

"It can see? You act like it's living," she scoffs.

"It was…"

"Okay, you're going to have to explain."

"It's Angel Dust."

"Wha—" Her mouth hangs open.

"When Angel's die we turn to dust, the particles return to Heaven reinforcing what you Secs call the Pearly Gates for protection."

"What?" She mutters again. "Secs?"

"Oh, um Seculars, people on the secular plane. Humans. The question is why didn't this return?" The question was rhetorical because he continues. "For it to be so protective of you, it means an Angel *died* to protect you. Their dust continues to do so."

"But who?"

"Well, that is the question, isn't it?"

"Just when I feel like I'm finally starting to get answers, ten more questions pop up."

"We will find your answers."

She breathes, "That's what I'm afraid of."

Nate pulls her closer, "There is nothing to be afraid of. After what I just saw, people should be afraid of you."

Sera finally smiles. "Okay." Finally allowing herself a moment of relaxation, she withdraws slightly leaning back into the headboard of the huge bed. Her common sense is telling her this is crazy, she only just met this guy. These dreams they are happening for a reason, and there must be a reason Nate is a part of them. Those strange gut feelings are telling her that they were to prepare her for this, for Nate.

Scooting out of the covers, she pulls closer to him on the bed once again grabbing his hand in hers. "I know this sounds crazy, but I feel like I have known you forever."

His face forms a smile now, one that reaches his eyes. He puts his arm around her bringing her close to him, the smell of pine tickling her nose, drawing her closer into the nape of his neck. She can feel how magical this moment is. That instinctual feeling inside of her is telling her that this is all she's ever wanted… and more.

Becoming overwhelmed with a new range of feelings, she opens her eyes to focus on something else, anything else. In front of her is a clock on the wall; her eyes focus on the time, half past eleven in the evening.

Her brain finally kicks in, and she jumps to her feet. "Oh my God. I have to go. I need to get home."

"Why?" He looks around alarmed.

"My parents, they are going to kill me. What am I supposed to even tell them? They already think I'm doing drugs." She stumbles around throwing on a shoe.

Not having a response, Nate grows quiet watching her slip on her other shoe. "You know Sera, I can't protect you twenty-four seven if you're still living at home."

She whips around to face him in complete shock while hunched over tying her shoe. "I'm sorry, I think I just blanked out for a second. What did you say?"

"You can't stay at home. Something is after you. I don't know who, and I don't know why, but wherever you are, you're in danger. If you are living at home, they are in danger, too. Plus, I've never seen someone harbor so much power before. We don't know what you are capable of. You are going to need some help honing your skills."

As much as she hates to admit it, she knows Nate's right. "So what do you suppose I do?" She finally looks him in the eye.

"Move in with me." He shrugs nonchalantly like it is the simplest decision in the world.

"What? Are you crazy?" she blurts out, "I mean what would I tell my parents? What would people think? How? Where would I...?"

"Sera," his calm voice cuts through her stammering. "This is the only way I can protect you." His eyes explore hers and plead.

"I know... I just, I just never really thought about it

before now. This is all happening so fast."

He drops his head, "I know." He releases a sigh before beginning again, "I want you to know that I made this home for *you*. This," he points about the room, "This is your room. I designed it exactly how you would like it." He reaches out tipping her face up to look into his, "It's always been yours. *I've* always been yours."

He finishes with a kiss on her forehead, and Sera glances away. He knew she wouldn't be able to stay with her family being part whatever-the-hell she is now. Deep down she knows she truly can't either. A possession was as close as her front lawn only a few short hours ago.

Leaning back, looking into Nate's deep blue eyes she states, "I'll think about it."

AGREEING TO THINK ABOUT moving in with him was all she had to say, before Nate agreed to drive her home. His sleek black car pulls down her dead end street. He hadn't even pulled into the driveway before he began lecturing her about how important it was that she moves in with him and begin training. Her eyes catch his gaze and she sits staring into those gorgeous blue eyes as he continues rambling on. Something in his eyes, she feels as though she can see into his soul. She can *feel* all of his emotions. It causes a shiver to tickle through her. Sera leans forward over the center console pressing her lips gently to his before pulling away.

"I said I would think about it, Nate. Goodnight."

The look of surprise on his face made her smile all the way to her door. She digs her keys out of her pocket twisting slightly when she catches sight of her father's truck in the gravel driveway completely restored to its original state. Actually, there is no sign of the struggle that occurred only a few hours earlier. *How is that possible?* She makes a mental note to ask Nate later. Her fingers turn the key in the lock and with a calming breath, she enters her house.

The lights are all extinguished. Her parents must be asleep already. Thank God. Carefully, she climbs the steps and slips into her bedroom.

She flicks the light on and begins to change out of her dirty work clothes and into sweatpants and a tank top before collapsing into the seat of her little vanity desk to remove her makeup. She blinks. Her reflection… it looks different. She comes closer to examine it. Her breath is causing condensation on the surface of the mirror when the face staring back at her begins to change, darken. In her reflection, eyes turn deep red, her hair black as night, the complexion white as a ghost and her cheeks sink in slightly. She pulls back in revulsion. Her reflected face begins to distort and twirl. Black swirling smoke is spiraling in the mirror in front of her until all she can see is a pair of beady red eyes.

The gut feeling comes again, followed along with that smell of garbage and burnt skin. It's so dense that she can barely breathe. The thought comes to her, Sera is in the presence of something wholly demonic.

"Seraphina," the voice calls to her. It's deep, just like the voice of the possessed woman earlier. "Seraphina," it repeats again, the way he mentions her name draws her closer, begging to be trusted.

"Yes," she finally responds but hesitantly.

"Will you join me?"

"Join who?"

His laugh echoes in the small room around her before he responds, "You are well aware of who I am."

"I want to hear it from you."

"You do not make demands of me."

"Then what is it you want from me?"

"Join me."

"Why? Why do you need me?"

"With you at my side, there will be nothing out of your reach. You will become the most powerful human on the planet. I can make the world bow at your feet, I can make you *invincible*."

"That doesn't answer my question, why do you need me?"

"You possess a power this world has never known. Only I can unlock it for you."

"And if I refuse?"

"Then you will be eliminated!" His tone sends a shiver down her spine, her senses going haywire around her. Goosebumps have sprouted all up and down her arms.

If Sera is such a powerful ally, then this is bigger than she ever could have imagined. Anna had warned her it would be as easy as good vs. evil. She decided in that very moment, whatever happens, she would never turn dark.

"I'm sorry, *Lucifer*," she emphasizes his name, "but I'm going to decline."

"You are making a grave mistake."

"You see, I don't think so. I think you need me. That means you wouldn't hurt me."

More dark laughing, "You are wrong, I can't kill you, but I can harm you all I like."

Sera gasps.

"Seraphina, you have made a terrible mistake. Everything you love will be obliterated until you come crawling back to me on your knees."

"No, you don't understand." She slams her palms down on the desk. "The old Sera is dead. You have no idea who I am or what I am capable of."

"You will regret this!" the voice in the mirror shrills before foaming back into the black smoke and disappearing. It vanishes, revealing Sera's real reflection angrily staring back at her.

Trying to process what had just happened, she turns away from the mirror and climbs into bed. Staring up at the ceiling above her, she can't seem to believe just how complicated her life has become. The alarm clock beside her flashes midnight. Just one week ago, she lay in the same position, depressed, lost, and *human*. Now, she's not exactly human anymore, powerful and exuberant. What a difference one week can make.

She had always felt as though she were waiting for something to begin, and now it turns out, she was right.

Maybe Jack was right; maybe this was God's plan all along. He could have reassigned Nate, on purpose. Knowing how he would've come to feel about her. The dreams of hers were all a plan to help her understand. This is all part of Sera's destiny.

Then the next thought hits her, she's going to have to move in with Nate now. It has become her only option. Lucifer knows where she lives, he will come for her, and he just threatened all that she loves. Plus, she needs to learn all that she is now capable of.

Scared out of her mind, she makes the decision to move into Nate's house—*her* house, *their* house. The thought causes her to smile. All the feelings from earlier reemerge and a warm feeling enters her heart. He built that house for her. He knows all there is to know about her. All her secrets, all her pain, and yet he gave up everything he knew… for her. Truly amazed, she finally allows herself to cry. Because even though her life is crazy and constantly under attack, she feels as though her life finally has meaning.

$\mathcal{E}$*pilogue*

$\mathcal{S}$UBCONSCIOUSLY, NATHANAEL finds himself walking along the main road of Angelica. A place known to locals simply as 'The Avenue.' He needs some time away from *her*. Every time he's around Sarah, his judgment clouds. He requires a clear head to think. This is a very dangerous path he's headed down. It's getting harder and harder for him to keep a level head. His life has become strange. On one hand, he has spent every waking moment with Sarah. He has gotten to know almost everything about her. Sometimes he thinks he might know her better than she knows herself. But, on the other hand, he doesn't understand why he *feels* this way. Why does he notice her like this? Guardians aren't supposed to be so close to their subjects.

It started out as curiosity. What's happening to this girl? What's she dreaming about? What's with the vial around her neck? But now, it's … more. His feet drag along the concrete sidewalk as the end of the empty street grows darker. The beat of his heart echoes in his chest. He doesn't remember hearing such things in Heaven, and it was so much quieter. Sarah's not the only one going through changes. The longer he remains on Earth, the more he… feels. He feels strange stirrings inside of him that he's not used to.

He can't seem to control anything. All these emotions are coming at him all at once. He's never felt such things before, and now to be feeling them all at once, it's unbearable. He wasn't trained for this. He's not adaptable like humans. How is he to cope?

What may have started out as curiosity has turned into fascination. Everything she seems to do is funny or amazing. From the way her nose crinkles a little when she smells something funny, to the way she can look angelic even when she is crying. Then there's the fact that he can't bear to be too far away from her.

Is this how Secs feel? Clammy hands, heart beating wildly, emotions he can't control that seem to come out of nowhere. Like the other night, with Jack. He witnessed one date, and it sent him into a temper tantrum like a child, tossing pots and pans around the coffee shop. Just now when he kissed her, it took everything in his power not to kill him. He had to rip himself away from her. Nathanael needs to get a grip on reality. No matter what it is that he is feeling, he will never be able to do all that Jack can.

Maybe, that's what he hates the most. He will never be

able to have any interaction other than protecting her. He will never hold her, touch her, feel her. She will never even know he's there. Eventually, he will have to watch her fall in love with someone else, and get married to someone else.

Shaking his head, he starts walking again. Nathanael comes to sit on a nearby bench. Beside him stands a post with a map on it. Is there nothing he can do about this? His options weigh heavy on him. It's not as if he can return to God and request another assignment. Sure that would go over well. He can picture it now:

Kneeling before the ivory throne, "Uh, God, you know that girl you sent me to guard? Well, I kind of fell in love with her. So would you mind sending her a replacement?

Then comes the feeling of disappointment from the Lord. The amusement plastered across Raziel's face.

He pauses for a second, wait, did he just say *love*? Is that what this is?

A large, long automobile stops before the bench. The doors fold open and a few people disembark before it continues off into the night. Nathanael still sits there staring into the road before him.

Love. I ... I love her. Good grief. This can't be good. There is nothing he can do about this. He will be forced to watch her from the sidelines always playing along in the background. He will never be able to feel her touch or to even hear her say his name. This is the most torturous form of punishment ever imaginable. What did he ever do to deserve this?

He climbs to his feet and screams at the clouds above, "Why?" he croaks before gaining some confidence, "What is the purpose of this? Why did you send me here?" He screams knowing exactly who would be listening.

No response comes. That's exactly how the Lord works. You only know what you are assigned. Anything more could change the course of history. Some Angels didn't like that idea. Some Angels have decided to live in a world in which their opinions matter and their deeds are rewarded here on Earth. Nathanael had never felt like that. He had always believed in God and his practices, but now… how could he ever be sure?

It has to be this place. It has to be *Earth* that is changing him.

His feet begin taking him back toward in the direction of town. He gets this ache in his chest. It's a pain he gets when he wanders too far away from Sarah.

If being in torturous agony is his cost for being able to stay with Sarah, he will pay it every time.

His wings extend as his mind decides it's time to head *home*. They flap twice before he rises from his spot on the pavement. They glide taking him back to Sarah. He flies over a few shops when he gets this tug in him to turn a different way.

It's another one of those strange feelings, one he can't seem to explain. It's like he's hooked onto the end of someone's fishing hook and is slowly being reeled in. He swoops low, gliding on the air down the unfamiliar street.

As he floats down closer, a form begins to appear in the middle of the road. His wings automatically retract at the sight. Nathanael lands on his feet with grace as a nervous feeling settles itself in the bottom of his stomach.

Everything around him slows as he puts one foot in front of the other and wanders toward limp figure. A tuft of red hair shines under the moonlight.

He's running now. His feet can't run fast enough, his wings don't seem to work. When he finally reaches the figure, his fears are confirmed. It's Sarah. He collapses to his knees and pulls her to him. Her lifeless body lies across his lap. He brushes her hair off her bruised face. Blood is dripping from her mouth, and he can do nothing but stare at her exquisiteness. *What have I done?*

This is his fault. If he had only been there, he could have protected her.

He's rocking back and forth now as he pulls her bloody body even closer to him. Something makes its way down his cheek. It tickles slightly before he reaches out to catch it. His hand comes back wet. He's ... he's crying.

He wraps her closer, allowing the tears to escape freely. Mumbling to her repeatedly that she's going to be okay. Even though she can't hear, see, or even feel him, it makes him feel slightly better knowing that she's not going to die alone. Someone who loves her is here for her.

The necklace at her throat glows softly, casting her in an eerie blue light. Once again Nathanael's fingers reach out for it. The closer he gets, the more his hand shakes. There's a power behind this vial that he can feel in his bones. His fingertips grow closer, closer still. They only slightly touch it when he feels it sear through his skin. Pain. Pain like he's never felt explodes from the tiniest part on his body.

"Ow." He pulls his hand away revealing a burn mark. It feels as though his entire skin is peeling back. "Ahh" Nathanael's voice screams to release some of this agony. It doesn't help. Not until the skin of his finger opens and a bead of blood appears to bubble up from it.

He blinks. The dots are finally connecting. One last glance at Sarah's limp form in his arms, and he knows what he has to do. Twisting her over the edge of his knee, He tilts her head back and allows his blood to drip into her mouth.

Nathanael didn't know how long he sat there with his finger in her mouth. The pain was nothing compared to the guilt inside of his heart. He stayed there in the middle of the street until the moon was high in the sky, until his skin healed over and the pain was only a distant memory.

When his brain finally clicks back on, he realizes he is still sitting in the middle of the street. He climbs to his feet with Sarah still in his arms, and his wings finally extend at his command. They lift them above the puddle of her blood and carry them away.

He reaches her house and the wood siding shimmers as he glides through the exterior wall with Sarah in his arms. He lays her in her bed and tucks her into the purple comforter. He barely has time to pull the covers over her when he hears it.

Nathanael.

"Yes Lord."

Report to the Throne Room immediately.

"Yes Lord."

On some level he knew this was going to happen. What he had done, it wasn't natural. He traces the back of his fingers down Sarah's cheek. She has gained some color back in her face. His fingers slide to her throat. A pulse is starting to thrum gaining its momentum with each beat. She will be okay. It's the only thought that makes him mildly okay with leaving her.

His wings take to the air. The roof of Sarah's house shimmers as he glides his way through the ceiling and then the beams of the attic. High and higher he soars. Those wings of his finally happy to get some real air once again. They flap beside him taking him closer and closer to a place that no longer holds the same significance as before. The air is different up here. Crisp and clean, it feels… fake.

Flying through the gates, St. Peter gives him a weird look before returning to the podium with his book before him. He continues over the pearly gates along the glistening River of Life. Cherubs pass him below and whisper solemnly to each other and point in his direction. There was no huddled masses waiting for Earthly gossip once his feet touch the clouds… something must be amiss. He comes before the entrance to the temple. His stomach twists when he sees Raziel proudly standing at the door. Preparing for the onslaught and humiliation, he walks up the steps with his head somewhat held high, although Raziel avoids his gaze. No insults, nothing but silence.

Something strange is definitely going on. He walks deeper through the white columned room. With each step, his anxiety raises. This is going to be bad, he can feel it. Racking his memory, he tries to think about the consequences of such actions. What could the Lord possibly say to him? Would he be demoted? Killed? Or worse…

He enters the Throne Room, knees trembling. It's been so long since he's been in the presence of God that the blinding light makes him fall before the Throne. Nathanael bows his head in respect. The bottom of the ornately sculpted ivory throne is all he can see facing downward.

Nathanael. The Lord's booming voice reverberates through him.

"Yes Lord."

Are you aware your actions are against our laws?

"Yes Lord."

There are consequences for your actions.

"Yes Lord"

So shall it be done.

Nathanael looks up just in time to see the Lord wave his hand dismissively at him. The gesture rips through him. Anxiety rises within him. He has no idea what is going to happen. His stomach twists inside of him with each passing second. Without warning, his wings seem to evaporate into thin air behind him. God is taking his wings? He wishes he could cry right now. It's like taking his manhood. It's taking a piece of who he is. Collapsing face first into the floor, he tries to tell himself that this is his punishment for failing. Failing both God and Sarah.

Then suddenly, the ground beneath him begins to shake. He tries to regain his balance when something on the far wall catches his eye. It must be the red hair that catches his attention first, then the eyes. Before he can process the gravity of what he is seeing, he's falling. Falling out of Heaven.

The ground beneath him has opened up and is sending him falling into oblivion. He's picking up speed now, falling faster and faster, until he notices land is coming into focus below him. *He's being sent back to Earth!* He can't help the smile stretching across his face as the thought of Sarah returns to his mind. *Sarah!* The picture! Just before he had fallen, he noticed the painting on the wall in the Throne Room. It bore a striking resemblance to Sarah. It doesn't make sense. Why would the Lord have a picture of a human adorning the holiest of rooms?

The ground is rapidly approaching now. Nathanael crouches, preparing for impact. When it finally hits him, he's smacked into the Earth creating a crater in the soil. The crash hit him so hard it knocks all the wind out of him. Rolling over onto his back, he lay gasping for air as the dust settles around him. That was definitely not expected. God may have taken more than just his wings. He lay in the dirt staring back up at the sky, sadly remembering all he had left behind as he tries to regain his energy. His whole life, everything he knew was up there. His wings! He realizes he will never be able to fly again. In Heaven, wings are such a huge honor, its one of the things that separate them from the Secs. In one moment, one action, everything has been taken from him.

Rising to his feet once his energy returns, he finds that he's breathing on his own. Actually breathing! Being an Angel of God he could breathe on Earth, but he didn't need to. Now he feels that he needs air to survive. Just as he's getting used to breathing in and out constantly, he feels a weird sensation in his stomach as well. Looking down at his abdomen, there doesn't seem to be anything wrong. He stands in confusion until he hears a gurgling sound coming from it. In that moment he realizes this must be what humans call hunger. Something he had never experienced before, when he was under the grace of God. Now that he's not, apparently he's subject to human feelings now. The gurgling comes again, more persistent this time. He's ravenous. It's like he's never eaten before, well, he hasn't.

Before he can focus on eating… there's something else he must do. Someone actually. He closes his eyes, he opens up his senses, he can feel her, *Sarah. His Sarah!*

There's no thinking involved, he has to make sure she's okay. He has to make sure she's still… her. Suddenly, another thought enters his mind, what if God steps in and tries to rectify what he's done. He breaks into a run, scaring the birds in the trees around him as he takes off in the direction he can feel Sarah in.

His feet are taking him as fast as he can, he's whipping

past complete towns and all types of scenery trying to get to Sarah before she awakens. He doesn't know what he's going to do or say, but he needs to make sure she's okay.

He's been running for hours, and he's starting to get that weird feeling in his stomach again like he's being pulled toward her. It means he's getting closer. The thought makes him push even harder. The wind is whipping through his hair, the sun on his face, the smell of Earth all around him, and he can't help but wonder why he's never been able to experience these things before. It's like he was immune to the beauty of the Earth until he had become a part of it.

A part of him feels bad for the other Angels who will never experiences these kinds of feelings and emotions. He has to say it's both good and bad, he can probably do without the nervousness and anxiety that is building inside of him the closer her comes to the town of Angelica. He just passed the green sign welcoming him, and he's starting to feel what Secs call butterflies in his stomach. He zooms past all the landmarks he's grown to know over the past few months. But, it isn't until he turns onto Sarah's dead end street that his feet stop working, and he freezes at the far edge of her street along the wood line. He's been thinking about this moment for the past few hours, and he has yet to come up with a scenario. He's staring at the blue farmhouse she shares with her parents and wondering what he could possibly say to her in a frozen stupor. He can't just fly through her walls, should he ring the doorbell? What would he say to her?

He's fantasized about this moment for months, but

never in his wildest dreams did he imagine it would ever come to pass. Suddenly, the pull in his stomach lurches. He turns to see Sarah running up the street toward him. Taken off guard, he reflexively ducks under the brush of the forest line. He peeks over the bush. She's wearing tight pants and a hooded sweatshirt, her red pony tail swishing from side to side as she comes down the street. She pauses on her front steps before twisting and collapses with her head in her hands. He wants to run to her, comfort her, help her get a hold on what is happening to her. But, that would make her even more confused, wouldn't it?

The fact that she was even able to leave her house this morning proves that she's gotten a hold of her senses already. He can't help but have this intense feeling of pride at how well she is adapting.

Even her appearance is altered since last night, her skin is flawless, her hair appears redder than usual, and her body still has those gorgeous curves he loves, but she appears taller and leaner. Angel blood agrees with her. He smiles. Even with his resounding guilt, he can't help but think he's created a goddess.

Without warning, she jumps to her feet, and he quickly jumps down out of sight. She notices the stir in the bushes. Slowly she studies them for the longest few seconds of his life. This is not how he wants to meet her. When she turns to walk inside the house, Nathanael releases a breath. He hunches over, sinking to his knees. Realization hits him: *she can see me!* Slowly he pieces back together the shards of his heart. He climbs to his feet and wipes the dirt off his tattered robes. He has a lot of work to do. IF he has even the slightest shot of being able to be with Sarah, he's going to do it the right way. The way she deserves, but first... he needs a place to live here on Earth.

A few hours later...

He finds himself parking his newly conjured car in front of a club called Chaos, deep in the heart of New York City where the pull in his stomach has taken him. It means Sarah is here, which is odd because she never used to go to places like this. This has Amanda written all over it. Everyone one knows that New York City is breeding grounds for demons. One sniff of her and they will never let her out of their sight. He needs to get her out of there before anything can happen.

He hops out of his car now, dashing up to the door about to head inside when an arm across his chest stops him. He turns to see a tall, bald man with a logo on his collared shirt.

"I.D.?" he asks of Nathanael.

He opens his mouth to respond when a petite little girl and her friend cut in front of him, passing what looks like a piece of plastic with her name and photo on it. The bald man allows them access to the bar. Nathanael realizes, he's asking for identification. Placing his hand in his pocket, he conjures a phony driver's license in his pocket before pulling it out to show to the man. Only then is he allowed to enter the building.

Nathanael enters the club and is immediately hit with alarm. This place reeks of evil. He closes his eyes and opens his senses to his surroundings. Evil doesn't seem to be present anymore, but it definitely was. He must find Sarah. He holds his nose as the remnants of the disgusting smell is poignant all over this place. He takes a step deeper inside when he catches sight of her bright red hair flowing down her back. She's sitting with her back to him at the bar. To the left of her is Amanda and some dude in a hat. To her right is that creep Jack. His fists clench.

Slowly, he makes his way to the bar. Nathanael moves his way to the corner of the bar for a better sight of Sarah. She looks so different. She's wearing make up, and it brightens up her whole face. That tight tiny black top, super tight jeans and knee-high boots are a sight to behold. To say this woman is sexy, is an understatement.

Jack is mumbling things into her ear. Nathanael's fists clench again. Jack and Sera throw back drink after drink. Although, she doesn't seem to be paying too much attention to the man on her arm. Her eyes uneasily glance around from time to time almost like she's looking for something. Her nervousness is making him nervous. Nathanael begins glancing around himself. Something definitely happened here. He rises to his feet, determined to figure out this mystery. He makes his way deeper into the club, once he gets to the hallway holding the bathrooms, the putrid scent of demon is all over this place. He opens the door to the women's bathroom. The smell is intense here, but he can't investigate because a bunch of girls are screaming and pushing him back into the hallway.

A little annoyed, he attempts to return to the bar when Sarah catches his attention once again. There's is no doubt she's the most gorgeous woman in this place. He watches from the center of the dance floor as random guys sneak glances over in her direction. No one seems to approach her while Jack is still at her side. Somehow, he finds a tiny shred of gratefulness at that little twerp. Although he doesn't trust him, at least he knows he's not demonic.

Nathanael makes a move closer. Sarah looks up. Their eyes meet. *This is the moment of truth.* She looks straight at him, and he freezes. He can't seem to catch a breath. His stomach is doing those backflips again. Never breaking eye contact, she climbs to her feet, dashes around the chair, and heads into the crowd toward him. Coming to his senses, he dodges to his side, ducking behind people, this is not how he wants to meet her. Not like this, not at this bar. He has been fantasizing about this moment for months, Nathanael wants it to be… special. He dodges behind an inebriated couple locked in a kiss, and he's able to sneak around her without being seen and heads out the front door.

He collapses into the front seat of his car. His mind goes over and over the moment their eyes met. It's almost as if she were heading toward him. Does she have the pull in her stomach that he does? What would he have even said to her?

"Hi, I'm Nathanael, former Angel of Heaven, nice to

meet you?" He shakes his head, that doesn't sound right. "Hi, I'm Nathan, nice to meet you." No, that's not it either. "Hi, I'm Nate."

Yeah, Nate. He likes the sound of that. This is different, exciting even. His heart is still beating out of his chest. He's never experienced anything like this. He can feel the adrenaline pumping throughout his entire body. It's taking everything in him not to return to that club. He's so lost in his thoughts, he almost misses her walk out of the bar arm in arm with a stumbling Amanda. He would just have to meet her some other way. How would she like to meet someone? Where is her favorite place? The coffee house!

Nathanael starts the car and drives down the New York City Street. The long ride home filled with fantasies and possibilities of what the coming days could bring.

The End

Acknowledgements

First off, I would be nothing without the love and support from my family and friends during the creation of this book. It's been a long road and I would be lost and probably would have given up a while ago without all of your help. Especially without my mother & father, who have become my biggest supporters. Thank you for all your constant support and editing.

My biggest fan, Miranda, Thank you for being the inspiration behind my Amanda character! (No, It's not a coincidence that your names rhyme) Words cannot express the thanks I owe you for always being there for me and giving me the confidence to pursue this.

For all the friends and fans that previously read the first edition – I'm sorry. It has come such a long way since then. Thank you for not giving up on the story.

I'm forever indebted to Sara at **Mad Hatter Press LLC** for turning my mumbling nonsense into an actual manuscript.

My cover is awesome because of Marisa at **Cover Me Darling**, thank you so much for making the mystery of Sera come alive. You can view more of her work at http://www.CoverMeDarling.com

A big shout out to Cassy at **Pink Ink Designs** for the Amazing formatting and design!

An extra special thanks to Starbucks for their addictive coffee that kept my fingers typing through the night.

Last but certainly not least, I want to thank God for giving me this insanely detailed dream, for putting it on my heart to write it down, and finally for instilling me with the creativity and patience to make my dreams become a reality.

About the Author

Sheena is a born and raised New Yorker, even her writing can't hide her hard sarcasm.

She claims destiny lead her to writing again. She constantly strives to be a positive role model and write stories that empower and inspire.

Sheena always roots for the underdog, believes in love at first sight, and that everyone should have their happily ever after. While God is currently writing her love story she continues to put all her time into her writing as she is constantly getting new inspiration.

For more on Sheena and her books visit her website
www.SheenaHutchinson.com

The Seraphina Series

Seraphina's Awakening
Book One

Seraphina's Initation
Book Two

Seraphina's Vengeance
Book Three

Also Note:
Seraphina Series coincides with the first two books in
The Discovering Trilogy

39042003R00196

Made in the USA
Middletown, DE
18 March 2019